SLOW ROAD TO LOVE

A MATURE-AGE CHRISTIAN ROMANCE

JULIETTE DUNCAN

A SUNBURNED LAND - BOOK 1

Cover Design by http://www.StunningBookCovers.com

Copyright © 2020 Juliette Duncan

All rights reserved.

SLOW ROAD TO LOVE is a work of fiction. Names, characters, and incidents are all products of the author's imagination or are used for fictional purposes. Any mentioned brand names, places, and trade marks remain the property of their respective owners, bear no association with the author, and are used for fictional purposes only.

THE HOLY BIBLE, NEW INTERNATIONAL VERSION®, NIV® Copyright © 1973, 1978, 1984, 2011 by Biblica, Inc.™ Used by permission. All rights reserved worldwide.

PRAISE FOR "SLOW ROAD TO LOVE"

"This is a beautifully story about a second chance at love. It is full of emotions and God's love. It will keep you turning the pages to see what happens next. This book was a joy to read and I highly recommend it." ~*Ann*

"I am so thrilled with this book. Once again Juliette Duncan has written a story that has inspired me from start to finish. It is so inspiring to read as two mature people who had previously experienced tragedy and heart ache begin to find love again. I love the references to scripture and as always with this author's book they give a hope for the future." ~*Judith*

"Such a moving story. I felt so bad for Maggie because she was still emotionally dealing with the baggage her ex-husband caused her. And the info on Station life was very interesting to me. I also cried when they finally told her how Frank's wife had died. The amazing faith this family had was very inspiring. If you like clean stories with each paragraph pulling you into the characters lives and you want to become friends, 'Slow Road to Love' is for you. I highly recommend!" ~*SJ*

CHAPTER 1

Darwin, Australia

It was a perfect sunny afternoon in Darwin. Temperatures hovered around 33^0 Celsius, relatively normal for this time of year. The small park across the street from Maggie Donovan's office was a hive of activity. Small children were playing in the adventure playground while their mums sipped coffee under the shade of the huge laurel trees. Businesspeople scurried through with their heads down, dodged by youths on electric scooters, and couples strolled along the pathways surrounding the duck pond and fountains.

One couple in particular caught Maggie's eye as she gazed out the picture window of the conference room, drawing her attention away from the staff meeting she was currently in.

The woman, a tall blonde with an athletic figure, stood next to a baby carriage and was rocking it slowly back and forth. An older gentleman in a well-tailored dark suit approached the woman. He was tall as well, with greying hair at his temples. As Maggie watched the couple share a romantic embrace and then proceed down the path pushing the stroller between them, she felt the slow burn of anger and jealousy in the pit of her stomach.

A long sigh escaped her lips as she reflected on her feelings. She hated that even after eighteen months she could still feel the pangs of jealousy and resentment over her divorce. It wasn't the couple's fault. They'd done nothing wrong. It was simply that they were a reminder that her husband of thirty-four years had left her for a younger woman, who so happened to be blonde and fit like the lady at the park. And Maggie had only recently found out that they were now expecting their first child together.

This news had torn open the old wounds. She could still remember the pain and shock when she first found out her politician husband was having an affair with a woman in his office. It was followed closely by the betrayal of being served with divorce papers. He wanted to move on and enjoy his new relationship with Mandy. That was her name. The woman who had come between her and her husband and broken up their family.

The infidelity by itself had been a great shock, but the fact he was so ready to throw thirty-four years away was even more so. He didn't even want to give their relationship a chance to be repaired. It was as if being caught in his infidelity had freed him from all his familial obligations. He had declared he didn't love her anymore and hadn't for a long time. That revelation alone had rocked Maggie to the core. It had shattered her heart and her confidence as a wife, as a mother, and as a woman. It had taken her months of therapy to begin to cope with her new life, and seeing that couple had brought it all back.

She pursed her lips, frustrated with her own reaction. She wanted to be over it. She wanted to be able to move on and had tried to convince herself many times that she had. But the truth was, she still struggled. Pretending it didn't affect her wasn't working. She needed a change. Something to focus on besides where she thought her life should have been instead of where it was.

Silently, she repeated the Serenity Prayer as she had done countless times before.

God, grant me the serenity to accept the things I cannot change,
Courage to change the things I can,
And wisdom to know the difference.

Only the sound of her name being called repeatedly pulled her from her painful trip down memory lane and self-recrimination.

"Maggie, is that okay, or were you hoping for a different assignment?... Maggie?"

The conversation had stopped, and all eyes were on her. Maggie quickly pulled her attention from the window. "I'm sorry, Suzanne, can you repeat the question?" Embarrassed at being caught not paying attention, she felt her cheeks colour.

"Of course." Suzanne smiled gently. Maggie's long-time boss and friend regarded her closely but said nothing about her preoccupation. "We were discussing the next issue's assignments and I thought you'd be a good fit for an article about women working on remote cattle stations in the Kimberley. More specifically, about how the women cope with the hardship of both the terrain and the lifestyle."

The assignment was definitely in Maggie's wheelhouse. She'd grown up on a small station just outside Darwin. It wasn't what she would have considered remote, but at least she had a good understanding of how hard the work was and how difficult it could be. Maybe God had answered her prayers, and this was the change she'd been looking for. This assignment would take her away from the city and from all the reminders of Cliff. It was the perfect opportunity to clear her head. Plus, she liked the idea of being able to highlight strong independent women who not only survived on these remote stations, but also thrived.

Although the Kimberley area was a full day's drive away, Maggie jumped at the chance. "I'd love to. Do you have some stations in mind, or do you need me to do some research?" The wheels in her brain were already turning with ideas for the story line.

"We have a few stations in mind that you could visit. Mike's already contacted Goddard Downs and spoken with the owner. They're located in a remote part of the Kimberley, and a couple of women there help to manage the station. I'd probably have you start there and work your way back," Suzanne said.

"Sounds great." Maggie's lips lifted in a smile.

"I'll set up a time with you and Mike tomorrow morning to go over the details."

"I'll look forward to it."

The rest of the meeting passed without incident as Suzanne continued doling out the remaining assignments. As Maggie was gathering her things to go, she felt a light touch on her shoulder and glanced up.

Suzanne's eyes were soft, as was her voice. "Are you okay, Maggie?"

They were the only two left in the room, so Maggie felt comfortable letting down her guard. Besides, Suzanne knew all about Cliff and Mandy and the baby, so Maggie knew she could be herself.

She stopped shuffling papers and looked her friend in the eye. "Yes, I'm sorry. I didn't mean to disrupt the meeting. I happened to glance out the window and spotted a couple on the path at the park. The man was older, and the woman was blonde and much younger. They were pushing a stroller between them and it caught me off guard."

"Ahh…now I understand what put that scowl on your face. Well, perhaps this assignment is just what you need. It'll involve a lot of travelling and considerable research, so it'll give you a chance to get away and help to occupy your mind with other things."

"That's exactly what I was thinking." Maggie nodded and smiled at her friend.

TWO DAYS LATER, when Maggie was talking to her daughter Serena about the assignment, Serena echoed the same sentiments. "I think this is perfect for you, Mum. It's about time you live a little. Get away for a bit. You've been wallowing far too long."

"I haven't been wallowing. And what do mean *live a little*? I live," Maggie argued as she balanced her mobile phone between her shoulder and ear while continuing to fold clothes and place them into her suitcase. She was leaving tomorrow to head to Goddard Downs and her daughter had called her right in the middle of her packing. She had wanted to take the call, because with her daughter's work, she didn't always know when she'd be available to talk.

Maggie was proud of Serena. She'd followed in her mother's footsteps and studied journalism and was now the lead foreign correspondent in Western Europe for the Northern Australian Broadcasting Commission. Currently stationed in London, Maggie didn't see her very often, and with the time difference, Darwin being eight hours ahead of London, she tried not to miss her calls.

"Mum, you haven't lived in years, even before the divorce."

"I take offense to that, sweetheart. I may not have lived an exciting life gallivanting across the world, but I've lived. I worked my way through school, got a Master's Degree in journalism and foreign policy, and happened to raise two upstanding children. Though, I'm beginning to rethink that last part," she said with mock indignation. She was only half-joking. She was extraordinarily proud of who her children had turned out to be, though she wished Serena would make better life choices when it came to her relationships.

"Don't get me wrong, I appreciate everything you've done for me, but you put everyone else first. Including Cliff."

"Don't call your father that," Maggie immediately corrected.

Serena still harboured anger towards her dad and had taken to calling him by his first name to put some distance between them.

"He stopped being my father when he betrayed our family. He can be a father to his new family now." Serena didn't even attempt to hide the bitterness in her voice.

"Oh, honey. He's still your father. That's not going to change just because he has a child with Mandy." Even as the words left her mouth, her stomach turned at the thought. But, she needed to set the right example for her daughter and show grace and forgiveness. She would never forgive herself if she didn't try to mend the relationship between her daughter and ex-husband.

"Mum, the man walked away from his family after thirty-four years, and for what? To start over with a new, younger, better family."

"Serena, it's not that simple." Maggie tried to argue, but even her arguments felt weak to her, too. "Our marriage was complicated," she finished lamely.

"It *is* that simple, Mum. And no, it wasn't that complicated. He had a wife who supported his political career from the very beginning, who put her dreams on hold to raise two kids, and what thanks do you get? He got tired of you and us and wanted something shiny and new. You need to stop making excuses for him. He left. That's what men like him do."

"Your father has some good qualities." Although right now, Maggie struggled to think of any. She tried to be patient, but Serena's words had stung, more so because she'd felt the same way. But she would never admit that to her daughter. She needed Serena to forgive her dad, but more importantly, she wanted her daughter to understand that not all men made the same mistakes Cliff had. "Not all men are like your father, sweetheart. Take David for example. He's a good man, supportive of you and your career."

"Mum, not this again. Long term is not something I'm interested in right now. What David and I have works for us. You don't need to try to change it."

Ever since the news of the infidelity had come out and her father had moved out to live with his lover, Serena had distanced herself from her relationships, keeping any boyfriend at arm's distance. She claimed she preferred to keep her relationships 'open and loose', but Maggie couldn't help but feel that was a lie. It seemed more like Serena was trying to protect her heart. Trust had been broken when her parents' marriage crumbled, and she was probably feeling insecure because if her parents' seemingly rock-solid marriage could crumble after thirty-something years, any relationship she was in could fall apart as well.

"I think David is good for you and you for him. Not every relationship will end up like mine and your father's." Maggie was met with a stony silence. She glanced at the phone to see if the call had been disconnected, but it still showed it connected. She waited another beat, but Serena said nothing. Her daughter could be stubborn when she wanted to be.

Not wanting to end the call on a bad note, especially when she would be in remote areas with very little coverage, Maggie caved. "Okay, honey. I'm sorry. I only want the best for you."

After another brief moment, Serena sighed. "I know you do, Mum. And I want the best for you, too, which is why I think this assignment has come at a perfect time. Live a little, let your hair down, dance with a stranger, put yourself out there."

Serena was intentionally changing the subject, but Maggie didn't press the matter further. "I don't know about putting myself out there, but I'll at least try to let my hair down."

"Come on, Mum, what about dancing with a stranger?"

"Let's take one thing at a time, okay, hon?"

Serena chuckled. "Fair enough. Take care and enjoy."

"I will. I'll call and email when I can. Love you."

"Love you back."

CHAPTER 2

The following day, Maggie set out before sunrise. Although she'd decided to take two days to do the long trip to Goddard Downs, she wanted to get an early start. Some of the roads she'd be travelling on would be unsealed and she wanted to make sure she hit those in the daylight. Not that she wasn't comfortable driving at dusk. She'd grown up on remote terrain, even learned to drive on it. Besides, her 4WD 2010 JK Wrangler Renegade was built to handle even the most rugged terrain. However, she'd had a step added so she could get in easily. At five-foot-four, she wasn't able to make the climb into the cab without it. Plus, the higher clearance would come in handy if she needed to travel over any rocky areas in the backcountry.

The night before, she'd double-checked her emergency supplies and ensured her spare tyre was in good form and properly inflated. The last thing she wanted to deal with was a flat and find out her spare was also faulty. Her first aid kit was fully stocked and up to date with fresh bandages, antiseptic creams, wipes, sunblock, and a host of other medical essentials. She had fresh water, non-perishable food items, blankets and two changes of clothes, one for warm weather and one for cold, stashed in the crate in the back. It was strapped in next to the spare fuel can.

She even had a satellite phone that Suzanne had insisted she take with her. Maggie appreciated the extra comfort, as she knew that mobile phone coverage in much of the area she was going to be travelling in was spotty and mostly non-existent. She couldn't assume that anywhere she stopped would have a landline either, so it was best to be prepared for anything.

She loaded the last of her luggage in the back, made sure everything was nice and secure and climbed in. Before she turned on the car to leave, she bowed her head.

Dear Heavenly Father, thank You for this lovely day and for the opportunity to set out on this adventure. I pray for safe travels on my journey. Place Your hands on mine upon the wheel and guide me. Grant me a careful and watchful eye so I may look out not just for myself but for others travelling on this day. I know that I don't travel alone and that I'm safe with You. In Your name, I pray. Amen.

The first leg of her journey was relatively uneventful. Because it was so early, she made it out of the city quickly, avoiding the morning rush hour. She stopped and grabbed a late breakfast in Katherine, the first large town she came to, and made a quick call to her boss to check on any last-minute updates. Suzanne said there was a station not far past Timber Creek near the Victoria River called Bullo River Station, and another, Mt. Elizabeth, which was further along the Gibb

River Road. Mike had been able to arrange visits to both places.

The latter was past Goddard Downs, so she could loop around after visiting there, but she could visit Bullo River on her way. Originally, she'd planned to stay the night at the El Questro station. However, it was more touristy and not as remote as what she would have liked for the assignment, although it was one of the most well-known stations and was directly en route to Goddard Downs. Suzanne's choice seemed to fit Maggie's taste better, so she decided to stay the night at Bullo River instead.

After she left Katherine, the terrain became more rugged and buildings of any shape or form were few and far between. Maggie let her mind wander as she thought about her assignment in more detail and reflected on what life might have been like one hundred years earlier, and all that had changed in the last century. One thing that hadn't changed was the beauty of the landscape. The diversity of her country never ceased to amaze her. The dense rainforests of the northeast, the snow-capped mountains of the Australian Alps in the south, the dry arid lands of the Great Victoria Desert.

Here, heading for the Kimberley, a region in north Western Australia known for its large areas of wilderness, rugged ranges, gorges, semi-arid savannah and largely isolated coastline, the road stretched ahead into the heat haze as far as the eye could see. It was deserted apart from the occasional 4wd or road-train, the huge semi-trailers that made her car wobble every time one passed.

Although arid, the landscape she was driving through was picturesque in its own unique way and begged to be photographed, but there would be time for pictures later. Right now, it was important for her to map out her article. Having grown up on a smaller station in a remote area, she knew of the work that went into running one. To some, life on a cattle station might sound fascinating and even glamorous. The movie *Australia* had helped romanticise the life, but it wasn't romantic at all. Although the landscape was beautiful, the land could be unforgiving and the work relentless. There was rarely a day off, rarely a holiday. Work began at sunup and finished at sundown.

With the nearest neighbour often a day's drive away or more, life on a cattle station could be isolating. Most had an airstrip where mail planes delivered mail and supplies, and sometimes that might be the only outside human contact for days or weeks at a time. Kids who grew up on a station didn't go to regular school. Their school was the 'School of the Air', which, in the past, was primarily done by radio and how it got its name. Nowadays, most lessons were done via computers and the internet, but it still could be an isolating experience.

Women on the station were expected to work just as hard as the men, but they weren't always given the same opportunities with regard to the type of work they were allowed to do. It was only a few decades ago that women were completely banned from stock camps, but now women were breaking barriers and shattering the misconception of what they were capable of. Women were flying the helicopters during roundups and managing the stations, but it didn't stop there. Women were also now becoming members of the various cattlemen associations, and even entering the political arena, something unheard of in the past. But, Maggie wanted to stay away from the political aspect of the cattle stations, at least for now. She would focus on the work that the women were doing on the stations themselves.

Speaking of stations, she glanced up just in time to catch a sign advising that the turnoff for Bullo River Station was coming up. The clock on the dash said it was just after four pm, so she'd made good time. She slowed as she came to the turnoff. Here she would leave the main highway and travel on a dirt road that wound through acres of countryside touching the northeastern side of the Kimberley region.

The photographer in her wanted to capture pictures of the rugged hills and the wildlife she knew it was teeming with, but there would be time for that later.

After more than half an hour, she reached the main house and parked in the front circle marked for guests. At the front desk, she was greeted warmly and told she was expected. As she waited to be checked in, an older gentleman appeared from the back office. He introduced himself as Hardy Jones, the station manager. He said he'd arranged for a special meal for her and some of the staff who worked on the ranch at seven pm. In the meantime, he offered to give her a tour of some of the grounds once she'd settled into her room. Maggie thanked him kindly and accepted the offer. He said he'd meet her back in the lobby in an hour.

That gave Maggie plenty of time to unwind from her long day in the car. Once in her room, she made a couple of quick phone calls, one to Serena that went straight to voicemail, but that wasn't unusual. She left her daughter a message saying she'd arrived safely and would call her later in the week. Her next call was to Suzanne, to give her an update on her ideas for the assignment. Suzanne was very excited about the angle of women breaking barriers in the cattle industry and agreed that Maggie should keep politics out of it for now.

Exactly one hour later, Maggie met Hardy in the lobby.

"I figured we would walk for the first part of the tour," he smiled at her congenially. "I imagine you probably want to stretch your legs after driving all this way."

"Yes, a walk would be lovely, thanks." Maggie was used to long car rides, but lately she found it took a lot longer to get over the stiffness. She wasn't exactly twenty anymore.

As they walked outside, Hardy pointed out different structures and paddocks and gave her some background on the station. They had four thousand Brahman cross herd cattle spread over their half million acres. The Bullo River station had been founded almost sixty years ago, when the pastoral lease had been granted to Raymond and Barbara Locke in 1960. It was surrounded by the dark tawny coloured waters of the Victoria River and rugged hills that were home to a vast array of fauna and wildlife, and also home to Aboriginal rock art.

The station was eventually sold to Charles and Sara Henderson in 1963. Charles passed away in 1986 leaving his wife to run the station with her daughter Marlee. At that time, the station was heavily in debt and Sara didn't know if they'd survive. But through sheer grit and determination and some clever business tactics, she and her daughter were able to turn it around. Sara was awarded Business Woman of the Year in 1990 for her management of Bullo River Station. Maggie was fascinated by the history and peppered Hardy with questions, not only about life on the station and the roles women played, but how life had changed since then.

It took very little time for them to make their way back to the main building. Hardy led her through the lobby into a small dining room set away from the main eating area. Several of the female staff were already there talking in small groups, obviously waiting for their guest of honour to arrive. Hardy did a quick round of introductions and then instructed everyone to serve themselves. The staff had laid out an impressive array of food, featuring the high-quality beef they raised on the station. There were beef kabobs, thick steaks and ribs, as well as lamb sausages, mustard coleslaw, and lamingtons for dessert.

After the long day, Maggie was famished and happily filled her plate with the delicious looking food. They all sat together family style at one giant round table. There was little discussion at first as they all dug in. Maggie imagined the women were just as hungry as her, if not more so. Several looked dusty and tired, like they'd just come in after a full day's work.

After the first few mouthfuls, the chatter began to increase. Maggie asked the women what Hardy had told them about her visit, and she filled in the blanks. The women seemed excited to be part of her assignment and were eager to highlight their contributions to station life. Most agreed they weren't concerned with breaking barriers. They simply wanted to do a job they loved and to be respected as good cattlewomen amongst their peers. They weren't looking to have their pictures in the paper, nor have accolades heaped on them. They were more concerned about taking care of their herd and their 'station' family. Maggie was touched by the camaraderie amongst the group.

She listened to their stories of hardship and triumph. Several hadn't grown up on a station but had been raised in the city. They'd felt a longing, a calling, to this rugged way of life. Maggie questioned them further about what it was like to leave city life, where everything was so easy, for this remote, challenging way of life, and how they'd adjusted. A couple said they'd considered quitting. Several others had quit before them, but it was the strength of the 'family' and the love of the job that kept these other women here.

After two hours of eating, talking, and laughing, Maggie had more than enough information. She'd filled five pages front and back with notes of all the stories they'd shared. She was pleased with the start and thanked the women for their willingness to let her go behind the scenes. There were lots of goodbyes and several hugs as Maggie bid them goodnight. As she lay in bed, she felt both lighter and more energised than she had in a long time.

CHAPTER 3

The next morning, Maggie didn't leave Bullo River quite as early as she'd planned. The second leg to Goddard Downs wasn't as long as the first, so she could take her time getting ready and enjoy the breakfast buffet the station had laid out for guests. After she ate and was packed and ready to go, she looked for Hardy to say goodbye. The front desk attendant informed her that he'd left at dawn to round up some stray cattle in the hills. She wrote him a quick note expressing her thanks for his hospitality and left her number in case he thought of anything else she might want to know for her article.

She made her way back down the access road and onto the main road. Hardy had been kind enough to fill up her tank the night before, so she didn't need to worry about stopping for fuel anytime soon. She drove for several hours, enjoying the wind in her hair and listening to her iPod through her Bluetooth speakers. She wasn't scheduled to arrive at Goddard

Downs until three p.m., and since she was running ahead of schedule, she decided to stop at the Keep River National Park and take an hour or two to photograph the unique sandstone formations that lay at the end of the gorge.

She took the gravel road that led to the beginning of the Jarnum Loop. Feeling restless, both physically and spiritually, she thought a hike in Mother Nature would be just the thing to lift her spirits. There wasn't enough time to do the full seven-and-a-half-kilometre walk, but she could do part of it. On a whim, she grabbed her pocket devotional and stuffed it in her hiking pack. Following the well-worn path, she listened to the white-quilled rock pigeons call to each other. Rock wallabies grazed in the shade of fat boab trees and Livistona fan palms and looked up as she passed. The track started to incline, and she began to think it would be a good place to turn around, but something made her keep going.

As she crested the top of the path, the ground levelled out and she broke through the trees. Before her was a breathtaking vista over the red and ochre ancient rock formations. Below, the savannah plains were framed by the dark, jagged outlines of ridges and plateaus.

It was here, in places like this, that Maggie truly appreciated God's power and majesty. Spying a flat outcropping of rock, she sat to take a breath and to be fully in the moment.

After a short while, she pulled out her pocket devotional and flipped it open, letting the pages fall as they wanted. It fell open to a devotion about taking time for the Lord.

Draw near to God and He will draw near to you.

She'd spent so much time being angry and hurt with the way her life and marriage had turned out that she'd forgotten to truly draw near to Him. To plant herself firmly in His Word. The verse spoke to her heart, as did the next.

Praise be to the God and Father of our Lord Jesus Christ, the Father of compassion and the God of all comfort, who comforts us in all our trouble, so that we can comfort those in any trouble with the comfort we ourselves receive from God.

Comfort in trouble... *Thank You, Lord. You've truly been my refuge these past months. Help me provide comfort to others who need it.*

Wait for the Lord; be strong and take heart and wait for the Lord. Wait for the Lord... *Yes, Lord. I wait for You.*

"For I know the plans I have for you," declares the Lord, "plans to prosper you and not to harm you, plans to give you hope and a future."

Hope and a future...that sounded wonderful. *Thank You, Lord. My hope is in You.*

Renewed in her spirit, she took a moment to capture the breathtaking beauty around her before heading back to her car. They may not be photos she could use for her assignment, but she would print a few to hang as reminders to always be right with the Lord.

Reaching her Jeep, Maggie put her camera in the bag and grabbed another bottle of water before setting out for the last few hours' drive to Goddard Downs. As she neared the station, she rattled through what she already knew. Most of the information she'd gleaned from a handful of articles on the internet. The station was owned by Frank Goddard. It was about a third of the size of Bullo River, but ran a thousand more head of cattle. That told her something.

The station had been in the Goddard family for multiple

generations going all the way back to 1906 when Frank's great grandfather Harold Goddard, a young newlywed of only twenty-five years of age, had bought the lease. At that time, the land had been completely undeveloped and extremely isolated. There was the hint of a scandal in one of the articles, but not much information to go on. Just something about the families of Harold and his young bride, Clara, not being thrilled about their choice to move thousands of miles north into unknown territory. She would make a note to ask about that in her visit.

There were no signs leading up to the station and she almost missed the turnoff. Only a small wooden sign painted in faded white letters about half a metre off the ground was all that indicated the station was to the right. Apparently, they weren't concerned about being found, unlike some of the other bigger, touristy stations.

That was one thing that set Goddard Downs apart from the other stations she'd researched. They were still primarily a cattle station. While others had succumbed to the lure of tourist dollars, Goddard Downs had remained steadfast. Despite the lack of fanfare, Maggie felt drawn to this place. There was a divine sense of peace even while being jostled about as she made her way along the rutted dusty road.

After another thirty minutes, she spotted a large ranch-style home up ahead. Not a fancy lodging like the Bullo River station homestead, but it had its own rustic charm. There didn't appear to be any designated parking area, so she pulled up to the side of the main entrance.

Removing her sunglasses after walking up the stairs, Maggie blinked several times while her eyes adjusted after being out in the bright sun all day. As her surroundings came into focus, she realised there was no lobby or front desk—she'd walked straight into someone's home. It must be the wrong building. She turned to leave when a voice from behind stopped her in her tracks.

"Hello. You must be Mrs. Donovan. Sorry, time got away from me and I didn't realise it was already three o'clock. It's a pleasure to meet you. I'm Olivia Carter, Frank's daughter." Tall and blonde with light brown eyes that were almost amber, she extended her hand.

Maggie shook it and was as impressed with the strength of her grip as she was with her natural beauty. Easily five-ten or five-eleven, Olivia had high cheek bones and a delicate nose and was so slim and elegant looking, she could have walked the catwalks in Milan. "Yes, please call me Maggie. Thanks for inviting me to stay on the station and for being willing to be interviewed," she answered graciously.

"Oh, it's no trouble at all. I must say, my sister-in-law, Janella, and I were excited when Dad told us you were coming and that you're doing a story about women. It's an honour to be included."

"The honour is all mine, really." Maggie couldn't help but smile at the warmth and excitement in Olivia's voice. It was clear the young woman was proud to be a part of the story.

"I imagine you've had a long day of travel. Let me show you to the guest house so you can freshen up. The fridge and pantry are fully stocked if you're hungry."

"Thank you, that sounds great." It had been a long couple of days and after spending the last few hours driving in the hot sun, a shower would be very welcome. "I'm parked out front. If you like, I can drive. Just tell me where to go."

"Sure, that'll save the trouble of getting the quad from the workshop."

They walked together to Maggie's Jeep. She started the vehicle and then looked to Olivia for directions, who pointed to the west. "We put you in the guest house overlooking the lagoon. It's a little way from the main house, but the view is spectacular. And it's peaceful and quiet in the evenings, which I thought would be good for your writing."

"Thank you. That's very thoughtful." They made idle chit chat as Maggie made the short drive to the guest house. When she pulled up, her jaw dropped. After seeing the basic ranch house, she'd expected little more than a bungalow or shack, but next to the crystal-clear blue lagoon stood a gorgeous log cabin with a wrap-around porch that faced the lagoon. Two rockers were on the porch for enjoying the sunsets. It was simply delightful. "It's beautiful," she said.

"Thank you. My grandfather built it. It took him six months because he hand-cut all the logs himself and he used the dovetail method. He was quite the carpenter."

Maggie didn't know what the dovetail method was but she could hear the pride in Olivia's voice. She followed her up the steps and, once ushered inside, was as impressed with the interior as she was with the exterior. It held an understated elegance, with handcrafted wood furniture accented with hand-woven blankets in traditional aboriginal patterns and framed landscapes of the local area hanging on the walls. Maggie could feel the love and care that had gone into the place and felt privileged to be staying there.

"There's a guest bedroom on this floor with a small half bath," Olivia said as she pointed down the hall past the stairs.

"But the real pride and joy is the master suite upstairs. It takes up the entire floor."

Maggie followed her up the stairs that emptied into to a large, loft-like room. With windows on every side, it offered an all-round view. A king-size bed faced the west and overlooked the lagoon, and there was a small rectangular table with one chair that would be perfect for her workstation. There was also a phone jack and modem connection. Perfect. She'd have wi-fi access—an unexpected luxury.

"Grandpa spared no expense for Grandma. It took six men to haul the claw-foot tub through the window of the bath area."

Maggie glanced to where Olivia was indicating. She was right. On the other side of a painted screen, a giant porcelain claw-foot tub, like one straight out of a western movie, filled the screened off space. Copper pipes and taps added elegance, and the view was amazing. The granite peaks of the Mirima National Park were clearly visible in the distance. Everything about the cabin spoke of relaxation and peace. It would be the perfect place to work on her assignment, and she voiced as much. "It's perfect. Thank you."

"You're welcome. I'll help you unload your gear and let you get settled."

Before Maggie could get in a word, Olivia was already headed downstairs and out to the Jeep. She'd already unloaded two suitcases and was about to grab her supplies crate when Maggie stopped her. "That stays in the Jeep. It contains my emergency kit and supplies."

Olivia nodded in approval. "Smart woman. Always wise to be prepared for anything."

"That's my motto. I'd rather have it and not need it, than need it and not have it."

"We're going to get along just fine." An infectious grin spread across Olivia's face. And with that, she headed into the cabin carrying Maggie's luggage as if it weighed nothing. Granted, Maggie was a light packer, but still, it would have taken her two or three trips to get it all up the stairs. She was grateful for Olivia's help.

"I'll leave you to get settled in. The phone on the kitchen counter has a direct line to the main house, so just dial #1 and it will ring directly to us. Dinner's around seven. We'd love for you to join us."

"Thank you. That would be lovely."

"Great, I'll swing by just before and pick you up."

CHAPTER 4

*D*inner was a relaxed affair. Maggie had initially worried that her presence might stilt the conversation or perhaps alter the family dynamics and she wouldn't be able to capture the family bond, but she had nothing to fear. The extended family and their children embraced her as if she were one of their own. She was seated between Olivia and Janella, and across from their respective husbands, Nathan and Julian. The children, ranging in ages from one to twelve, were seated at their own table but were as much a part of the conversation as the adults.

Maggie took time to observe, not just the women, but the men at the table as well. Julian, the oldest Goddard sibling, was married to Janella, an olive-skinned attractive woman. He resembled the typical first-born, holding himself as a leader in his mannerisms, though he didn't sit at the head of the table. That seat was reserved for Julian and Olivia's father, Frank Goddard, although it currently remained unoccupied. Olivia had apologised for her father's absence and said that he'd join them shortly—there was an issue with one of the calves. Maggie didn't mind. She'd meet him soon enough, and besides, she wasn't here to interview him.

Joshua, the youngest of the Goddard clan, held himself slightly aloof from the conversation. He was polite when personally addressed, but was less engaged with the family and the conversations flowing around him. Maggie wondered if this was his normal demeanour, or if perhaps something was going on that caused him to be this way. It didn't matter much either way since she was here to focus on the women, and they already seemed more than willing to be open and honest about their feelings and thoughts about station life.

Olivia, the only daughter, had just finished talking about the history of Goddard Downs when heavy footsteps sounded in the hallway. Choruses of 'Grandpa' filled the dining room as the head of the house joined them. Maggie's first thought was that Frank Goddard was an imposing figure, a tall man whose broad shoulders almost filled the doorway. He sported a full beard speckled with grey, and he would have been intimidating if his blue eyes hadn't twinkled at the sight of his family.

He gave the children a wink before sweeping off his hat and apologising for being late. "Sorry, everyone. The new calf was having difficulty feeding, but she's okay now."

When he turned those blue eyes to Maggie and gave her a nod, she felt a wave of recognition wash over her, but she struggled to place him. How could she have forgotten such an imposing and formidable figure? But as hard as she tried, she couldn't recollect where she might have known him from.

She stood to greet him, but he stopped her. "Please don't

get up on my account, 'specially not in the middle of your dinner. There'll be plenty of time later for formalities." He gestured to the plate of food in front of her. "Nice to meet you, Ms. Donovan," he said as he sat at the head of the table. "And welcome to Goddard Downs."

"Thank you," Maggie said as she settled back into her seat and placed her napkin on her lap.

Conversation resumed around her as Frank filled his family in on the condition of the calf. Apparently, she had some kind of cleft palate which made it difficult to eat. Maggie had grown up on a farm outside of Darwin, but they'd farmed crops not raised cattle, although she understood it would be critical for a newborn calf to be able to feed to get the nutrients it needed in order to survive.

While Frank carried the conversation, she scrutinised his face, willing herself to remember where she knew him from. She wasn't given long to brood before the conversation turned back to her.

"I understand my children gave you the rundown of the history of Goddard Downs?" Frank asked, those blue eyes holding hers with a friendly gaze.

"Yes, that's correct," she replied quickly, glancing down at her plate before looking back up to answer. "I found it fascinating that Harold and Clara took a chance on such an isolated place, especially back in those days."

"Yes, it was quite newsworthy at the time, so I've heard, but more so because neither of their families supported their decision to leave Sydney, but they were pioneers who loved a challenge. It caused a rift in their families for a time, but eventually relationships were mended. The station's been in the family now for more than a hundred years."

"That's truly remarkable." Maggie smiled and dabbed her mouth with the napkin. "Did you always want to work on the station, or did you have a yearning to see what city life was like?"

Frank leaned back in his chair. "I had a taste of the city once. My parents didn't think the School of the Air was enough, so they sent me and my sister to boarding school in Darwin."

"Oh? What boarding school did you go to?" The wheels began to turn in Maggie's mind. She'd also gone to boarding school in Darwin and it was too much of a coincidence for their paths not to have crossed at some point. Darwin wasn't a large city. Even smaller back then. And boarding school kids tended to hang out with each other. She wasn't sure how old Frank was, but he looked around her age, so it could be possible they'd run in the same circles.

"I went to St. John's All-Boys and Sarah went to the Haileybury Rendall School across town."

Maggie's eyes widened. "I went to Haileybury, too."

"Why, that's where my late wife Esther went as well!"

"Esther?" The name sounded familiar. She leaned forward. "What was her maiden name?"

"Williams. She was a year younger than me. I graduated in '77. She graduated the year after in '78'."

Maggie sat in stunned silence as realisation hit her. She didn't only know Frank, she'd known his wife. She and Esther had been in the same school and the same grade. They hadn't been the best of friends, but they'd known each other and had some of the same friends. That's how she knew Frank, or Franklin as he'd been called back then. She'd seen him with Esther. They'd dated through the last two years of secondary school.

"You're Franklin," she said.

Frank chuckled as a broad grin spread across his face. "Well, I haven't been Franklin in a very long time. Only to the nuns at school, and to my mother when I was in trouble."

"I knew Esther. We were in the same grade."

His face lit up. "You knew my Esther?"

"Yes, I knew her, though not well."

Frank regarded her closely, as if willing himself to remember. "I'm sorry, I don't remember a Maggie Donovan. But back then I only had eyes for Esther. It was love at first sight. Nobody else really existed."

Maggie's heart constricted. To be loved so deeply, the way Frank had so obviously loved Esther, was something she'd not truly experienced in her own marriage. "Well, I was Maggie Johnson back then." She smiled, trying to put thoughts of her failed marriage aside. "Actually, Margaret Johnson to the nuns. And please don't apologise. Esther and I were only school mates." Realising that sounded a bit harsh, she clarified, "I mean, we were in the same grade and shared some of the same friends, so we knew each other, but we didn't see each other outside of school."

"What a small world."

"Yes, it is."

AFTER DINNER, Olivia drove Maggie back to the guest house.

On the short drive, Maggie tried to think of a tactful way of asking what had happened to her mother, Esther, but wasn't sure how to bring it up. Thankfully, she didn't have to.

"I'm glad you decided to come to Goddard Downs. My mother would have been tickled pink at the idea of an article featuring the women who live and work here. She was very proud of our station and pulled her weight alongside my dad." Olivia grew quiet and Maggie sensed a deep sadness as the young woman slowed the vehicle and then stopped in front of the cabin.

"I would have loved to have met up with your mother again after all these years."

"She would have liked that too," Olivia replied, offering a small smile, although it didn't quite meet her eyes.

"If you don't mind me asking, how long has she been gone?" Maggie asked quietly, chastising herself for not knowing.

"It's been almost six years since the accident."

"The accident?"

"The east arm of the Ord River overflowed in the floods. My niece and nephew got caught in the raging waters and my mother braved the currents to rescue them." Olivia paused and blew out a breath before continuing. "She got them to safety, but she was swept down river."

Six years ago she and Cliff had been overseas. Cliff had been a foreign diplomat for a time, and when they returned, the Ord River flood was old news, explaining why she hadn't heard about Esther's death.

Maggie's heart wrenched for the young woman who'd had her mother taken from her too soon and in such a tragic manner. "I'm so sorry for your loss. I can't begin to imagine what you must have gone through. All I can say is that God's love provides comfort even in our darkest hours. I lost my mother to cancer almost a decade ago, but there are days when I still miss her as if it were yesterday."

Maggie reached into her purse and pulled out a wrinkled piece of paper. One that had been folded and refolded a hundred times over. "Here."

"What's this?" Olivia asked as she unfolded it and began to read the words quietly. "The Lord is close to the brokenhearted and saves those who are crushed in spirit. Psalm 34:18."

"It was given to me by a close friend at my mother's funeral. I pull it out every now and then when I'm struggling. It gives me peace and reminds me that I'm not alone."

"It's very kind of you, but I can't take it." Olivia tried to hand the paper back to Maggie.

Maggie pressed it back into her palm and closed her fist around it. "Keep it. I want you to have it. May it give you as much comfort as it's given me."

"Thank you," Olivia said, leaning over to give Maggie a quick hug.

"You're more than welcome."

Before she bid Olivia good night, the two women made plans for the following morning. Although Maggie said she could drive herself, Olivia insisted on picking her up at five a.m. and driving her to the main house for a quick breakfast before Janella took her on the morning rounds, something Maggie was looking forward to.

CHAPTER 5

Five a.m. came too soon for Maggie. Although she was an early riser, she was rarely up before the sun and now she'd done it twice in one week. She stifled more than one yawn when Olivia collected her and drove her to the main house. Thankfully, Janella had a steaming mug of coffee waiting when she and Olivia arrived for breakfast. They feasted on scrambled eggs, thick slabs of bacon, and homemade buttery biscuits before Janella took her on the morning rounds.

Frank and his sons were already out working, and Olivia was staying back at the house to do some bookkeeping and paperwork for the upcoming auction while looking after her two young children, a three-year-old daughter and a fifteen-month-old son, so it was just Janella and Maggie for the first part of the morning. Janella's children, Caleb and Sasha, were busy with their School of the Air lessons under Olivia's supervision.

Maggie appreciated the one-on-one time with the woman and the opportunity to gain a different perspective. Janella had married into the family and into station life instead of being born into it.

Maggie learned that Janella and Julian met when they were teenagers. Janella's family had moved to Kununurra, the nearest town to Goddard Downs, and her father was looking for work. Life hadn't been the easiest for Janella, growing up with an aboriginal father and a white mother, and at times she'd experienced discrimination from both sides of her heritage. She wasn't white enough for her white family and not dark enough for her aboriginal family. But things took a turn for the better when they landed at Goddard Downs where the family was immediately accepted.

Despite her father being aboriginal, he and Frank hit it off straight away. They'd both had extensive experience raising cattle, and her dad had worked with farm animals most of his life. Frank had been seeking another hand to help with the cattle and to help reclaim some of the land for additional crops. The two men bonded over eco-friendly farming techniques, but her father cemented the friendship when he helped Frank save two yearling calves that had gone astray and were caught in a dangerous ravine. The loss of two yearlings would have been extremely costly, but together they'd managed to get the two calves out before the rains came and drowned them.

Janella and her family had lived on the station since then. She and Julian had initially kept their relationship a secret for fear that Frank might not approve, but they couldn't have been more wrong. Upon discovering their relationship, rather than forbid it, he embraced it. His only condition was that they not hide it, and he encouraged them to put the Lord first. Frank's unconditional love and support had made the young couple's bond that much stronger. They married when Julian was twenty-two and Janella was nineteen. They'd been together since and were now the proud parents of twelve-year-old Caleb and ten-year-old Sasha.

Caleb, Maggie remembered from the night before, was Olivia's nephew who'd been rescued in the flood by Esther. She wondered how her death had weighed on the young boy, but she didn't feel it appropriate to bring it up. She would let Janella tell her, if she felt comfortable. Instead, she focused on Janella's life on the station. For subtext, she thought the aspect of discrimination from both the gender and the racial perspective would add extra depth to the article, but for now, her focus was firmly on the work aspect of station life.

Janella took Maggie to the chicken shed first, where the chickens were cared for from the beginning of their life cycle to their end. Eggs were either gathered for the breakfast table or left for the creation of more chickens. They looked in on the peeps to ensure they were warm, well-fed, and had plenty of water. New hatchlings were born about every ninety days or so, depending on the breed of chicken. At Goddard Downs, they raised Sussex, Rhode Island Reds, and Leghorns.

All aspects of the process were done in situ, and because they weren't a commercial breeder, they weren't restricted by government regulations. That didn't mean they cut corners though, Janella asserted. Both her father and Frank were advocates of sustainable and humane farming techniques.

This meant that the chickens were given free rein over the farm during the day and were only put in the coops at night to protect them from predators. They ate the bugs in the vegetable gardens and their droppings were used as compost in the soil. The meat was butchered and used to feed the families that lived and worked on the station, and whatever wasn't used was sold to other stations or the local market. Nothing went to waste.

Maggie took plenty of pictures while Janella talked and worked. It was hard work, prepping the chickens for slaughter, but Janella handled it all with ease. She was patient and kind with Maggie as she peppered her with questions or asked her to pose a certain way for a photograph. Once they were done with the chickens, they headed to the pig pens.

The sun was already high in the sky and Maggie had to wipe her brow several times. Arriving at the pig pen, the smell was overwhelming at first. Janella suggested covering her nose and mouth with her bandana until she became accustomed to it. Maggie did as instructed, and it made the smell somewhat more bearable. Unlike the lighter, more delicate work with the chickens, here the work was brutish.

Maggie watched in awe as Janella worked alongside the men as they mucked out the stalls and replaced them with fresh hay. She got some good shots of Janella with her biceps straining under the weight of the slop buckets as she fed the pigs. Although Goddard Downs was known mostly as a cattle station, they also only had a hundred head of pigs, mostly Large White, but a couple dozen Berkshire as well. The pigs surrounded the workers as they went about their business. Janella wasn't a large woman by any means, but she manoeuvred them out of her way as if they were ten kilo sacks of flour.

The action shots Maggie took would be great talking points for the article.

After the pigs were the alpacas and sheep. At Goddard Downs, both were mainly raised for their wool, although they did occasionally butcher a sheep for mutton stew, but it was a rarity. Here, Maggie had the opportunity to get her hands dirty and help out firsthand. Janella showed her how to herd the animals into the different corrals depending on their age and the length of their coat. Not wanting to miss an opportunity, Maggie asked one of the younger workhands if he would capture the tutorial with her camera. The young man readily agreed, seemingly happy to take a break. She gave him a brief introduction to her camera and how to focus the lens, then told him to snap away.

It took several tries before she could get a clean row of wool sheared off, but she was determined to get it right. She wasn't nearly as quick as Janella or the others who could shear a full adult sheep in under two minutes, but she felt proud and accomplished when she finally finished hers.

Once all the shearing had been completed, they gathered the wool to be skirted. This, Janella informed her, was the process of removing the 'tags,' or the wool that was too dirty and full of manure, to be used. The fleeces were then sorted into their various types, from fine to coarse and from short to long. After just an hour of skirting, Maggie's arms felt like dead weights. Who knew wool could be so heavy?

Once the skirting was done, they took a break. Janella showed Maggie where she could get cleaned up and wash the muck from her hands and face. Skirting was dirty work and Maggie was grateful for the reprieve. She retrieved her camera from the young man and proceeded to capture the workers and Janella as they loaded the wool into a big truck. Janella drove the bobcat like she'd been doing it all her life, manoeuvring in and out between the other men with ease and scooping up large piles of wool without dropping any. In no time at all, they had it loaded onto the truck and on its way to the processors. There it would be cleaned, teased, carded, roved, and finally spun into yarn to make blankets and clothes.

"Time to head back for lunch," Janella said. She told Maggie she often brought a packed lunch with her to eat as she worked, but Olivia had arranged for a sit-down meal today. Maggie was eternally grateful. It was barely past noon, and she wasn't only starving, but drop dead tired. How on earth did these women do this day in and day out? Granted, they were a lot younger than her, but still, the fortitude and grit they had to not only keep up with the men, but to outshine them, was amazing.

As the ladies enjoyed a light lunch of cold cuts, pasta salad, and ice-cold lemonade, Janella and Olivia shared stories from when they were younger and what life had been like growing up on the station. Janella had a slightly different perspective, since she came when she was thirteen, but Olivia had been born and raised on the station and working as far back as she could remember. Except for her short time at university, she didn't know any other way of life.

"What were you studying?" Maggie asked.

"Business. I like numbers and had a head for it, so it seemed a good fit."

"But it wasn't?" Maggie asked, hearing the slight hesitation in Olivia's voice.

"No, it wasn't that." There was a sadness in her eyes when she answered. "I came back home after Mum passed away. I couldn't bear to be away from my family...not after we lost her so suddenly."

"I'm so sorry. I didn't realise the timing. That was careless of me."

Olivia gave her a weak smile. "It's okay. There wasn't any way for you to know. Besides, it's in the past and I'm happy now. I love working and living on the station. It's fulfilling work. I have everything I could need or want right here."

"And I'll be forever thankful for that." All three heads turned as Frank's voice sounded from the entryway.

"Dad! We didn't hear you come in," Olivia said, smiling broadly.

He laughed as he gave the shoulders of his daughter and daughter-in-law a squeeze when he reached the table. There was genuine affection in their connections with each other and Maggie's heart warmed at the sight. It was clear that Frank had much love for his family and they for him.

But such closeness was also bittersweet. It made Maggie miss her kids, even though they were grown. It made her long for the tight-knit family that would never be. Cliff had ruined that dream for her. For them. But, if she were honest, even if he hadn't had the affair, they wouldn't have had what Frank had with his children. Cliff had never fully connected with any of them. They were a piece to the perfect puzzle, his perfect political family. His career had always meant more to him than his family. It was only in hindsight that Maggie had realised that. All the missed holidays and birthdays, the excuses she had made for him to the kids.

Frank spoke. "I thought I'd take Maggie for a tour around the station this afternoon. I have to run fence lines and it would be a good chance for her to get a lay of the land, take any pictures, and ask whatever questions she may have."

"That's a great idea," Olivia said. "Do you want me or Janella to come along too?"

"No, but thanks for offering. After I show Maggie the boundaries, I'll pick Caleb up and bring him out with us to help repair the fences. I need the extra set of hands, and it'll be good experience for him. Maggie can see firsthand how the youngins help out around the station."

"He'll enjoy that," Janella said.

"And so will I," Maggie said, smiling in appreciation. "Seeing more of the station will give me some great photo opportunities and help me understand the scale of the entire operation."

Frank gave a short nod. "I'll grab the truck and get what I need while you ladies finish eating." He checked his watch. "Can you be ready in thirty minutes?"

"Of course." Maggie smiled as she answered, though her stomach fluttered as if butterflies had been set loose. She wasn't sure why the idea of being alone with Frank Goddard made her nervous, but it did. She would reflect on that later, because right now she had to finish eating quickly. She didn't acknowledge the fact that she also wanted to hurry so she could take a few moments to freshen up before they left.

She would reflect on that later as well.

CHAPTER 6

Frank was right on time. Thirty minutes later, on the dot, he pulled up in his truck in front of the main house. He jumped out and walked around to the passenger side and held the door open for Maggie as she climbed in, thankful she was wearing shorts and boots, and for the handle she could use to pull herself up with. She was sure her ascent was less than elegant. It was nice to know that good manners were still valued even in remote areas. When she said as much after Frank joined her in the cab, he chuckled.

"My great-grandmother would roll over in her grave if she discovered I didn't hold the door open for a lady."

"She sounds like quite the character."

"She was at that. She was a pioneer of her time, with only grit and faith in God to help her not only survive in this remote area, but to thrive and prosper."

"I wish I could have met her. I can't even fathom making

the courageous choices that she did. I'm not sure I could have done it."

"Oh, I don't know about that," Frank said as he regarded her closely. "I think you'd be surprised at what you could do. I bet you're made of sterner stuff than you think."

Maggie felt the warm heat of a blush creep up her neck at the surprise compliment. "Thank you," she said, lowering her gaze. A moment of awkward silence fell between them. Maggie started fiddling with her camera lens to give her hands something to do.

With a small cough, Frank started the truck and headed down the main road. He talked as he drove, pointing out various landmarks of the station. "Goddard Downs is approximately one hundred and fifty thousand acres, or roughly two hundred and thirty-four square miles." He turned to her and grinned. "Now, we won't be driving the entire perimeter today, but I'll show you the highlights."

Maggie grinned at his jovial manner, the earlier awkwardness completely gone. They got on easily as Frank talked about his land. He spoke with passion. It was obvious he loved the station, its heritage, and what it represented to him. "We're lucky in its location. We're bordered on all sides by conservations and national parks. Harold and Clara couldn't have picked a better spot."

They stopped on a hilltop that had a gorgeous three-sixty-degree view. Maggie jumped out to take some photos.

He pointed to the east. "Over there is the Keep River National Park. You can see the sandstone formations in the distance."

Maggie followed the direction he was pointing and could

just make out the reddish rock outcroppings. She dug into her bag for her telephoto lens, thankful she'd brought her long-range lenses for just such an opportunity.

After she'd taken half a dozen shots, he pointed to the west. "Here, we're bordered by the Goomig Conservation Park, and a little to the north is the Jemarnde-Wooningim Conservation Park. To the southwest, there's the Barrbem Conservation Park. They're all part of the CALM Act."

"I've heard of that act, but I'm not overly familiar with it."

"It stands for the Conservation and Land Management Act. In addition to several other acts, it was introduced to help provide for the conservation and preservation of native flora, fauna, and wildlife. The Conservation Commission and the local Aboriginal tribes work together to help preserve their natural and cultural heritage, as well as enriching cross-cultural awareness."

"So, that means you can't be built out."

"Exactly. We'll never have to worry about further development. No big city hotelier or developer can come in here and decide to build a flux of resort hotels or clear the land for a super-highway. It will always be as it is, as God intended it to be."

There must be peace in that knowledge, Maggie thought as she gazed at the beautiful landscape before her. So many things in this world had been irrevocably changed by mankind, and there was something incredibly humbling about being in the presence of something that had been so totally untouched, just as it had been since the dawn of time.

When she said as much, she could tell her words had

touched Frank. His light blue eyes shone, and he nodded his head in agreement. "You get it. I couldn't have said it better."

They stood there for a long time, neither speaking, both simply enjoying the moment together, but eventually, it was time to head back and pick up Caleb. It took twenty minutes to reach the sheep paddock where Caleb had been helping shear the rest of the sheep with his father.

As the truck came to a stop, Frank honked the horn and waved his arm to get the boy's attention. Even from a distance, Maggie could tell that Frank's grandson took after him. At only twelve, he was already taller than her. He had broad shoulders and long arms like his grandfather, though he still had the slenderness of youth. He also had the awkward gait of a boy not yet used to his size.

Maggie made a move to the back seat, but Frank reached out his hand. "That's okay, Caleb can jump in the back. He's used to it."

Looking at Caleb's size with some scepticism, Maggie said, "So long as you're sure."

"I'll be fine." Caleb's voice broke as he spoke to Maggie, clearly showing the signs of transitioning from a boy to a man. His olive skin grew slightly pink as he ducked his head, deflecting Maggie's gaze.

Frank put the truck in gear and headed out. She settled into her seat and enjoyed the scenery while he chatted with his grandson. It was obvious to her that he had great affection for the boy, and vice-versa.

Frank headed southwest of where they'd been earlier that afternoon, pulling up next to a couple of trucks where two other men were hauling fence supplies out of the back. Caleb jumped out to help before the truck had barely stopped moving.

"Here we are," Frank said as he opened Maggie's door and offered his hand to help her down. She figured his hands would be coarse and rough, given the nature of the work he did on the station, but to her surprise, his hand felt both strong and soft against hers. An unfamiliar warmth spread under her skin at his touch, catching her off-guard, and she lost her footing. "Oh goodness," she cried as she fell into Frank's arms.

"Whoa, there." He caught her around the shoulders and held her upright. "Are you okay? You didn't hurt anything, did you?"

Caught unawares, all she could do was stare into those pale blue eyes. He continued to look back at her in silence until his brow furrowed with concern and she realised he'd asked her a question.

"Yes...yes, I'm fine, thank you," she managed to stammer after collecting her wits. It had been some time since she'd had a man's arms around her. Longer than that, really. But this wasn't a romantic embrace, simply a helping hand, and yet her stomach was aflutter.

Realising that not only were his arms still around her, but that they also had an audience, Frank stiffened. The eyes of the other two men and Caleb were on them. The two adults looked on with smirks on their faces, but Caleb's eyes were wide.

Taken aback by his reaction, Maggie quickly stepped back and smoothed an invisible ruffle on her shirt. She pointed to the materials the men had just finished unloading and asked him what they were doing.

"We're replacing this section of fence," he replied, obviously relieved to be talking about work.

Maggie squinted at the fence but couldn't see any holes or gaps. "But there doesn't look to be anything wrong." Sure, it was a bit rusted and sagged in a few areas, but it was intact. It seemed like a waste.

Frank seemed to read her mind as he answered her unspoken question. "With so many acres, we have miles and miles of fence row. I found, or I should say, Julian figured out that it was more cost effective and less time consuming if we kept to a schedule of fence repairs."

Maggie was puzzled. "I don't understand how it saves money to replace a fence that isn't broken."

Frank chuckled. "I had the same question when Julian first suggested it. But then he had Olivia show me the numbers to back it up. She always did have a good head for business," he said proudly. "But getting back to your question, the cost comes into the lost cattle and the deterioration of the integrity of the fence that ends up causing even more damage."

"Okay, so I understand the lost cattle, but I'm not sure I get the integrity of the fence."

"The fence is barb wire, and barb wire rusts over time, right?"

She nodded, wondering where he was going with this.

"And the fence is all connected, right?"

Again, she nodded.

"All that tension is spread out across a long distance rather than on one spot." He paused, making sure she was still with him. "So, over time, the wire will rust and start to decay, or a storm takes out a section, or what have you. When we only repaired the fence if it was broken, not only did we lose out on any cattle that escaped, but we wouldn't always know when the holes occurred. The added stress on the fence sections between the holes caused the fence to become less stable and wear out faster. We found that over time, more and more sections were failing faster than we could keep up with. So, Julian came up with the idea of doing a scheduled fence repair as preventative maintenance rather than a reactive maintenance, as he calls it."

"And changing miles and miles of fencing that hasn't failed yet is still cheaper?" Maggie couldn't hide the scepticism in her voice.

Frank laughed at her expression. "I didn't believe it either until Olivia showed me the expense numbers. It was true that it was more costly that first year, but then, as the plan began to unfold and we started changing out sections on a schedule, the numbers flattened out. It also made things easier from an accounting perspective. Instead of having a large influx of unexpected expenses that we didn't know how to plan for, we now have a virtually flat rate expense that we can budget for each month. The only time it fluctuates is if the price of the wire goes up or down."

"Wow, that's really quite clever, especially from a business perspective. I never would have believed that would work, let alone have the courage to try it."

"Sometimes all you have to have is a little faith." Frank's eyes twinkled.

"Amen to that." Maggie chuckled.

CHAPTER 7

Maggie and Frank spent several hours travelling down the fence line making the necessary repairs. It was time consuming and tedious work as they pulled all the fasteners from the posts to remove the fence, then rolled it up, tied it off, and loaded it in the back of the truck. Maggie was intrigued to discover that they were able to recycle the fence. Nothing went to waste on the station. That was Frank's great-grandfather's motto and he abided by it as well.

For the first hour or two, Maggie had hung back and watched, and took plenty of photos of both the work and the surrounding landscape, as well as quite a number of candid shots of Frank and Caleb. She'd captured a few good ones of the boy smiling at his grandfather's praise. It was clear there was a special bond between the pair. She marvelled at Frank's patience as he explained the process to Caleb and showed him how to use the tools to remove the fasteners.

The other men weren't impatient either when Caleb struggled for a bit as he learned to use the tools correctly. They simply gave him tips and words of encouragement and let him carry on as if he were an equal crew member. And that's what he was, Maggie realised. She recalled Olivia's words... 'Everyone plays their part on the station, no matter how big or small, nor how old or young. We're a team.'

Nothing could have proved that more than when Frank invited Maggie to join in. Everyone was a team player, he reminded her. He gave her a pair of Janella's gloves that were in the truck and showed her how to use the gun that shot the staples into the fence posts to hold the barb wire in place. Not much for physical labour, Maggie struggled with the gun. It was big in her small hands and packed quite a punch. She missed the first few times and tried to hand the gun back to Frank because she didn't want to be wasteful.

"Nonsense. You can do it. I'll help you steady it," he said as he walked around behind her. "I'll hold the wire and the gun steady, and that way you can focus on pulling the trigger with both hands."

Maggie was very aware of Frank's physical presence as he put one hand around her to hold the barb wire in place on the post and then used his other to help her guide the gun. She could feel the heat of his body through the back of her shirt and her pulse jumped in response. Shaking her head, she tried to refocus on the task at hand. She was no quitter and was determined to get this right.

"Steady now," he said as her hand shook with the weight of the gun.

She took a steadying breath and squeezed with all her

might. *Thwack!* The gun would have knocked her back if Frank hadn't been behind her.

When she opened her eyes to see if she'd hit the mark, she let out what could only be described as a girly squeal as she realised she'd done it.

Behind her, Frank chuckled at her glee. "See, I knew you could do it," he said with genuine encouragement.

She turned around and grinned. "Thank you! That was amazing. Can I do it again?"

This time, Frank let out a full belly laugh as he waved his hand at the rest of the fence posts. "You can fire away until your heart's content or your hands give out. Whichever comes first."

Maggie's smile broadened. It felt good to have someone believe in her and support her the way Frank did. Cliff had never been supportive of anything she'd done or wanted to do unless it benefitted his political career, and even then, he would more often than not sneer and make derogatory comments that her efforts weren't good enough. She hadn't realised how tired she'd been of the constant criticism. To have someone, a virtual stranger, be so encouraging was both amazing and eye-opening.

Frank helped her with the next few until she got the hang of it, then he let her hold the gun by herself while he held the fence in place for her to tack it in. She worked for about thirty minutes before her hands finally gave out. "Ugh," she said as her arms sagged with exhaustion. "I can't even feel my fingers anymore."

"You did well," he said as he took the gun from her shaky hands. "Better than I expected from a city gal."

Maggie feigned offence, but his eyes twinkled with mischief and she realised he was only toying with her. Relaxing, she joked along with him. "Hey, city girls can hang on the station."

"Well, *you* certainly can. That's for sure."

She pulled off her gloves and rubbed her sore hands as they made their way to one of the trucks to grab some water. Caleb was already there, leaning against the truck, his baseball cap low over his face. Maggie tried to engage him in conversation while Frank stopped to talk with one of the men, but all she could get out of him were one-word mumbled responses. After a few tries, she gave up. The water was ice cold and a welcome treat to her parched throat. She hadn't realised how hard she'd been working until they'd stopped. She was grateful for the respite.

Just as Frank joined them for a drink, one of the other men called over to him. "Hey, Frank! Rob called and said there are some loose cattle on the lower east side."

"Not again!" Frank's face twisted in frustration. "This is the third time this month."

"Jim and I can finish the fence line if you want to take Caleb and Mrs. Maggie to help Rob round them up."

Maggie thought it was endearing that the man had referred to her as Mrs. Maggie. Apparently, the manners extended beyond Frank and his family and was ingrained into his crew as well. That impressed her immensely.

"Whereabouts on the lower east side?" Frank asked.

"Down by the river…" The man scratched his head, hesitating slightly before continuing. "Near Ivanhoe Crossing."

Maggie wasn't sure why the man hesitated or what the

significance of Ivanhoe Crossing was, but as soon as Frank heard the location, he stiffened. "That's okay, Mike. Why don't you let Caleb stay here and help finish the fencing?" Frank gave his grandson a squeeze on the shoulder. "I'm sure Maggie, Rob, and I can round up a few wayward cattle."

Befuddled, Maggie glanced from Frank to the man called Mike and then to Caleb who was staring down at his boots, scuffing them in the dirt. Something was going on, but she had no idea what.

Frank finished giving the men his instructions and then led Maggie back to the truck. She climbed in wordlessly as he held the door for her again. She watched as he walked around the front, climbed in, and started it with a stony expression on his face. He waved in the direction of Caleb and the men and then took off down the track. Maggie sat quietly with her hands folded in her lap as she wondered if she should ask the questions that were on her mind. She argued with herself for a good minute before curiosity finally got the better of her.

"Excuse me for asking, but what was that about?"

"Huh," he said as if she'd pulled him from deep thoughts.

She repeated the question. "Back there, what was that all about?"

He didn't reply, and his gaze remained firmly fixed on the track ahead. She didn't get it and wondered if she'd done something wrong by asking. But finally, he spoke. "You saw that, did you?"

Maggie nodded. "It was kind of hard not to."

He let out a heavy sigh. "Do you know anything about how Esther died?"

Maggie gulped. Oh dear. She'd opened a bag of worms. She hadn't meant to. Should she tell him that Olivia had told her some of the details? She didn't want him to be upset with his daughter, but she couldn't lie to him, either. "A little. Olivia mentioned there was an accident and that Caleb had been there."

They came to a wide river crossing. Frank stopped the truck on the bank and turned the engine off. They sat in silence, staring at the water for a long moment before he began to speak. His profile was sombre. "There *was* an accident, and Caleb was there, and it did take Esther's life...but there's more to it than that."

Maggie's journalistic inquisitiveness made her sit up. She was sure that what Frank was about to reveal would be heartbreaking, but maybe she didn't need to know, after all. She barely knew the man, and here he was, about to tell her how his wife died. Facing him, she touched his arm lightly. "You don't have to tell me if you don't want to."

Slowly, he turned his head and looked at her. His eyes seemed clouded with visions of the past. "It's okay. I'm happy to tell you. You knew her, after all."

That was true. And if she were honest, she would like to hear the story, but it still made her feel like she was intruding. Crossing a line.

He blew out a heavy breath and stared at the river. "It was the rainy season of 2013. The boys and I were moving cattle to higher ground and Esther had taken Caleb and his little sister to get supplies before the roads closed. They stopped on their way back to help a young family whose car was stuck in the mud. They didn't have a four-wheel drive and had foolishly tried to drive through water-soaked roads. It took Esther a bit to dig them out and winch them back onto the road. The kids had begged to be let out of the Jeep and Esther finally relented, but she made them promise not to go far. The Ord River was in view, but they were a safe distance away. Or so she thought."

He paused to inhale deeply.

Maggie felt the beginnings of tears as the story tugged at her heart.

"Esther turned her back for only moments while she waved the other family on. When she turned around, the kids were gone. She searched everywhere but couldn't find them. It wasn't until she heard Caleb screaming for help that her worst fears were confirmed. She raced to the river. The children were clinging to branches as the water raged below them. As Caleb tells it, Sasha had wanted to see the river, and being the big brother, he said he'd show her, but they had to be quick. Sasha was only four at the time and a curious sort. Caleb looked away for an instant, and that's all it took. Sasha was swept away in the current almost immediately."

Maggie closed her eyes as she felt tears building. Those poor children.

"Both children knew how to swim, but they weren't a match for the strong current. Sasha was swept downstream but managed to get caught in a tree. Caleb tried to rescue her but got swept away, too. He got caught up in debris in an eddy and broke his leg. Esther managed to reach him and carried him to safety. We always keep rope in the Jeep for emergencies, but Esther had left it behind in her haste. She waded into the raging river with nothing. No life jacket, no lifeline."

Frank's voice caught as he struggled through the rest of the story.

"She got to Sasha and started to swim back with her, but she could barely keep Sasha's head above water, let alone her own. Caleb sat on the bank of the river watching helplessly as his grandmother and sister were drowning."

He cleared his throat before continuing.

"To this day, I don't know how she managed to swim across that mighty current and get to Sasha, but she did. And she somehow managed to swim back across. She made it to the edge of the riverbank and was trying to set Sasha on the edge when a large tree trunk broke free of the debris and knocked her off her feet. In a last-ditch effort, Caleb said she threw Sasha towards him before they were both taken down river. Somehow, even with his broken leg, Caleb was able to crawl to his sister and pull her to safety."

He turned and faced her. "It was only by the grace of God that I didn't lose both my grandchildren that day too. It was hard enough to lose my Esther."

"I'm so sorry, Frank. I had no idea." An ache like she'd not felt in a long time tore through Maggie's heart. When she was a young journalist, she'd covered some horrific stories, but this one...this one. She sat in silence and bit back tears.

Both remained silent for a few moments before he said, "I'm sorry. I didn't mean to dump all that on you."

She turned her head and met his gaze. "I appreciate you trusting me with your story. It couldn't have been easy for you."

"We mostly avoid talking about it these days, for Caleb's

sake, but I think I needed to talk about it. You're a good listener."

"Are we going near where it happened?"

"The exact spot."

CHAPTER 8

It took Maggie, Frank and Rob almost two hours to round up the lost cattle, an experience that was both fun and frustrating. The young calves were adorable and playful, and not the least bit inclined to give up their freedom to be corralled into a cattle truck. Maggie had started taking pictures and capturing some of the mishaps, but when Frank asked if she could give a hand, she jumped at the chance. Through the lens of a camera, it looked easy. She soon found out that rounding up wayward cattle was a lot like herding cats —almost impossible.

But eventually, they successfully rounded up the last one and got it in the truck. Maggie was sweaty, tired, and dusty from head to toe. She was also famished. So, when Frank said it was time to head back and prepare for dinner, she was more than ready.

They sat in companionable silence as he drove them back. They hadn't talked any further about Esther's drowning, but the entire time they'd been at the spot, Maggie had been picturing the scene in her mind, and it tore at her heart. She couldn't imagine what Frank felt. No wonder he hadn't wanted Caleb to come.

Sitting quietly in the truck gave her the opportunity to reflect on her time so far at Goddard Downs. She was learning a lot about the station and the strong women who were part of its success, but she was also learning a lot about Frank, and she was also learning a lot about herself.

She wanted to be open to God's plan for her life, whatever that might be, but these unexpected feelings scared her a little. After Frank had shared with her about Esther's death, something had changed between them. She was still very aware of his presence, but there was an ease between them that hadn't been there before. Sharing something so deeply personal and heart wrenching had forged a bond between them. She didn't feel the nerves she had earlier, and there wasn't any awkwardness, either. She wasn't sure what to do about this newfound revelation, so she tucked it away in the back of her mind. For the time being, she enjoyed the ride and the wind in her hair.

When he pulled up in front of her cabin, she waited for him to open her door and help her down. This time when his hand touched hers, it didn't feel foreign. It somehow felt right. She smiled at the thought, and he looked at her quizzically.

"Penny for your thoughts?"

For some reason, she laughed. She was grateful he couldn't see inside her head. There was no way she was going to share what she'd been thinking. At least not right now. So, she simply told him she was thinking about the days' mishaps with the cattle.

He grinned and then walked with her to the cabin.

She turned when she reached the steps. "Thanks for everything, Frank. It's been such a memorable afternoon. I especially enjoyed learning how to shoot a staple gun." She flashed him a playful grin.

That statement made him laugh. "Well, it was my pleasure."

She'd wanted to thank him again for sharing about Esther. It couldn't have been easy, and it meant a lot that he'd felt comfortable enough to share something so deeply painful with her. In the short time she'd been at the station, she'd gained so much respect for the life he and Esther had built for their family and the obvious love they'd shared, but she didn't want to stir up painful memories again. Instead, she simply said, "I'd better go in and get cleaned up for dinner."

Frank nodded. "I should probably do the same. The women run a tight ship, and there's no way they'll let us within ten feet of the dinner table with this dust. I'll swing back a little before seven to pick you up."

"Oh, there's no need, Frank. I can drive myself."

"I won't hear of that. You're our guest, and I'm more than happy to escort you."

"Okay. I won't argue. Thank you." Maggie gave a smile that bordered on a grin and then headed inside the cabin, blowing out a breath. She closed the door and sank against it as a new and unexpected warmth surged through her. Could Frank be feeling some of the same things she was?

∽

As FRANK DROVE AWAY from the cabin, he had two women on

his mind. Esther, and Maggie. They were different from each other. Esther was the strong, country type, whereas Maggie was more feminine. Dainty. Yet, she'd rolled up her city girl sleeves and jumped right in, not balking or batting an eye when he'd suggested she have a go at the fencing or helping round up the calves.

Something about her made him feel at ease, which is how he ended up sharing about Esther. Normally he kept his feelings to himself. He wasn't sure what had come over him, but sharing with her felt like a release.

He didn't have to pick her up for dinner, but he wanted to. Plain and simple. In the short time he'd known Maggie Donovan, she'd managed to get under his skin. And not in a bad way, which surprised him.

∽

THIS TIME GETTING ready for dinner, Maggie took much more care with her appearance. This was her last night at Goddard Downs, and she wanted it to be a memorable one. She brushed her hair until it shone and applied her makeup carefully. She didn't want to look like she'd put in an effort, but she wanted to do a bit more than tinted moisturiser, so she added a bit of colour to her cheeks and used some lip gloss instead of Chapstick to give her lips a slightly deeper colour as well. She added a small, modest strand of pearls to accent her black wrap dress. After all the years as a politician's wife, she still remembered how to look both polished and understated at the same time.

She'd just slipped on her sandals when she heard a knock at the door. Glancing at the clock, she had to grin at Frank's punctuality. It was six forty-five on the dot. She gave herself one last glance in the mirror before dashing down the stairs to answer the door.

Her eyes widened. She hadn't been the only one to take extra care with their appearance. Frank's hair was still damp. In the times she'd seen him, he wore a wide-brimmed cowboy hat, but now he was hatless, and his hair was neatly combed. Instead of jeans and a work shirt, he was wearing a pair of khaki trousers and a royal blue polo shirt that brought out the colour in his eyes. She also caught a subtle whiff of cologne. The fact that he'd also taken time with his appearance warmed Maggie's heart. It also further confirmed that he might also be experiencing the same feelings about her that she was about him. The thought lifted her spirits and made her as giddy as a teenage girl on a first date.

"You look lovely," he said as he held out his elbow.

Maggie smiled as she took the offered arm. "Thank you. You don't look too bad yourself."

When they arrived at the main house, Frank again opened her door and held his arm out to help her down. This time, he didn't remove it once she was down and Maggie made no move to remove her arm from his. They walked up the steps arm in arm and stayed that way until he held the door for her. As she passed through, his hand touched the small of her back. The touch was gone before she'd barely registered it, but the sensation sent tingles of awareness down her spine.

The family was already seated at the table when they entered. There was a chorus of greetings, and Maggie did her best to acknowledge them all even though her attention was on Frank. He pulled her chair out for her and helped her scoot in before he took his own seat. If anyone noticed anything out of the ordinary, they didn't say. Conversation continued to flow around them.

Once Frank was seated, he said grace and they all dug in. Maggie kept sneaking glances across the table at him, only to quickly look away when their gazes met. After about the fifth time, a small giggle escaped her lips, and she quickly tried to cover her mouth to hide it. Judging by the twinkle in Frank's eye and the smirk on his face, she wagered he knew what she was laughing about. They were too engrossed in each other to notice whether anyone else at the table was watching their interaction.

As dinner wound down and the children shifted to a play area in an adjoining room, the adults lounged in their chairs and discussed the events of the day. They all had a good laugh as Frank recounted the mishaps that occurred when they were herding the stray calves. When Julian asked how the fence repairs had gone, Frank was especially complimentary of Maggie's assistance. She felt herself blush as he raved about how well she did on the fence line.

"Oh, it was nothing really. Caleb's lines were much straighter," she said, trying to deflect the attention. "He's such a hard worker."

"That he is," Frank praised, obviously proud of his grandson.

"Do you have any children, Maggie?" Julian asked.

She nodded. "Two grownup ones. A boy and a girl. Jeremy's the oldest at thirty-four, and Serena is thirty-one," she answered. "Jeremy lives in Darwin with his wife Emma and their son Sebastian. He's a bank manager and Emma is pregnant with their second child. She's due any day now. Serena's a foreign correspondent with the Northern Territory Broadcasting Commission and mainly travels in Western Europe."

"And what does your husband do?" Julian lifted a brow and pinned her with his gaze. It was years of training that allowed Maggie to maintain her outward poise. Being a politician's wife, she was used to awkward questions. There was a thump under the table as if Olivia had tried to kick her brother, but he was undeterred. His gaze remained fixed on Maggie's as he waited for her reply.

"Don't be rude, Julian." Frank's voice was steady and firm.

"It's a fair question, Dad. I'm simply asking Maggie about her family. You know, to be polite."

"It's okay," Maggie said. "My ex-husband, Cliff, is a politician."

"So, you're divorced." Julian said it more as an accusation rather than a question.

"Yes," she said simply. She wasn't sure what she'd done to offend Julian, but it was obvious by his tone and the way he sat ramrod straight in his chair with his arms folded across his chest that she had.

There was a brief pause in the conversation. She didn't know what else to say. She didn't want to go into the particulars of her divorce or mention that her ex-husband had remarried, not when that wound was still too raw. So, she simply sat there staring at her food, praying someone would say something to steer the conversation away from her.

Someone did say something, but it didn't do what she'd hoped. Instead, it focused it directly on her.

"So, besides being a reporter for The Country Life's

Women's magazine and being an avid photographer, what do you like to do for fun, Maggie?" Janella asked the question in a kind voice. Maggie didn't miss the sideways scowl she threw Julian before she turned her attention back to Maggie.

"Oh, I don't know. I'm a pretty boring individual." She gave an embarrassed laugh. She wasn't used to being the centre of attention. Cliff had expected her to be seen and not heard most of the time. She was to fade into the background and not take the spotlight from him. And as a journalist, she was the one who asked the questions, not the one being asked. Having someone genuinely interested in her and her life was unusual.

"Oh, I sincerely doubt that. We spent plenty of time together today, and I wasn't bored in the least," Frank said, winking at her.

If only the floor would open up and swallow her. If Frank was wanting to stir up his eldest son, he was succeeding. She tried to smile, but her heart wasn't in it. The atmosphere in the room had changed from jovial to almost downright hostile, at least from Julian's direction. And it was clear that everyone in the room felt it too as they made awkward attempts at lightening the mood. But the damage had been done.

A short while later, Maggie excused herself from the table, claiming to be worn out from the long day. Frank jumped up and offered her a ride back to the cabin, but she politely declined, saying she'd like to walk off the meal, though in reality, she'd eaten very little.

He followed her to the door and stopped her. "I'm sorry about what happened in there. It was uncalled for."

She shrugged. "It's fine. Really."

"It's not. I'll have words with him."

"Please don't. It's not a big deal."

He pursed his lips as if he wanted to argue. Instead, he said, "Well, let me walk you home, at least."

His offer was tempting. She was flattered by his concern and felt eager affection coming from him, but she didn't belong here. She was simply a sojourner on the road who would be leaving in the morning. She drew a deep breath and smiled. "Thanks, I appreciate the offer, but I think I'd like to walk alone. I hope you understand."

The disappointment in his eyes tore at her heart, but she remained resolute. "I'll see you in the morning before I leave."

But as she walked back to the cabin, her heart was as heavy as her footfalls.

CHAPTER 9

The next day, Maggie rose early to pack. Part of her was sad that it was her last morning at Goddard Downs, but part of her also felt relieved. Despite what she'd said to Frank, Julian's sudden coldness had hurt and she'd struggled to sleep.

She also couldn't keep thoughts of Frank off her mind. She chastised herself for the romantic notions she felt, but the pale blue eyes that had looked at her with such concern last night when he offered to walk her home had stayed with her all night, haunting her. She needed to leave.

After she threw her things together, she walked out onto the dock to take some more pictures before she left. She'd go up to the main house later, once everyone else had eaten, and grab a banana or muffin before she went on her way. After last night, she had no great desire to see everyone again this morning.

She shivered a little in the chilly morning air. A light mist had rolled in and hovered over the lagoon. It was uncommon for this area, but it was quite beautiful.

She didn't know how long she'd been on the dock snapping photos before a voice from behind startled her. She would have dropped the camera into the water if she hadn't been wearing the strap. She turned around.

It was Olivia. "I'm sorry," she said as she approached. "I called your name a couple of times, but you didn't seem to hear."

Maggie had recovered from the slight start and gave a warm smile. "Yes, I'm sorry. I often get lost in the beauty of nature and lose all sense of time."

"It's fine." Olivia smiled and held up a small picnic basket. "I noticed you didn't come up for breakfast and thought you might be hungry."

As if on cue, Maggie's stomach let out a loud rumble. She chuckled. "Ha, I guess I am."

"It's nothing much, just some muffins and jam, boiled eggs, and some fresh fruit."

"Thank you, that's very kind of you," Maggie said as she accepted the basket.

Olivia shuffled her feet. Despite not really wanting the company, Maggie couldn't bring herself to be rude. "I was about to head out, but I can stay a bit longer. Would you like to join me? Even if you've already eaten, I could make some coffee."

Olivia smiled. "I'd like that. Thank you."

The two women strolled into the cabin. Maggie began to prepare the coffee as Olivia opened the basket and spread the contents on the table. Maggie placed the mug of coffee on the table in front of her and sat down.

Olivia wrapped her hands around the mug. "I wanted to apologise for my brother."

"You don't have to apologise," Maggie said. It wasn't her fault her brother was impolite.

"Yes, I do. He was rude and purposely so, and that was inexcusable."

"I think you're making too much of it. It didn't bother me. It was just a little awkward, that's all."

"I think when Julian noticed Dad was paying you attention, it took him by surprise," Olivia said, tears suddenly welling in her eyes. "Even though it's been six years since Mum died, sometimes it feels like yesterday."

Maggie reached across the table and laid her hand on the back of Olivia's. "Losing a parent, whether it's divorce or in death, is hard."

Olivia sniffed as she gave Maggie a warm smile. "For what it's worth, I'm really glad you came. I hope Julian's actions haven't soured your visit."

"Not at all. I've loved being here and seeing the love you all have for each other. Your father is a good man. I can see that by the way he is with you and the grandchildren, and especially Caleb."

Olivia nodded. "Yes, Dad's so good with him. It's been exceptionally hard for Caleb because he blames himself for Mum's death. He feels if he'd been a better brother and kept a better eye on his sister or been a better swimmer that Mum wouldn't have died. He's suffered so much. Nightmares, depression, anger over her death. But Dad's never blamed him. Not once."

"I can't begin to imagine what it's been like for Caleb to go through that ordeal and then carry that kind of guilt through his childhood. He's lucky to have your dad in his life."

Olivia nodded. "We all are."

MAGGIE WAS TEMPTED to leave without saying goodbye to Frank, but that would have been cowardly, not to mention, discourteous. If anything had been ingrained into her, it was that manners mattered. So, despite the awkwardness, after she hugged Olivia, she drove up to the horse stables where Frank was working to say goodbye.

He, too, once again apologised for his son's behaviour. She waved it off and left with an open invitation to come back and visit any time.

It was that open-ended invitation that she contemplated now as she headed towards the next station. Although nothing had been verbalised, she sensed that a thin, delicate thread had been formed between her and Frank, and she recalled the tingle of excitement inside when he squeezed her hand before she left.

In the last eighteen months since her divorce was finalised, she'd been too focused on her own pain and the betrayal that she hadn't thought about her own healing or how to move on. But maybe it was time she started thinking about her life and moving forward, like Serena had encouraged.

She couldn't deny that she wanted to see where this 'thing' with Frank might go, but she needed to leave it with God. She needed to trust Him to lead and guide, to pave the way, because on the surface, it would be an impossible relationship. She sent up a prayer and asked for peace.

With her mind and heart lighter, she focused on her next destination.

Mt. Elizabeth Station was quite different from Goddard Downs. Not only was it three times the size at half a million acres, in addition to raising cattle, it also offered tourist attractions like camping and hiking, and it even had a bed and breakfast on site. Upon arrival, Maggie met with Emily Martin, one of the owners. Emily and her husband, Jensen, had managed the station with their three children for the past year. With his background in raising cattle and hers in tourism, it was the perfect fit.

Emily told Maggie the history of the station, which was quite fascinating. It was one of the oldest working cattle stations in the Kimberley, founded in 1945 by the Frank and Theresa Lacy family. The station was situated about halfway between Derby and Kununurra. The property boasted an array of landscapes, from the white sandy beaches of the gorges, to rivers and waterfalls, to the harsh, wild landscape of the Munja Track. Like Goddard Downs, Mt. Elizabeth also had an amazing collection of Aboriginal rock art sites. The diversity of the landscape was what made Mt. Elizabeth a popular destination for tourists.

Maggie found the history of the station interesting, but she found Emily's story more so. It was fascinating to her that Emily had come over from the UK as a real estate agent and left the commercial world behind to work, live, and raise a family in the middle of the Kimberley. The writer in Maggie could see there were parallels between her story and Clara Goddard's story. Both women hailed from the city and had left that life for a completely different one in the desolate terrain of northern Australia. They were both pioneers; Emily a modern-day one. It made for an excellent theme for Maggie's article. It didn't hurt that both women had chosen the lifestyle for love. The magazine's readers would lap up the drama and romance.

Emily was an easy-going woman, and Maggie felt comfortable in her company. They spent the next few days exploring the grounds, although this time, rather than getting out and experiencing firsthand what it was like to work on a cattle station, Maggie remained a spectator and took pictures and notes. She was sure Emily would have let her join in, had she asked, but Maggie didn't have the same desire to experience things firsthand like she'd had at Goddard Downs. There the station had been more family focused, and everyone joined in.

Although it was family owned, Mt. Elizabeth was a much bigger operation and ran like a well-oiled machine. Maggie didn't want to get in the way of their processes. Besides, she had plenty of information and pictures for her article. She would combine her firsthand knowledge and experience from the more informal Goddard Downs, and the notes and pictures from the more process-oriented Mt. Elizabeth, to give her readers both perspectives.

She'd been staying in one of the bunkhouses where the workers stayed, but on her last night there, Emily suggested she get the full tourist experience and stay in the bed and breakfast. It was yet another perspective for the article, since

Mt. Elizabeth relied on both cattle raising and tourism to keep it going.

The next day she was scheduled to drive to Rosewood Station near Lake Argyle. The fact that she would have to pass by the road that took her to Goddard Downs did not escape her thoughts as she headed off.

She capitulated for over an hour, trying to decide if she should stop by again or not. She could always get some more information and interviews for her article, but deep down, she knew the only reason for wanting to return to Goddard Downs was to see Frank. Deep in thought, she didn't see a long branch straddling the road until it was too late. When she jammed on the brakes, the Jeep dug into the dirt and skidded, but there wasn't enough time to stop before hitting it. Her heart pounded as she gripped the wheel tightly waiting for the impact.

Thankfully, the branch was dry and crumbled beneath her tyres. When she brought the car to a stop, she sat for a few minutes to settle herself and to offer a prayer of thanks to the Lord for keeping her safe.

Once calm, she climbed out to inspect the damage. All the tyres seemed to be okay. None were visibly flat, but she inspected each one and listened for any hissing noises that would indicate a puncture. She grabbed a flashlight from her safety kit and bent down in front of the Jeep to inspect the undercarriage. There was one superficial scratch on the heat shield, but nothing else that she could see. Although the extra height of the vehicle made it difficult for her to get in, she was now glad for it, since that height had probably kept the undercarriage from becoming damaged.

She did one more cursory glance around the Jeep to ensure all was in order and shifted the tree off the road as much as she able, before climbing back in and starting the engine. This was not an area she wanted to be stuck in. She hadn't seen another car for over an hour. She needed to get closer to civilisation in case something did go wrong, although she prayed nothing would. The vehicle started straight away and the engine sounded just fine. She drove the next few kilometres slowly, listening for any strange noises, but nothing came. The Jeep drove normally, and there was no pulling to one side or the other. No emergency lights came on either, so she figured she was in the clear. After about an hour, she turned the radio back on and relaxed.

Four hours later she neared the turnoff for Kununurra and Goddard Downs. In a split-second decision, she indicated right and took the turnoff for the station. Her pulse throbbed double time as she neared the outbuildings. She almost turned around. What if Frank had only said she'd be welcome any time just to be polite? They'd had no contact since the day she left, and she hadn't called ahead to let him know she was coming. She was simply turning up out of the blue. It was a stupid idea.

But maybe she could ask Frank to check the Jeep for her. The road to Rosewood Station, her next destination, was supposed to be quite rough. She could say she stopped by to see if he could take a look at the Jeep to make sure everything was okay for her to make that trip. After all, she did hit a pretty large tree branch, and even though she couldn't find anything wrong with the Jeep at the time, she wasn't an expert. During her time at Goddard Downs, she'd picked up that he was mechanically inclined. In fact, almost all the men on the stations were. They had to be because they were so remote—there weren't mechanics on every corner like there were in the city. If something broke, he, or one of the men, had to fix it.

As luck would have it, he was coming out of the main house as she approached. Her heart pounded, but the broad grin on his face told her she had nothing to worry about.

"Well, hello stranger." He greeted her warmly on the driver's side as she pulled up. "To what do I owe the pleasure? Olivia didn't say anything about you coming back so soon."

Maggie felt a little flush of guilt at not having called first but tried to ignore it. "Sorry, no. I didn't call. I probably should have."

"No, no, that's perfectly fine. No need." He waved off her concern. "You're always welcome. What brings you here?"

She swallowed hard. "I was heading to Rosewood Station, and I ran over a tree."

His face creased in a mixture of amusement and concern. "You hit a tree?" He stepped back and gave the vehicle a quick once-over before returning his attention to her.

Maggie tried to smother her laughter. "No. I didn't hit a tree. I ran over one."

He cocked one brow and waited while she explained.

"A tree had fallen across the road. I came around a curve and was going too fast to avoid it. I slowed as best I could, and then I just…" Maggie shrugged her shoulders, "drove over it."

"Well, alrighty then," he said with a laugh. "You aren't injured, are you?"

"No, I'm fine. It was an old, dead tree, and it was quite brittle." Then she quickly added, "I checked the tyres and the undercarriage to make sure nothing was damaged. There's nothing I could see, and it didn't make any funny noises on the way. But I thought I'd stop by and have you take a look just to be sure. I probably should have called first to make sure you had time. I didn't mean to interrupt your day." She was talking too fast but couldn't stop herself. It was a silly decision to have come.

"Of course you aren't interrupting. Besides, you don't want to head down the road to Rosewood if you think something might be wrong. It's desolate territory during the day and worse once the sun goes down. As it so happens, I have time. If you'll drive me over to the shop, I'll take a look at it now."

"Are you sure? I don't want you to change your plans because of me."

Frank put a hand over his heart. "I solemnly swear that you are not interrupting, or that I am changing my plans to accommodate you. Scout's honour."

He struggled to keep a straight face under her scrutiny. The corner of his mouth was twitching, and she couldn't help but laugh when his blank expression folded into an impish grin.

"Okay, okay. I give up. Thank you so much, I really appreciate it," she said.

"It's my pleasure."

With that, he hopped onto the passenger seat and gave her directions to the station's workshop, a large steel building with four oversized bays. He opened the second bay and had her pull in. One of the station's trucks was on one of the four lifts, attended to by a hand she didn't know.

Frank came around to the driver's side and held her door as

she climbed out. She was acutely conscious of his physical presence, and the very air between them seemed electrified.

"I'll give it a thorough inspection, so it might take a bit of time. You can wait here, or I can have one of the men drive you to your cabin if you'd be more comfortable there."

Maggie liked that he'd called it *her* cabin. She would have loved to spend more time there, but she wanted to be here. With Frank. She wanted to spend time with him, even if it would be underneath her Jeep. She smiled into those pale blue eyes, her heart beating a crescendo. "Thanks, I appreciate the offer, but I'd rather stay here with you." She gulped. She hadn't meant to say that. Quickly, she added, "I mean, in case you find anything, so I know what to watch for."

"Uh-huh, sounds logical." But it was clear he didn't believe her flimsy excuse. He chuckled to himself with that familiar twinkle in his eye as he turned his attention to the vehicle.

What could have probably been done in half an hour turned into a two-hour inspection from top to bottom. Though they chatted back and forth as he worked, his focus was on her Jeep. He was thorough, she had to give him that. And she appreciated that he was taking the time and care to ensure she was safe.

But she also wondered if perhaps he was dragging it out on purpose. She didn't want to speculate about his intentions, but the thought that he might be as happy to see her as she was him made her as giddy as a schoolgirl. It was a nice feeling.

Although he didn't find anything wrong with the vehicle, he replaced the fluids and changed the oil. He also thoroughly checked each tyre, including the spare. It was late afternoon when he finally declared her Jeep was in tip-top shape.

"I guess I'd better be on my way, then. Like you said, the roads are tough to navigate during the day, but more so at night." She glanced at the sun, now low in the sky. "Looks like I won't get there until after dark."

"Why don't you stay tonight? You haven't eaten since you arrived and you must be hungry. Stay in the cabin and make the journey in the morning."

She hadn't been looking forward to making that drive in the dark, and the thought of spending more time with Frank was too tempting to pass up. Besides, he was right. She was starving. While she had protein bars and jerky in the Jeep, she couldn't pass up the opportunity to eat one of Goddard Downs' home-cooked meals. She smiled and replied, "Thank you, that's very kind. I'd love to stay."

"Well, I'm glad that's decided. Let's get you settled in."

CHAPTER 10

*D*inner that night was not what Maggie had expected. The older children had opted for a pizza and movie night and were outside on the front lawn with some of the other children from the station watching a movie on a projection screen. With memories of her last meal at Goddard Downs still vivid in her mind, Maggie had been a little anxious when Frank collected her for dinner, worried that Julian wouldn't be pleased by her surprise visit. However, she had nothing to worry about since he was in town on station business. Joshua, the youngest, who said little to her the last time she was there, was in Alice Springs at a rodeo trying to qualify for Nationals.

Only five adults sat around the table. Janella, Olivia and Nathan, Frank and Maggie.

While they ate their roast dinner, Maggie sensed tension between Olivia and Nathan. It wasn't overt, just the occasional look between them, and Olivia in particular wasn't joining in on the conversation like she had on previous occasions. Janella chatted to Maggie and quizzed her about her time at Mt. Elizabeth Station, almost like she was trying to cover for Olivia. Maggie shared a little about Emily's story and asked if Janella knew her.

"No, but I've heard of her. She's got a reputation for running a tight ship."

Maggie couldn't agree more. Although she'd liked Emily and was impressed by how well run the Mt. Elizabeth station was, it lacked the warmth of Goddard Downs. Although, right now, she was starting to wonder if perhaps Janella and Olivia had presented a more glowing picture of their life on the station than it actually was.

Once dinner was over, Frank offered to walk her back to the cabin. This time, Maggie accepted the offer gladly, happy for the chance to spend more time with him after the somewhat strained dinner.

The evening was balmy, and Maggie was glad she hadn't over-dressed. The last time she'd walked back, she'd been wearing heels that kept getting stuck in between the small rocks in the gravel track. This time she was wearing ballet flats, but they made her feel tiny beside Frank.

As the lights from the house slowly faded, the stars became brighter and Maggie's heart swelled with contentment. She began quietly humming one of her favourite hymns, 'How Great Thou Art'. The only other sounds were from the crunch of the gravel and the occasional hoot of a boobook owl.

They walked in companionable silence, although Maggie wanted to ask him so many things. Since the day Frank told her the story of Esther's death, pain had squeezed her heart whenever she thought of it. It must have been such a horrid time for the family and she could barely think of it without tears welling in her eyes.

She wanted to know how he'd coped after her death. If he'd truly dealt with his grief or if he'd simply put on a stoic face and pushed on because that's what they did out here. She also wanted to know how Caleb was truly doing. Experiencing something like that could have long term emotional and psychological implications. Yes, he had loving family around him, but she'd sensed he was carrying scars that perhaps were more visible to an outsider than his immediate family. She also wondered about Sasha. Now that she was older, was she secretly carrying guilt as well, since she was the one who'd instigated the misadventure? But Maggie didn't ask. It was too personal, too intrusive, so instead, she simply said, "It's so peaceful out here."

"It is. It's the most peaceful place in all of God's creation."

She smiled to herself. "And how do you know that?" She somehow doubted Frank had travelled any further than Darwin.

"I just do. I don't need to have travelled far to know it." He turned to her and winked. "Although I have seen a few places in my time."

"Oh yes? Where have you been?"

Frank told her he'd taken Esther to New Zealand for their honeymoon, and to Fiji for their twenty-fifth anniversary. "They were wonderful places, but there's no place like home."

They reached the cabin and Maggie stifled a yawn, not because of the company, only because she was tired. Frank stood and looked at her for a long moment, something akin to longing in his eyes. Her pulse quickened, wondering if he was going to share what was on his mind, but he simply smiled and bid her goodnight, promising to be around in the morning to say a proper goodbye. She thanked him again for looking over her car and for his hospitality.

As he walked away and disappeared into the night, a twinge of disappointment settled on her heart. Maybe she'd imagined there was something between them. Or perhaps it was simply that neither knew how to cross that imaginary line separating friendship and something more.

It was a warm night, so she left the windows open when she climbed into bed a short time later. She loved the sounds of the night, the deep ribbit of frogs and the calming hoot of owls.

She'd almost fallen asleep when she heard raised voices. Curious, she slipped out of bed and went to the window. She pulled back the curtain and vaguely made out the silhouettes of two figures on the dock. The moonlight wasn't strong enough to see them clearly. However, as their voices floated up through the window, she recognised them as Nathan's and Olivia's.

At first, Maggie thought she was intruding on a romantic interlude, but it became quickly apparent that they were arguing.

"It's been six years, Olivia!"

"I know how long it's been, Nathan," Olivia said with obvious frustration in her voice. "It was MY mother who died. I miss her every day. I don't need a reminder of how long it's been since the last time I got to see her."

Maggie quickly dropped the curtain. They clearly thought they were alone, and she didn't want to intrude on a private conversation. She thought about closing the window, but it had squeaked terribly when she'd opened it earlier. She was afraid it would make a ruckus, and she didn't want them to know she'd heard them.

Quietly, she tiptoed back to bed and laid down, hoping they'd walk back to the main house. But much to her dismay, they continued arguing right outside the cabin.

"I'm sorry, that's not what I meant. I know you miss her and feel her absence every day. But my point is, when do we move on? When do we start *our* lives?"

"What do you mean, when do we start *our* lives? We got married, didn't we? We have two beautiful children that we're raising surrounded by a loving family. How is that not starting a life?"

"You're purposely twisting my words, Olivia! I mean, when do we start living out *our* dreams and not your dad's? I never thought this would be our permanent home. I understood that you needed to be with your family when your mum died, and I supported that. But I thought we'd eventually move back to the city and raise our family there, and you'd want to finish your degree."

"Of course I want to finish my degree. That's not fair. You know what it means to me, but Dad needed me here. Needed US here. You AND me."

"Needed, being the operative word, Liv. Past tense. And he may have needed you, but he never needed me. He has Julian and Joshua. I'm just his daughter's husband. A figurehead, but that's beside the point."

"You're not just a figurehead. You can take a more active

role in the station. All you have to do is say something, Nathan."

"But I don't want that. I never have. I'm a city boy, born and raised. This is *your* family's dream, not mine. Are you even listening to me?"

Maggie cringed at his tone. She'd heard it many times in her husband's voice. But where Cliff's had just been cold and accusing, Nathan's was laced with hurt and frustration.

"Of course, I am! But what do you expect me to do? Pack up and leave my dad and brothers, just like that? What do you want from me?"

"I want you to put me and the kids first…"

Maggie shut her eyes tightly and put her hands to her ears to block out their voices. She couldn't take the pain and despair that was threaded through every word. It was heartbreaking to hear the young couple's strife. To distract herself, she hummed one of her favourite tunes, 'I Can Only Imagine' by Mercy Me. The chorus always gave her strength and chills at the same time. In the worst of times, she would sing this to herself, and it would bring her hope. Knowing that one day she would walk with the Lord gave her peace and strength. She often wondered what she would do when she was surrounded by His glory. Would she dance for joy in front of him, or like the song said, would she 'in awe of You be still?'

She didn't know how many times she hummed the song, but sometime later the voices faded. She guessed Olivia and Nathan had returned to the main house. Her heart went out to them. She couldn't imagine the struggle they were going through, Nathan living a life he never wanted but trying to support his wife and her family in a difficult time, and Olivia torn between being loyal to her dad and family and to her husband. It was a difficult spot to be in for them both and Maggie didn't envy their position. Silently, she prayed to the Lord to guide them in these troubled times.

Dear Heavenly Father, I come to You in prayer, not for myself, but for Olivia and Nathan. You know each one of Your children's hearts and You know the strife on these two. I pray that through this difficult time they can lean on each other and on You. Remind them they're not alone and that together, through You, they can overcome anything.

Open their hearts and minds to Your guidance. May they share in the belief that You have a plan for them and grant them both courage and peace as they work this out together. I pray all these things in Your blessed name. Amen.

It was a long time before Maggie fell asleep. Even after praying for the young couple, her heart and mind were heavy. Try as she might, she couldn't help but think about her own marital struggles. Her only hope was that their fate would have a happier ending than hers and Cliff's.

MORNING CAME MUCH TOO SOON and it was a struggle to get out of bed. Even after two cups of coffee, Maggie couldn't stave off the exhaustion from the night before. This didn't bode well for her journey that morning, as it was still quite a long drive to Rosewood Station. She'd have to make a point of stopping every hour to get out and stretch and get the blood flowing since she needed to be alert.

When she drove up to the main house just before seven to say goodbye to Frank, Olivia was standing with him on the verandah, the two children playing nearby. She frowned as Maggie got out of her Jeep and walked towards them.

"Maggie? I...I didn't know you were still here." She stumbled with her words as she shifted her gaze between Maggie and her father.

Maggie could all but see the wheels turning in the young woman's mind. She must have been so distracted last night at dinner that it didn't register that Maggie was staying. "Yes, I was just coming up to say thanks to your dad and to say goodbye...again."

Totally unaware of the brewing situation, Frank smiled and said, "We were glad to have you. Besides, I'm always pleased when the cabin can be used."

How she wished Frank hadn't mentioned the cabin. She'd hoped she could skate on without letting Olivia know she'd been out there last night. That Olivia wouldn't find out at all, or at least, not until Maggie had already left, saving her the embarrassment. But it was too late. Frank had let the cat out of the bag, and by the looks of it, Olivia instantly realised that Maggie would have overheard her and Nathan last night.

She visibly paled, and her gaze swung to Maggie's in alarm. Maggie couldn't think of anything to say to alleviate her mortification. All she could think to do was smile apologetically, say a quick goodbye, and get into her car and leave.

As Frank walked with her to the Jeep, she made him promise to look her up if he found himself in Darwin.

"I might just do that," he said, tipping his hat as she climbed in.

As their gazes held, her heart fluttered and she hoped he might say more. He closed her door and nodded. "It was good to see you again, Maggie. Safe travels. And no more running into trees, okay?"

She chuckled and started the engine. "Okay. No more trees. I promise."

Her heart was heavy as she drove away. Maybe she'd imagined the connection between them. She must have, because Frank had given her nothing other than a smile. She turned on some worship music and focused on her next destination and determined to put Frank Goddard to the back of her mind. For now, at least.

Rosewood Station was the smallest of the stations Maggie was visiting, but it was breathtakingly beautiful. About one hundred kilometres southeast of the town of Kununurra, it was situated on the eastern side of Lake Argyle and was currently managed by Brian and Karen Douglass, but had been founded by the Kilfoyle family in the early 1880's.

Brian and Karen employed traditional methods in the raising of their cattle, using horses where possible instead of vehicles and modern-day equipment. It was a throw-back to how the property had been run when the land was first settled, and Maggie appreciated their genuine effort to adhere to the traditional ways. It also gave her a different narrative for her story.

Brian and Karen both held the view that anyone could do any of the work, regardless of gender. They raised their children, both sons and daughters, to help with all types of chores and work. The girls knew how to ride, rope a steer, and how to birth, wean, and castrate cattle. And the boys were skilled in cooking, baking and sewing. They also took their turns cleaning and scrubbing the house.

Maggie found the children's perspective on their lives and the work they did insightful. Being isolated on the station and doing their schooling via the School of the Air, their thoughts and beliefs weren't tainted by society's notions of what boys and girls should or should not do. The sons didn't think it at all weird or beneath them that they could bake a pie, as good, if not better, than their sisters. In fact, they took much pride in that. They considered it a life skill, and to them, the more life skills they had, the better off they would be.

Spending time with the Douglass family was refreshing. They were warm and kind and genuinely enjoyed each other's company and doing things together. It may have been a simpler way of life, but it was just as fulfilling. It forced Maggie to reflect on her own upbringing and think about her perceptions or notions. While married to Cliff, she had been so preoccupied with the 'idea' of what a politician's wife should have been that she forgot to look in her heart and see who she really was, or focus on what God meant for her to be, instead of on what society expected her to be. Two entirely different things.

In her travels to the stations, she'd filled three notebooks with interviews, notes, and her own journal entries. It was more than enough for her article for Suzanne. It was more than enough for several articles. In fact, she could even do a collection of pieces on station life with all the material she'd collected. Maybe she could write a book.

She didn't know where that last thought had come from. At first, she quickly dismissed it. Old criticisms reared their ugly head. Cliff had never encouraged her career. He'd put down her work and called it a hobby. One night he'd even gone so far as to say that the only reason her articles were published at all was because she was his wife. The implication that her writing was subpar, or that people were only paying lip service to her because they wanted to get in his good graces had hurt her confidence deeply.

But she wasn't that woman anymore. During the long drive back to Darwin, she thought more about it. She had plenty of material already, and she could do research on the internet, but the story that grabbed her heart the most was that of Clara Goddard.

Maybe she would write that courageous woman's story. She would at least pray on it.

CHAPTER 11

Two weeks had passed since Maggie arrived back in Darwin. She'd been holed up in her home office for most of that time, writing away. Suzanne checked in with her every couple of days to see how the writing was going and offered encouragement for her to continue. Suzanne's enthusiasm was catching.

Maggie had been a little hesitant when she'd first returned. She hadn't been able to sleep the night before she met with Suzanne to outline her ideas and broaden Suzanne's initial suggestions.

Even though Suzanne was one of her most trusted friends, she was also her boss and the chief editor of the magazine. Maggie had questioned whether or not she would appreciate her taking liberties with the assignment. However, she quickly learned she had nothing to worry about. Suzanne had been over the moon about her ideas for the initial article and even more so about the subsequent ones.

"Are you sure you're not just saying that because we're friends?" Maggie had asked, self-doubt creeping in.

Suzanne hadn't taken too kindly to that remark. "I'm offended you would even ask that," she'd said.

Maggie's immediate reaction was to apologise, but Suzanne stopped her. "I'm not Cliff. I don't expect, nor do I want, you to apologise the moment we have a disagreement."

"I'm sorry, old habits die hard." She internally chastised herself for reverting to the old Maggie.

"I get that, but I'm not kidding when I say I'm excited about your ideas. Yes, I'm your friend first and foremost, and yes, I'm also your boss. But I can be both and still be objective. And as both, I absolutely LOVE your ideas and the areas you want to cover that I hadn't even considered. I think it will be an amazingly impactful piece."

Since that conversation, Maggie had been relentless in her writing. The words just poured out of her, as if she'd been hit with a fever. She simply had to get all her thoughts down. It was an intense feeling, but also most fulfilling.

She saved writing about Goddard Downs until last. When she got to the notes and interviews with Olivia and Janella, her mind wandered to Frank. As she read over her journal entries, she was surprised at how much she'd written about him. She hadn't realised how much he'd dominated her mind, her thoughts, and her feelings. It was as if he'd awakened something inside of her. She clutched a hand to her chest as she read her entry about the first moment they'd met.

Frank Goddard is an imposing figure. Not only because of his size, but because of his presence. He fills the room and commands your attention, but he has the kindest eyes and the softest spot for his family. Nothing is more impressive than a man who adores his family.

She blew out a breath and shut the journal for a moment as she closed her eyes and replayed that moment in her mind. But before she could consider her feelings for Frank any further, feelings she knew she would eventually need to put aside, her attention was diverted by the ringing of her phone. It was Serena. Finally. She hadn't talked to her daughter in what seemed like weeks, although in reality, it was only days.

"Hi, honey," she said.

"Hi, Mum. Sorry, the connection may be spotty. I'm at the airport." Serena's voice came through, but it was choppy.

"The airport? Where are you going? A holiday with David?"

"No, not on holiday. Just off to Paris."

"Paris? Really?" A flicker of apprehension coursed through Maggie. She'd heard about the recent unrest in the city.

"Yes. Work's sending me over to cover the terrorist attacks and the political unrest over there."

Maggie's heart immediately dropped to her stomach. Normally, being sent to Paris would be a welcome assignment. She herself had been there several times as a young correspondent, but never in such dangerous times. It had been more for the women's movement and other far less chaotic and controversial events. Now, what had started as a peaceful political protest concerning the increase in fuel taxes had quickly escalated into riots. The 'Yellow Vest Movement' had spurned zealots and fanatics who had wreaked havoc and devastation across Paris and other major cities in France. It was a mother's worst fear.

With concern etched in her voice, she pleaded with Serena.

"Oh, honey, are you sure you should accept this assignment? Couldn't you cover it from London, or at least somewhere safer, like Lyon?" Although she knew the answer to her question, she secretly hoped her daughter would be swayed.

"Mum, you know as well as I do that I can't cover a story from four hours away. If I ever want to be a respected journalist like Christiane Amanpour, I've got to cover the tough stories. And I have to be right in the mix. You know that."

And it was true. Maggie knew that. What she was asking her daughter to do was impossible, not to mention, an unfair request. But it was instinctual for her to want her daughter to be as far away from danger as possible.

"I'll be fine. We're staying in a hotel away from the centre of the riots, and the station has hired private security for all of us. Besides, the rioters aren't interested in hurting the media. They want their voices heard, and I can give them that. We'll be perfectly safe."

Despite her assurances, Maggie didn't feel the least bit mollified. She knew that she would be in a constant state of worry for her daughter, but she couldn't discourage her from pursuing her passion, either. She didn't want to stand in the way of her dreams. She wanted to be that support for her that she hadn't had while she was trying to pursue her own career.

"You're right, honey. I'm sorry. I shouldn't have tried to discourage you from going. I know it's an important assignment and that covering it will help you further your career. It was a knee-jerk motherly reaction to want to protect my children. But you aren't a kid anymore and I know you'll be careful and safe. But for my sake, can you please call, text, email, or carrier pigeon me a note every day so I know you're okay?" She meant the last part to come off as more of a joke, but deep down, she really did hope her daughter would check in with her as often as possible.

A loud, muffled noise sounded in the background, covering most of Serena's following words. Maggie couldn't make out any of it. "What did you say, honey? There was background noise, and I didn't get that."

"Sorry, Mum. My flight's being called for boarding. I've got to go," Serena said in a rush.

"Okay, honey. Please call when you can or at least have the station check in with me regularly."

"I will, Mum. I really have to go. I love you."

"I love you, too," she said, but Serena had already disconnected.

Maggie sat there for a moment, trying to calm her racing heart and reassure herself. It wasn't like Serena was being sent to some war-torn country like Bosnia, Iraq or Syria. But it did little to alleviate her fears. It was still less safe for a woman to be out in the streets covering major controversial issues like these than her male counterparts. Maggie hated to think that way, but her thoughts drifted to the few horror stories that had plagued the news recently of newswomen and anchor-women being attacked and harassed on live TV. She didn't want that for her daughter. But she had to have faith that her daughter would make good and responsible decisions and that the NABC and her fellow crew members would also look out for her.

On a whim, she closed her computer and drove to her church. Although she knew God would hear her prayers from wherever she happened to be when she prayed, she felt the need to be in church, to be in God's house where peace might be found for her troubled mind.

It was nine p.m. when she arrived and the church appeared deserted. It was a Thursday evening, and there were no other cars in the car park, but that didn't mean no one was inside. Located in the heart of Darwin, the church was within walking distance of several of the more popular neighbourhoods and was open twenty-four hours a day for anyone who wanted to pray. When Maggie walked in quietly, only one other person was in the sanctuary, a woman, and she sat upfront with her head bowed. She didn't stir when Maggie settled herself in a pew at the back.

It had been a while since she'd attended church on a regular basis. After her divorce, although she hadn't lost her faith, memories of attending religiously every Sunday with Cliff left a bitter taste in her mouth. He hadn't attended because he was a devoted believer. It looked good to his constituents if he and his wife were seen there together. Half the time, he was busy on his phone during the entire sermon and barely listened. He would stay around after the service to get 'facetime' with the pastor and be the upstanding citizen his constituents believed him to be. But like his devotion to his wife and family, his devotion to Christ had also been questionable. She'd changed churches after her divorce to avoid facing all the memories each time she attended.

But she didn't want to dwell on that. She didn't want to come into church with anger in her heart. Right now, she wanted to focus on her daughter's safety. She closed her eyes and bowed her head, settling her spirit and heart before she prayed.

Dear Heavenly Father, I come to You in prayer, asking You to watch over Serena and her colleagues as they travel to Paris.

I feel anxious about her going. Please help me to trust that You'll watch over her. But Lord, more than that, I pray that she might know Your presence in her life. She's strayed from You, Lord, but I know You love her and that it grieves Your heart to have her living her life without You as Lord and Saviour. Do a work in her heart, Father, even as she's in the midst of danger.

I pray all these things in Your Son's precious name. Amen.

As she raised her head and opened her eyes, she saw that she was alone. The other woman must have left sometime during her prayer. Now, the chapel was eerily quiet yet peacefully calm. Maggie rose to leave but then sat back down and bowed her head again. There was more on her heart than her daughter.

Lord, I feel I'm at a crossroads in my life and I don't know where I'm going. I don't want to be stuck in the past any longer, hampered by bitterness and regret. I want to move forward, but I feel restless. I want to move on. I want to live. She paused. *And if I'm honest, I want to love again. Or perhaps, I simply want to believe in love again.*

But more importantly, I want to live my life for You. For so long I allowed Cliff to control my thoughts and actions, but now I'm free to follow You. To love You. Teach me Your ways, dear Lord. Show me what You have for me. If that involves Frank, I'd be ecstatic, although the thought of starting over makes me anxious.

Lord, I give You my heart. My life. Lead and guide me, I pray. Help me draw closer to You and learn to trust You with every aspect of my life. In Jesus' precious name. Amen.

As warmth, like that of a hand resting on her shoulder,

spread through her, she turned around, but no one was there. Her heart filled with peace and assurance that she was not alone, and there was no doubt in her mind that God was with her, leading and guiding her.

Whether you turn to the right or to the left, your ears will hear a voice behind you, saying, 'This is the way; walk in it.'

She smiled and nodded her affirmation. "I will, Lord. I will."

CHAPTER 12

Life on the cattle station didn't change much day to day, season to season. There were always crops to grow or harvest, cattle to be weaned or culled, horses to be broken, fences to be mended. Life went on much the same as before Maggie had visited, or at least Frank tried to tell himself that as his thoughts continued to wander to the interesting woman who had wormed her way into his life.

It had been more than three weeks since Maggie Donovan left Goddard Downs to return to her life in Darwin, but by the way he was missing her, he would have thought it was yesterday. He'd found her creeping into his thoughts now more than ever. He'd rewrapped this bale of hay at least twice already and would have to do it a third time if he didn't start paying attention to the task at hand.

"Something on your mind, Dad?"

Frank looked up to find Julian eying him with curiosity.

Julian tipped his head towards the hay bale and looked back

at him with his brows raised. "That's the third bale of hay you've had to rewrap at least twice. What gives?"

Maggie is what gives, Frank thought, but he wasn't prepared to admit to his son that he couldn't get her off his mind. He wasn't ready to share his thoughts about her to anyone just yet. And his eldest son wasn't ready to hear it, anyway, of that he was sure. Not after the way he'd acted towards Maggie at dinner that night.

Julian's tartness towards Maggie had surprised him at first, but in hindsight, Frank realised he shouldn't have been. Although it had been six years since he'd lost Esther, he'd shown no interest in other women nor given even the smallest indication that he might want to move on and find someone else. Truth be told, he really hadn't given it much thought. As time had passed and the pain of losing his beloved had eased, he'd simply continued on with station life. Until he met Maggie. Ever since he'd set eyes on her, he'd been entertaining the notion of moving on a lot more.

He hadn't been against the idea of starting anew with someone else. It was more that the opportunity hadn't presented itself. Since he spent the majority of his time on the station, the only females he met were either related to him or were of the bovine variety. So, he'd never given it much thought. But now, he was thinking about it, or rather *her*, almost every day.

"Earth to Dad. Hellooo…" Julian's voice cut through Frank's thoughts, and he realised his son was now openly staring at him.

"Sorry, son. Got a little lost in my thoughts."

"You aren't still worried about the meeting with the officer from the DPI, are you?"

Although Frank hadn't been thinking about the meeting with the Department of Primary Industries' rep right then, the changes to the live cattle export rules and regulations were never far from his mind and often kept him awake at night.

When he didn't correct Julian's assumption, Julian continued, "I told you we'd be fine. We're in compliance with all but one of the changes, and we should be able to get an exemption for this year and be grandfathered in. Are you sure you don't want me to come with you? I'm well-versed in all the requirements."

"Yes, I know you are, son. And I greatly appreciate all the research you've done for me and for the station. It will definitely come in handy when I talk to the officer, but I have this one. Besides, I need you to handle things for the upcoming auction while I'm gone. Especially since Joshua isn't back yet."

"You know the others can handle the auction if you need them to," Julian argued. "Besides, you hate leaving the station for more than a day or two. What's up? Is there something you aren't telling me about this meeting?"

Under normal circumstances, Frank would have completely agreed with Julian. However, having noticed some underlying tension between Olivia and Nathan of late, he didn't think it was the best idea to let them handle everything right now. He couldn't put his finger on it, but he sensed something was up between the two of them, but any time he tried to broach the subject with Olivia, she was quick to change the topic and skirt the issue.

He could try talking to Nathan, but he'd never been very

close with his only daughter's husband, no matter how hard he'd tried to connect with him. Nathan did anything that was asked of him, but had never quite warmed to Frank, and Frank always felt a little bit at arm's length with the young man. He'd never pushed the issue, but now he was second-guessing as he tried to establish a closer relationship with him.

It was also true that Frank hadn't much cared to travel far from the station these last few years. He much preferred the quiet of the country to the hustle and bustle of the city. And he loathed all the formalities the government had started to incorporate into cattle raising and exporting. If it had been up to him, people would have been allowed to farm and raise cattle without all this red-tape and bureaucracy. However, it wasn't up to him, and he had to comply with the regulations. Which was why he had a meeting scheduled with the DPI officer in Darwin in a few days' time.

Normally, he left those kinds of things to Julian, but Frank saw this trip as an opportunity to visit Maggie, although he'd also visit his sister and her family while in Darwin. Visiting Bethany and Graham would help to justify the few extra days he was planning on staying.

"I'm not doubting their ability to handle things," he said, pausing to lift his hat and wipe his brow. "On the contrary, I think they're all more than capable. However, I thought that since I'll be in Darwin, I'll spend an extra day or two and visit with your Aunt Bethany."

"And stop by and see Maggie?" Julian raised a brow.

Frank stiffened momentarily and then turned his gaze to his son. Instead of the animosity or disappointment he expected to see, all Frank saw was a big sheepish grin on

Julian's face.

"Uh...well, the thought had crossed my mind," he admitted slowly.

"It's okay, Dad, really," Julian said. "I know I handled things poorly at dinner that night when she was here and I'm truly sorry for that." He ran a hand through his thick dark hair. "I was caught off guard to see you interested in anyone...you know, since Mum died. But the next time I see Maggie, I promise I'll apologise to her. It was uncalled for."

"I'm sure she'd appreciate that, as do I. However, I think we both understood how you were feeling. Although there's nothing between us, then or now. She was just a nice lady who happened to grab my attention for a moment."

"Are you sure about that, Dad?" Julian's eyes narrowed.

Frank let out a small chuckle. "Maybe not."

"It's okay, Dad. We want you to be happy. It might take us a while to adjust to the idea of you being with someone else, but we will."

Frank walked over and laid a hand on his son's shoulder. "Thanks, son. That means so much. If anyone would have told me a month ago that I could entertain the thought of being interested in a woman again, I would have laughed them off as crazy. I don't know what God has in store for me. It may be nothing, but I think I at least want to see where this might go."

Julian nodded. "She seems like a nice woman, Dad. You have my blessing." Then he let out a little chuckle and added, "You have Olivia and Janella's already. They've been talking about you and Maggie non-stop for the last few weeks."

"Have they just?" Chuckling, Frank leaned against the shed wall, out of the direct rays of the sun. "Glad to know the women have been gossiping about me. And what about Josh? What will he think?"

Julian's eyes narrowed again. "I don't honestly know, Dad. He's been distant, almost angry, of late. I think he's going through his own struggles right now. I don't know that he'll have an opinion one way or the other. But I can help him get around to the idea if you need me to."

"I appreciate that, son. But I think I'll have a chat with him myself about it when he gets back. Hopefully, he'll be home by the time I return from Darwin."

"Okay. Make sure you let me know how the meeting goes." He paused and grinned. "I mean, the meeting with the DPI officer, not Maggie."

Frank clapped his son on the back good-naturedly. "How about I tell you about both?"

TWO DAYS LATER, Frank set out for Darwin at the crack of dawn, just as the sky was starting to lighten. He planned to do the thousand-kilometre trip in one day, much to the chagrin of Olivia and Julian who tried to convince him it was folly for him to drive that far on his own in one day at his age. He'd brushed them off. He might be in his sixties, but he was quite capable of driving that distance. He'd gone on all day and night cattle rides, so he could easily handle the country roads in his four by four. His children didn't have much argument after that and let him be, although Olivia did make him promise to call as soon as he arrived.

He chuckled to himself as he pulled onto the main road. His kids meant well and loved him dearly, and he them. And maybe they did worry about him a little more since their mother died in such a freak accident. He couldn't blame them. He worried about them just as much as they worried about him.

With a twelve-hour drive ahead of him, Frank had time on his hands. As the miles slipped by and red dust clouded the air behind his truck, his mind wandered. It was true what he'd said to Julian the other day. He would have thought someone crazy if they'd told him that one day soon he'd meet a lady who captured his mind, and his heart, almost as much as his Esther had when they'd first met over forty years ago.

He'd been in his twelfth and final year of school and had been horsing around with his buddies after class the day he met her. His best friend, Jim, had a car and he'd driven Frank and two other friends to the square in downtown Darwin where most of the boarding school kids hung out after school. Normally Frank had to work, but he'd been given an unexpected afternoon off when the hardware store he worked at had developed a plumbing leak, and Old Man Rivers had to shut it down for the day to clean up the mess.

Esther had been with a group of girls strolling through the mall, stopping every now and then to look in the shop windows. She was dressed simply in her school uniform, but he remembered the bright yellow ribbon in her hair, which had fluttered in the breeze and come loose and landed at his feet. He'd grabbed it before the wind carried it away and walked it back to her.

She'd smiled at him, her soft brown eyes warm and friendly, and he'd lost his heart even before she spoke. She had the voice of an angel. Her tone was soft and gentle. She'd thanked him kindly for catching her ribbon, but he'd been too dumbstruck to say much of anything. Just stood there with the ribbon in his hands and his mouth hanging open like a fool. Frank chuckled at the memory.

But instead of giggling or making fun of him like his friends had, she'd simply smiled and asked his name and if he was from around there. He'd finally gotten his wits about him and answered her question. Then he remembered, he still held her ribbon, so he gave it to her. Their hands had touched for only the briefest of moments, but electricity shot straight to his heart. They'd been almost inseparable from that moment on. Until that fateful day.

They'd shared thirty-five years of marriage and had three wonderful children together and four beautiful grandchildren, two that Esther had never met. The good Lord had been kind to him and blessed him with a beautiful family and a beautiful life, although he'd be lying if he said his faith hadn't been tested when He'd taken Esther home to be with Him that day. Many a night Frank recalled railing at the Lord for taking her too soon. But, eventually, the Lord had calmed his spirit and healed the wounds of his heart.

It was his heart that he thought about now as he continued his drive. Even after his wounds had healed, it had never occurred to him that he might find someone else he could love. He certainly hadn't thought about looking, not that the opportunity ever presented itself on the station. But even if he'd had the opportunity, he wasn't sure he would have entertained the idea. For so long, he'd believed it was meant to be just him and Esther, and he'd thought he could live happily enough on the station watching his family grow. That had been enough for him…until he met Maggie.

There'd been something about her that had captured his attention from the moment he'd met her. It wasn't quite the same tingling sensation of his youth when he'd first met Esther, but there'd been something. An awareness, like a kinship that had been there all along, just waiting to be discovered.

He found it both odd and coincidental that Maggie had gone to school with Esther. Try as he might, he couldn't remember ever having met or even seeing Maggie back then. Of course, it made sense because he'd only had eyes for Esther. Back then, he'd been smitten with her and hadn't paid attention to anyone else. But now, Maggie had his full attention, although he wasn't sure how to feel about that.

Excited, but perhaps also cautious. Maybe even scared, if he were honest. He'd only ever truly loved one woman, and the idea of opening himself up to love another was daunting. It was in times like these, when he felt the most lost or unsure, that Frank turned to prayer. This time was no different. While he drove, he kept his eyes fixed on the road, but his thoughts were directed to the Lord.

Heavenly Father, I come to You with a concerned heart. I'm truly thankful for the time You gave me with Esther. You know how much I loved her, and the grief I felt after I lost her, when I felt I couldn't go on. But You were there, holding me, carrying me. You've healed the wounds of my heart, although not a day goes by that I don't miss her. But Lord, I've found someone else who's captured my heart in a similar manner, but I'm afraid. Afraid to trust my heart again. Afraid to allow these thoughts and feelings to grow.

Lord, give me guidance as I struggle with them. And if it's Your will, Lord, that these new feelings develop into something more, I ask that You grant me an open heart and an open mind to follow the path You've set for me.

I pray all these things in Your Son's precious name. Amen.

CHAPTER 13

Frank made good time and arrived in Darwin just after four. It had been several years since he'd been to the northern capital, and he was surprised by how modern it had become. He was staying at the Hotel Tropicana on the waterfront, and when he pulled into the entrance, he couldn't believe it was the same place he'd stayed at last time he'd been in town. He vaguely remembered newspaper articles mentioning a billion-dollar project to revitalise the Stokes Hill Wharf area, including the Hotel Tropicana, but he could barely believe his eyes. Instead of an older style hotel with brown brick and old-fashioned arches, in its place stood a building with marble tiles, huge expanses of glass that made it look and feel spacious, and it had a tropical rainforest in the entry.

Back when he was a kid, the wharf was a popular place to explore, but as he'd driven through, he'd noticed the changes. Gone were the fish shacks and shanties and small mum and dad restaurants that had bordered the pier. Now, in their place was a huge convention centre that played host to concerts, plays, and numerous other entertainment acts. Grand hotels, including the Hotel Tropicana, dotted the waterfront and there were not one, but a host of five-star restaurants and shopping areas as well. It was quite a departure from the quiet simple life he lived in Goddard Downs.

He checked into his suite without much ado, although his mouth dropped at the size of his room. He hadn't given it much thought when the concierge at the front desk had told him they'd upgraded him to a suite free of charge. He figured that meant he had a little pull-out couch in the room, but this was something straight out of one of those fancy magazines.

The sitting area was as big as his bedroom back home. An elegant rattan sofa with large, colourful cushions faced a wall-mounted flat screen television and looked like an inviting spot to rest his weary body. And there were not one, but two bedrooms to choose from, both with queen sized beds and bathrooms and balconies with views over the harbour. It was a bit extravagant for his tastes, but he wasn't one to look a gift horse in the mouth. He made a mental note to thank Henry, the concierge, for his thoughtful gesture after he freshened up.

He felt better after a shower, but he was a little restless so he decided to take a stroll along the boardwalk alongside the waterfront before dinner. Stopping by the front desk, he thanked Henry for the upgrade and also asked him for recommendations for dinner.

"Are you planning on dining alone, or with somebody?" Henry asked.

Frank was about to answer 'alone' when he thought of Maggie. It was short notice, especially when he hadn't even told her he was in town, but perhaps, just perhaps, she'd join him for dinner. The thought made his heart beat erratically. He drew in a slow breath and asked for recommendations for two. Just in case.

"Seafood on Cullen is the most well-known restaurant in town. The food is excellent but it can get noisy. If you're looking for somewhere quieter, I'd recommend Pearls, but I suggest making a reservation as soon as possible."

"Thanks, Henry. Pearls sounds great."

"Shall I make a reservation?"

Frank hesitated. He didn't want to be presumptuous, but he didn't want to miss the opportunity either. Taking a chance, he said, "Yes, please. Make it for seven o'clock."

The concierge made the necessary arrangements and Frank left the hotel lobby to call Maggie. His hand shook as he pulled up her number in his contacts list. He was as giddy as a schoolboy and just as nervous as one, too. It had been many years since he'd asked a woman on a date.

His heart pounded as he listened to the phone ring. Part of him wished it would go to voicemail, but after four rings, she answered. Her voice was just as he remembered...soft, friendly. He relaxed straight away.

"Hi, Maggie. It's Frank. Frank Goddard."

"Frank!" She sounded surprised, but not in a bad way. At least he didn't think so. "It's so nice to hear from you. How are things at Goddard Downs? I hope everything is okay."

"Yes, yes, everything is fine here. I mean there."

"There?"

"I'm not at Goddard Downs right now. I'm...I'm in Darwin."

"Darwin?"

"Yes. On business."

"Oh." He wasn't sure, but he thought she sounded disappointed.

"I know this is short notice, but I was wondering if you'd like to have dinner with me tonight?"

Silence. Had he misread the signs? His heart thumped so loudly he was sure she could hear it. "If...if you have other plans, it's okay..."

"No, Frank. No other plans. I'd love to have dinner with you."

"You would?"

"Yes, I would."

He blew out a relieved breath. "That's wonderful. I can pick you up, unless you'd rather meet me at Stokes Hill Wharf."

"I have a few errands to run first. Why don't I meet you at the wharf at six-thirty?"

"Sounds perfect. I'll be wearing my cowboy hat so you shouldn't miss me."

She chuckled. "Great. I'll look forward to seeing you then."

FRANK WALKED the entire length of the wharf twice to get rid of some of his pent-up energy before heading back to the hotel to get ready. He was thrilled that Maggie had said yes to dinner. It had been a long time since he'd been truly excited about something, and he was definitely excited about dining with her.

Wanting to look his best, he dressed with great care, and at six, he headed downstairs to the hotel gift shop to buy a small bouquet of flowers. He looked at the roses, but not wanting to be too cliché, he decided against them. He was about to give up on the idea when a bunch of wildflowers in the back of the case caught his eye. The clerk looked at him as if he were crazy when he asked for them. The young woman told him they were filler flowers for other bouquets and not really a bouquet on their own, but he thought they were perfect. After some cajoling, she agreed to wrap them for him.

He made it to the wharf about ten minutes early, but thankfully he didn't have long to wait. Maggie arrived within a few minutes and waved as she approached. She was wearing a floral print wrap dress with a pearl necklace and matching drop earrings. She was as pretty as a picture and he felt an unfamiliar stirring in the pit of his stomach as their gazes met.

He smiled and kissed her on the cheek. He wasn't sure he should have done that, but it seemed the right thing to do. "It's good to see you, Maggie." He handed her the flowers. "For you."

Her face lit up. "Why, Frank, you shouldn't have. But they're gorgeous. Thank you."

"You're more than welcome." He cleared his throat. "I hope you like seafood. I made a reservation for us at Pearls."

Her brows lifted. "I'm impressed. That restaurant is usually booked up several weeks in advance. And yes, I love seafood."

Frank would have to thank Henry again it would seem. The man must have pulled some strings to get a same day reservation.

"Shall we?" Frank asked as he offered his arm.

Nodding, Maggie smiled and hooked her arm through his before they strolled down the wharf to the restaurant.

Henry had been right about the ambiance. Pearls was a

classy restaurant but not overly stuffy. Some diners were dressed in formal attire, while others were more casual. In their smart clothes, Frank and Maggie fit right in.

The maître d' greeted them kindly and escorted them to a table for two tucked in the corner. It was private enough to hold a conversation without having to shout over the din of the other tables, but not so private that it was uncomfortable. The maître d' handed Frank the wine list and then proceeded to provide the specials for the evening.

Frank opted for the trio of oysters for an appetiser, and Maggie chose the seafood chowder. She passed on the wine, stating she rarely drank alcohol and would prefer a lemon and lime soda. He ordered two. He asked Maggie what she would like for a main course and was pleased when she suggested they share the seafood platter for two. That way, they could sample all the different types of seafood. He liked that she wasn't afraid to voice her opinion or show her appetite. He'd never understood women who deferred everything to their partner or who only nibbled their food, almost as if it were impolite or wrong to enjoy eating. Esther had been a healthy woman and was unafraid to state her opinions. It was one of the things he'd loved most about her.

As they sipped their drinks, conversation flowed easily between them. It was as if they'd been old friends for a long time and could seamlessly pick up where they'd left off.

Frank leaned back in his seat but kept his gaze fixed on her. "Did you always want to be a journalist?"

Maggie nodded. "Yes. Current affairs fascinated me and I loved hearing people's stories. I was editor of our school magazine for most of my high school years." She shrugged. "It seemed like a natural progression."

"I always knew that once I finished school I'd go back to the station," he said.

"So how did you manage to see Esther?" Maggie angled her head, her eyes twinkling with curiosity as she swirled the straw around her glass.

He chuckled. "I drove all the way into town every other weekend to see her. Twelve hours there, twelve hours back. It was such a long way, but I was young and in love." He chuckled again at the memory. "During the middle of her senior year I proposed, and three weeks after she graduated, we were married. Her parents had been hesitant about us marrying so young, but I convinced them I was serious about their daughter and would provide a good and proper home for her on the station. We settled into life at Goddard Downs with the eagerness of two young, bright-eyed newlyweds."

He sensed Maggie wanted to know more, but the waiter arrived with their platter, interrupting the flow. As much as he loved reminiscing, he didn't want to spend his time with Maggie talking about Esther, so he returned his attention to the woman sitting opposite him. Maggie...

CHAPTER 14

The seafood platter was almost large enough to feed an army, and Maggie and Frank didn't come close to finishing it. When asked if they'd like dessert, he deferred to her, who emphatically declined.

"I think I'll explode if I eat another thing. Thank you. It was lovely."

"You heard the lady," Frank told the waiter with a chuckle. "We can't have her exploding."

The waiter smiled politely and went to get the bill. As he did, Maggie fretted about whether she should offer to pay half. When Frank called, she'd been so delighted and surprised to hear from him, she'd jumped at his dinner invitation and assumed it was a date. Frank seemed to be treating it as if it were, but what if she were wrong and he'd only asked her as a friend? In that case, she ought to offer to pay her share. But if she did, would he be offended? He was probably old school and would be expecting to pay.

Frank must have read her mind because his forehead creased. "What are you fretting over, Maggie?"

When she didn't answer immediately, he raised a brow. "I can see the wheels turning in that mind of yours. What is it? Did I do something wrong?"

"Oh, no, no. It's not you." She quickly rushed to assure him, because the last thing she wanted was for him to think she wasn't having a good time. In fact, she'd been having a wonderful evening and didn't want it to end. But could she tell him what was on her mind? Would he think her silly?

"Then, what it is it?"

She blew out a breath. "Okay, but you're going to think I'm silly."

"Never." His pale blue eyes held not one hint of amusement, just one hundred precent sincerity, easing her mind greatly.

"Well, I was sitting here trying to figure out if I should offer to pay half the bill."

An amused grin spread across his face.

"See, I said you'd think it was silly."

He shook his head and chuckled. "It's not silly at all. I'm sure out of touch with date etiquette, and I'm guessing you might be, too."

She swallowed hard. He said date. She hadn't gotten it wrong. Relief flowed through her, followed quickly by joy. They were on a date. So carried away by her response, she didn't see the waiter approach until he was standing beside them. He discreetly placed the bill folder on the table in front of Frank before asking if there was anything else he could do for them.

Frank reached into his wallet and produced a handful of

notes. He tucked them into the bill folder and handed it to the waiter. "No, that will be all. It was a wonderful meal. Thank you."

The waiter nodded graciously. "It was my pleasure. Please come and see us again."

When the waiter left, Frank faced Maggie and grinned sheepishly. "I hope you don't mind that I took care of that."

She laughed. "No. Thank you, Frank." She grew serious. "Thank you for being so kind and thoughtful. And understanding." She meant every word.

Their gazes held for a moment and the very air around them seemed electrified.

"I'm not sure what to say to that."

She smiled and then shrugged. "You don't need to say anything."

"Well then, how does a stroll sound?"

"It sounds lovely."

Frank stood and helped her out of her chair and then offered his arm. As she tucked her hand into the crook of his elbow, she felt blissfully happy.

A light breeze picked up as they strolled along the pier. Maggie was wearing a shawl, but she still shivered.

"Here," Frank said as he shrugged out of his jacket. "You must be feeling a bit chilly."

"Thank you," she said as he helped her into it. The jacket dwarfed her and she couldn't help but laugh at the spectacle she must look. Her hands didn't even come close to reaching the ends of the sleeves.

Laughing with her, Frank rolled up the sleeves so at least the tips of her fingers were free. A thrill of awareness flowed through her as his hands grazed the inside of her wrists while he cuffed them. It had been a long time since she'd felt that familiar tingle. Long before her marriage was officially over.

The coat was still warm from Frank's body heat and Maggie could smell the faintest hint of aftershave. It wasn't overpowering like some could be, just a very soft woodsy scent. It suited him.

They walked together in silence for a few minutes, simply enjoying the night air. Above them, the sky had turned from light blue to black, and a few stars had popped out. It was a pleasant walk, unhurried, and with no pressure. Frank was easy to be with, and Maggie didn't feel like she had to be 'on' around him. She could truly be herself, and that revelation was freeing.

They came to the end of the pier and Frank suggested they sit on one of the benches. She chose one nestled against a fish shanty so they could be out of the wind.

"So, tell me about your children. If I remember correctly, you have two," Frank said.

"Yes, that's correct. A son and a daughter. Jeremy is the eldest. He lives here in Darwin and is married to a lovely young woman named Emma. They have a son who's two and a half, and they have another child on the way. A little girl this time."

"And your daughter? Does she live in Darwin as well?"

"Sort of."

At Frank's quizzical expression, she explained further. "Serena shares an apartment with her boyfriend—when she's home."

He angled his head. "When she's home?"

"She splits her time between London and Darwin at the moment."

"Wow, that's quite a distance."

Maggie smiled. "Yes, it is. She's a television journalist for the Northern Australia Broadcasting Commission. She's their Western Europe correspondent which is why she's based in London."

"You must be proud of her."

"I am. Nothing surprised me more than when she told me she wanted to follow in my journalistic footsteps. However, it wasn't always that way." Maggie smiled as a memory flashed into her mind of Serena as a little girl with a plastic play microphone. "When she was little, she wanted to be a singer, but poor girl, she couldn't carry a tune to save her life."

"Kids say the darndest things, don't they? When Joshua was four, he swore he was going to be the first man on the moon. I didn't have the heart to tell him it had already been done. Later, when he found out about Neil Armstrong, he was crushed."

"Sometimes I wish Serena had been able to sing. It would definitely have been safer."

"Safer?"

"She's in Paris right now," Maggie said by way of explanation, but she could see that Frank still wasn't making the connection. She guessed it was difficult to keep up with current affairs being so remote. "She's covering the Yellow Vest Movement and the riots."

"Ahh," he said. "You're worried about her."

Maggie nodded. "Very much so."

"That's only natural. I worry about Joshua constantly."

Maggie's forehead creased. "Really? Are you afraid he'll get hurt in the rodeo?"

"There is that, but it's more his unquenchable thirst for adventure that worries me." Frank pulled at his beard as if in deep thought. "His nature is to be wild and reckless, and he pushes the limits, putting himself in harm's way. It's a complete disregard for his safety that worries me the most."

Maggie knew a little of what that felt like. Serena wouldn't, or couldn't, acknowledge the danger her job put her in. She was always so confident that nothing would go wrong, but Maggie knew better. She'd lived long enough to know that things didn't always go as planned, and that at the drop of a hat, your life could be flipped upside down. She guessed Frank knew that as well, having lost Esther in the blink of an eye.

"I can see how much this worries you. I'll add your Serena to my prayers," Frank said.

Maggie's heart warmed at the kind gesture. "And I'll do the same for your Joshua. One can never have enough prayer."

"Amen to that."

They sat quietly for a moment, enjoying each other's company, until Frank broke the silence. "Maggie, will you tell me about your ex-husband?" His tone wasn't demanding in any way. More caring than anything.

She'd been expecting that question sooner or later but had secretly been hoping it would be later. She couldn't avoid the subject forever, especially if she wanted their relationship to develop. "Sure. What would you like to know?"

He shrugged. "How long were you married?"

"Thirty-four years."

"That's a long time."

She nodded. "Yes, it is…or it was. I thought we'd have forever." She wasn't sure what made her admit that. She hadn't planned to and didn't think it was something that Frank would want to hear, but the brutal honesty didn't seem to bother him.

"I imagine you did. I don't think anyone gets married expecting it to end before its time."

"True, but it wasn't my choice. And I didn't get a say in the matter." Maggie clenched her hands in frustration as old wounds opened and insecurities and pain reared their ugly head. "I felt so, so stupid and blind."

"You don't have to talk about it if you don't want to." Frank took her hand. "But I want you to know that I'm here for you, if you need someone to listen. Just like you did for me."

She smiled and soon found herself opening her heart to Frank like she'd never done with anyone before, not even with her kids. She'd tried so hard to remain impartial about their father, never wanting to be that woman who painted the ex-husband as a terrible person and tried to ruin his relationship with his children. Although, he'd pretty much done that on his own.

Frank was amazing. He sat quietly, holding her hand as she vented the last eighteen months of pent up frustration. He even wiped her tears as she became overcome with emotion. He didn't say a word, or try to make excuses for Cliff like so many others had. He simply listened. No judgment, no unwanted advice. It was exactly what Maggie needed.

When the last word had been spoken, the last tear spent, instead of feeling embarrassed at spilling all her anger and resentment to a man she barely knew, Maggie felt new. Not quite whole, but clean. Like the ugly film of the last year had washed away.

"Better?" Frank asked softly as he gazed into her eyes.

"Yes, actually I am." And she genuinely meant it. "Thank you, truly."

His smile was so warm and tender she wished he'd wrap his arms around her and hug her. Instead, he simply replied, "You're more than welcome."

Nothing more needed to be said on the matter. They both now knew about their previous spouses. The air was clear between them.

Maggie glanced around the pier which was now practically deserted. She had no idea how long they'd been sitting on the bench, but the moon had come out and it shone a brilliant light across the calm water. The breeze had also dropped, and all of a sudden she felt warm. Hot, even. She sat forward and shrugged out of Frank's jacket. He took it from her and then folded it over his arm.

"It's late," she said. "We should probably get back." Although she made the suggestion, she could easily have sat there all night with Frank.

"You're right. It's been a long day and I've got another one tomorrow. I'll walk you to your car."

"Thank you." After they stood, it felt completely natural for her to slip her hand into his as they walked back to the car park near the restaurant. Theirs were the only two cars left, as the restaurant had closed and the workers had all gone home.

At her car, Maggie paused before getting in. "I had a lovely time tonight, Frank. Dinner was amazing and I really appreciated your company."

His eyes twinkled as he took her hands in his. "I had a lovely time, too. Thank you for coming."

She didn't want the evening to end, especially when they didn't have much time before he'd be leaving to go home. To Goddard Downs. Twelve hours' drive away.

His thoughts must have been mirroring hers because he asked what she was doing over the weekend. "I have meetings tomorrow and Friday, but I'd love to see you again before I head home on Monday."

She sighed. "I'd love to spend the whole weekend with you, but Saturday's already booked up. We could meet on Sunday and go to the Mindil Beach markets. Have you been there lately?"

"Not for many years."

"They're really impressive now. So many vendors and there's live entertainment. Lots to see and do."

"It sounds perfect."

"Wonderful. They don't open until mid-afternoon. Perhaps we could meet at the front pavilion at three?"

He smiled, his pale blue eyes melting into hers. "I'll look forward to it."

"Great, I'll see you then." She struggled to pull her gaze from his without success.

Her pulse skittered as he lifted his hand and touched her cheek before kissing her lightly on the lips. "Good night, Maggie."

"Good night, Frank."

She drove home to her apartment floating on cloud nine.

CHAPTER 15

The following day proved frustrating for Frank. Yesterday, particularly last night, had been amazing and he'd gone to bed feeling at ease and light-hearted after his date with Maggie, but today he was filled with tension and impatience. He was meeting with a potential cattle buyer from Indonesia. It seemed they did things far differently there than he did on the station. He was used to business negotiations being direct and to the point. He traded and bartered with other station owners and feed vendors in a matter of minutes.

A couple of hours had already passed, and they hadn't begun to discuss the type or quantity of cattle Mr. Tamala was interested in purchasing. He'd insisted on meeting Frank at a restaurant for lunch, and after ordering their drinks and food, Frank had launched into the details about the station and what kind of cattle they offered.

Mr. Tamala had stopped him cold and said there would be

plenty of time for business discussions later, and it 'caused indigestion' to discuss such matters over a meal. When Frank pointed out that they'd yet to receive their food, the look he was given would have quelled lesser men. Uttering a silent prayer for patience, Frank tried to relax and 'go with the flow' as Joshua would say, but it was proving much more difficult than he'd anticipated.

Mr. Tamala was a firm believer in enjoying each course and was very specific with his instructions to the waiter about when to bring out each part of the meal. By the time they finished eating, two hours had elapsed. Once the waiter had finally cleared the plates, Frank again tried to start business negotiations, only to be halted for a second time. It seemed the restaurant was not a private enough place to discuss business.

Mr. Tamala had reserved a private conference room at his hotel for the discussion. Anxious to get to the room, Frank hurriedly paid for the meal and headed to his car to follow the man, but Mr. Tamala had other ideas. "Come with me, Frank. It would be rude of me to expect you to drive yourself." He wanted Frank to accompany him in his rental, and even when Frank assured him he was fine to drive, he wouldn't accept no for an answer.

Not wanting to insult the man, Frank reluctantly agreed.

The driver took them on a scenic route to the hotel, and at first, Frank was a bit miffed by the continued delay. But as Mr. Tamala commented on the beauty of the city and the amazing scenery, and genuine joy filled his face at the sight of a mob of wallabies bounding alongside the road when driving through the East Point Reserve, Frank felt humbled. There was merit in appreciating the simple things of life. In taking things slowly.

He was reminded of a scripture his father used to tell him when he was young and bull-headed about things.

Whoever is patient has great understanding, but one who is quick-tempered displays folly.

It was true that Frank was in a hurry to complete the negotiations with Mr. Tamala, but what did it hurt if it took two hours or the whole day? The result would be the same, of that he was sure. Everything was in God's time and in God's plan. Frank needed to let go of his timing for this meeting and relax.

Once he did, he began to enjoy Mr. Tamala's company. They shared stories of their youth and discovered they had quite a lot in common. They each had fathers and grandfathers who'd built their cattle businesses from the ground up and passed them onto their sons. There was a mutual sense of pride in what their families had accomplished and carried forward into the next generation. These newfound commonalities reduced the tension between the two and once they reached the hotel conference room, helped to speed up the negotiations.

Although Mr. Tamala liked to take his time with mundane things, when he was ready to talk business, he was ready to talk business. He already had a draft of the agreements prepared. As Frank perused the draft, he was impressed with the amount of research the man had done on Goddard Downs. He knew with accurate detail the number of individual head of cattle the station ran, the breeds, and a range of selling prices for the last five years.

He was a shrewd businessman and an even shrewder negotiator, but Frank was no spring chicken. He hadn't built Goddard Downs into what it was today by being a pushover.

The two men spent the better part of an hour going back and forth on pricing and numbers. At the end, both sides were satisfied with the negotiations.

"You are a canny negotiator, Mr. Goddard," Mr. Tamala said with a nod of appreciation.

"Please, call me Frank. And you weren't so bad yourself." He chuckled, leaning back on his chair and stretching his arms. "I was impressed by both the extent and accuracy of your research."

The man grinned. "I like to know who I'm going into business with."

"I couldn't agree more," Frank said as he stood and extended his hand. "I look forward to doing business with you, Mr. Tamala."

"You may call me Rafi. And I look forward to the same. Would you care to celebrate this new partnership with a drink at the bar?"

Frank glanced at his watch. It was already five o'clock and he'd promised Bethany and Graham he'd meet them for dinner. He'd like nothing more than to accept Rafi's offer, however, he would have to pass. Frank hoped he would understand. "Any other time, I would love to. However, I promised my sister and her husband I'd meet them for dinner. I don't come to the city often," he said by way of explanation and apology.

"Say no more. Family comes first. I respect that. Perhaps, another time."

Frank smiled. "Yes. I'll look forward to it."

. . .

Rafi had his driver return Frank to his car, and Frank had just enough time to freshen up and get to the restaurant by six. Dinner was a relaxed affair. He and Bethany were only three years apart—he was the older sibling, and they'd been close as kids.

They were still close as adults, although distance kept them from seeing each other often, but when they did, it was as if no time had passed at all. She and Graham had recently retired and were enjoying spending time on their boat and taking extended vacations to Europe and southeast Asia. Graham had been a successful solicitor in the corporate sector and Bethany had enjoyed her own success as an artist.

She still painted, but now it was when the mood suited her rather than at the beck and call of the art galleries. Frank envied their laid-back lifestyle, but he wouldn't trade station life for anything. He enjoyed the occasional day off, but if he had too much time on his hands, he'd get bored. To him, the station wasn't work, it was his passion. His life. He supposed if it ever became a chore, he would know it was time to hand over the reins completely to his children. But that day had yet to come.

Altogether, it was an enjoyable evening and Frank couldn't wait to see the new boat the following morning. Upon retirement, Bethany and Graham had splurged and purchased a thirty-eight-foot deep sea cabin cruiser. Although he didn't go fishing often, Frank enjoyed the sport and was looking forward to catching some barramundi, cod or maybe even some salmon.

As they finished their coffees, Frank yawned. The long days

were finally catching up with him. He bid them goodnight and headed back to the hotel, hoping for a good night's rest in preparation for the day of fishing.

As he settled into bed and was turning the light off, his phone pinged. He picked it up and smiled. It was a message from Maggie. *Hope you had a successful day. Looking forward to Sunday. Maggie.*

He replied, *Yes, the negotiations were successful...finally. Thanks for asking. Looking forward to Sunday, too. Frank.* And he was. He truly was.

THE NEXT MORNING, he met up with Bethany and Graham at the docks bright and early. He let out a low whistle as he spied the boat. It was a beautiful specimen. Graham wasted no time having Frank come aboard and the two men spent a good twenty minutes talking about all its features.

"Come on, you two," Bethany finally said. "The fish aren't going to catch themselves!"

Laughing, the men made quick work of preparing the boat for cast off and they were soon on their way, navigating through Fannie Bay to the open waters of Beagle Gulf. It was a beautiful day, not a cloud in the sky and the seas were calm. Graham found a good spot to anchor, and the trio settled in for a morning of fishing.

They were successful, catching a number of good-sized threadfin salmon before midday. The cruiser came equipped with its own galley kitchen, and while Graham was downstairs preparing lunch, Frank sat on the upper deck with Bethany.

They chatted about everyday things for a while, simply enjoying each other's company while sipping on ice-cold soda. Bethany talked about her eldest son Adam's love life and how he was feeling lost and hesitant to start over again after he and his partner had recently separated.

"I can understand his hesitancy. It's not easy starting over," Frank said, his thoughts drifting to Maggie and how it had taken him a couple of weeks to even get used to the idea of being interested in someone.

Bethany nodded. "Yes, but he and Andrea were only together for three years, not thirty-plus like you and Esther."

"Give him time. Sometimes it takes months, even years, to move on."

She quirked a brow. "Do I detect some underlying meaning in that response?"

Frank rubbed the back of his neck and grinned. "Maybe."

Bethany sat taller, her face lighting up. "What do you mean? Have you found someone?"

He gave a low chuckle. "I think I have," he admitted slowly.

"Oh, Frank! That's wonderful!" She jumped up and hugged him tightly. "I'm so happy for you."

He held up his hands. "Now, don't go getting all excited just yet. It's new. Very new."

"I'm sure it is. And I don't mean to overreact. I'm simply happy for you."

"I know you are, and I appreciate it."

"So, what's her name? How did you meet?"

He gave her a summary of how he and Maggie had met and mentioned that she was divorced. He didn't talk about Cliff's infidelity, nor that he was a local politician, since Bethany would be sure to know of him straight away. She didn't pry. She was good about things like that. Instead, she simply wished him all the best and said she'd be praying for him.

CHAPTER 16

Later that evening, after returning to the hotel, Frank fell asleep as soon as his head hit the pillow and he didn't wake once during the night. It had been a long time since he'd slept that well. Only the shrill ring of his morning wakeup call woke him from deep slumber the following morning.

Groggy, he turned the coffee machine on to percolate while he showered, and soon the room was filled with the rich aroma of brewed coffee. Today he was meeting with the Department of Primary Industries officer to discuss the possibility of being grandfathered into some of the newer regulations and license requirements and he needed to have all his wits about him.

As he sipped his coffee, he studied the information Julian had prepared. Frank had to admit as he scanned the notes that Julian had been thorough and organised. Everything was summarised neatly for him to follow.

Before leaving for the meeting, Frank bowed his head in prayer. He couldn't go into such a big meeting on his own.

Heavenly Father, I come before You as Your humble servant asking for wisdom and guidance. Please give me the right words to negotiate a true and just agreement. I ask for Your advocacy on behalf of my family. I commit this day to You. In Your Son's precious name, I pray. Amen.

He was filled with optimism on his way to the meeting with Officer Shepherd, a short, balding man with spectacles. However, ten minutes into the meeting, despite his prayers, he could already tell it was not going his way. He'd barely gotten through the introduction and the first set of points Julian had prepared before Officer Shepherd stopped him.

"I'm well aware of the rules and regulations governing the export of cattle, Mr. Goddard, as it was my office that was responsible for writing most of them." His tone was patronising and full of disdain. "I don't need a lecture on them."

"My apologies, Officer Shepherd. It wasn't my intent to lecture you." Thrown off his plan, Frank was unsure where to go to from here. He would have to tread very carefully. "It was my hope to secure a stay for the new Health Certification for next year and be grandfathered into the requirement. As I understand it, there can be certain concessions made for hardship."

Officer Shepherd leaned back in his chair, steepling his hands under his chin as he regarded Frank for a long moment. Frank dared not speak. The man was sizing him up. Being under such intense scrutiny made him uncomfortable, but he remained silent and watchful.

"That's correct. If the station can prove undue hardship, a

stay MAY be granted." His emphasis on the word 'may' did not go unnoticed by Frank. "However, hardship is not a guarantee for such things. One must take other factors into consideration."

His last statement was confusing. From everything Frank had read and from what Julian had researched, the only qualification for a stay was hardship. "What other factors?" he asked as he rifled through his notes. "I wasn't aware of any other factors."

After a prolonged silence, he looked up from the papers. Officer Shepherd was leaning back in his chair, rubbing his thumb and fingers together with a smirk on his face.

Frank's eyes narrowed. Surely it wasn't what it seemed... He knew under the table dealings were not a new thing. In fact, they probably happened more often than people were aware of, but not for him. He'd always been a rule follower, never one to stray from the right path. If Officer Shepherd was looking for some kind of monetary contribution to sway his decision, he'd picked the wrong man.

Narrowing his eyes further, Frank held the man's gaze for a long moment. Tension filled the room. Finally, he tore his gaze away, gathered his papers and stood. "I think we're done here, Officer Shepherd."

Shepherd leaned forward in his chair and crossed his arms on the desk. "When I make my decision, I'll let you know. Call if you have any questions."

Frank couldn't respond. He couldn't even shake the man's hand.

He returned to the hotel, barely believing what had just happened. He'd been brimming with optimism and hope, but now felt confused and dismayed. He'd been so certain he could present their case and be given the stay. Now it seemed the only way to do that was to succumb to a bribe. Pay Shepherd money. Money they didn't have, even if he'd consider such a thing.

And would he?

That he was even thinking that way scared him more than anything. He'd always been a man of uncompromising faith, but the threat of losing his family's station was real. More real now than ever before. There'd been rumours going around for years about the potential ban on live cattle exporting because some of the buyers were mistreating the animals. That ban would cripple Goddard Downs if it ever went into effect, but it had always been just rumours. Until now.

Instead of an outright ban on live exporting, the Australian government had passed rigorous licensing and certification requirements to prevent such cruel behaviour from happening. It was those requirements that Frank was trying to fulfil, or in their case, be granted a stay for a year so they could have time to fully comply with the stringent laws, which in itself would prove costly.

Julian had tried to warn him about the costly measures some time ago, but he'd dismissed his son's concerns. Julian had come up with what Frank had originally considered harebrained ideas for alternative forms of income. But as he sat there in the hotel with his head in his hands, he realised that he might need to take his son's suggestions a lot more seriously.

Julian had first tried to persuade Frank to not worry about the new licensing and instead transition their station to a tourist destination. Several other stations had opened their land and their home and invited strangers in to be workers for a day. What befuddled Frank was that people actually paid money to work. Station work wasn't glorious or glamorous. It was dirty, difficult, and went on night and day, rain or shine. It didn't sound like a relaxing vacation to him.

But what was the alternative? Ignore Shepherd's 'suggestion' and risk the chance of losing an opportunity for a stay and be required to obtain the proper licensing and certifications sooner than later? To do that, they'd need to extend the mortgage on the station, something he wasn't keen to do. But if they didn't, they'd lose the sale to Mr. Tamala. A sale that was intended to keep the station afloat for at least another year. Or he could compromise his faith and his integrity and offer the man some money, but that would cost him far more than dollars and cents. And even then, the costs for the licensing and certifications were still daunting whether he had to pay them now or in a year from now, especially with an uncertain market.

Selling the station wasn't an option. Goddard Downs had been in his family for generations. He refused to except that as a possibility, so there was no alternative. He'd have to consider other options, such as Julian's suggestion. He felt the Lord was testing him. Maybe not like Daniel in the lion's den or Shadrach, Meshach, and Abednego in the blazing furnace, but he knew his faith was being tested. Being a man of faith and knowing he was being tested, he turned to the Lord for strength and guidance. He bowed his head and drew a steadying breath.

Heavenly Father, I come to You not knowing which way to turn or what path is the right one to take. I know which one is the wrong one, yet I struggle with the desire to not follow that path. Forgive me for entertaining a thought I know is wrong.

You never promised that life would be easy, and I know You're bigger than any storm I might face in this world, but Lord, I'm struggling right now, as I don't see any way forward.

James 1 verse 5 says, If any of you lacks wisdom, you should ask God, who gives generously to all without finding fault, and it will be given to you. So, Lord, I'm asking You now for wisdom. Show me what to do, which way to go. I ask all of these things in Your precious and holy name. Amen

LATER THAT EVENING, after he'd eaten dinner in the hotel's waterfront restaurant, Frank took another stroll along the pier, wishing Maggie was beside him. He could sure do with a friendly ear right now. So much was going through his mind and she was a great listener. But that wasn't the only reason. Despite everything else that was going on, she was still uppermost in his mind, and he found himself thinking about her often. When he was with her, everything seemed brighter. Happier. Although they barely knew one another, she lit up his world in a way no one since Esther had. Not even his children.

He'd love to call her. Hearing her voice would cheer him. But would it be too forward? He deliberated for minutes and had decided to call her when his mobile phone rang. It was her. He quickly answered it. "Maggie! I was just about to call you."

"Really? How funny is that!"

"Yes." He let out a small chuckle.

"I hope I'm not disturbing you."

"Not at all. I'm just out enjoying a walk after dinner."

"I was calling to see how the meeting went today."

He grimaced. "Not good. But it's okay. I'm trusting God for the answers."

"Do you want to talk about it?"

"You know what? I'd rather not. I'd rather hear about your day and what you've been up to." *And not give Officer Shepherd and his underhanded deal another thought.*

"Well, I worked all day. Not much to tell."

Frank stopped walking and leaned his elbows on the railing while he gazed out across the water. Maggie chatted on, and he found her voice soothing. She didn't seem in a hurry to end the call, so he asked her about her favourite music, what she liked to do, places she'd been to or wanted to visit. He was surprised to discover that although she quite enjoyed the outdoors, she'd never been camping.

"Cliff wasn't much of an outdoorsman. His idea of camping was staying at the Park Hyatt in Sydney," she said with bitterness in her voice. "His idea of fishing was renting out a yacht and eating whatever the deckhands caught that day. I would have preferred to have caught them myself. I think it would have been fun."

"It's never too late to start."

"Oh, I couldn't do anything like that now. I'm far too old."

"Nonsense," he retorted. "We go camping several times a year as a family. The grandkids love it and so do I. You should come some time. I'm sure you'd love it, too."

"Hmmm...perhaps I would," she answered non-committedly. There was a pregnant pause before she spoke again. "Actually, the reason for my call is to invite you to something."

"Oh..." Frank's curiosity was peaked.

"Well, I know we planned to meet on Sunday afternoon, but I was wondering if you might like to join me for church beforehand. We could grab a bite to eat afterwards while we wait for the markets to open."

"That sounds good. I normally worship with my sister and brother-in-law when I'm in town, but I'm sure they won't mind if I go elsewhere. Can I let you know tomorrow after I've talked with them?"

"Sure, not a problem. Just give me a call."

"I will." When the call ended, he wore a big grin. Maggie was a breath of fresh air and he couldn't wait to see her again.

CHAPTER 17

Frank arrived bright and early at Bethany and Graham's home the following morning and shared a quick breakfast with them before they all headed to Manton Dam, about an hour's drive south of Darwin, to do some early morning kayaking and bird watching. Bethany and Graham had a double kayak and a single Frank could use.

It was a perfect morning to be out on the water. There wasn't a cloud in the sky, and with the sun still low, it wasn't yet unbearably hot. Being an avid outdoorsman, Frank loved trying to spot rare and endangered species and he had high hopes of spotting a Tiwi Hooded Robin. He had no such luck, although he did see quite a few Crested Terns, some Little Friarbirds, and a Red-necked Stint.

The trio spent a little over an hour kayaking leisurely along the banks of the lake, enjoying the peace and quiet. However, as the sun rose higher, so did the noise. Manton Dam was a favourite spot for water sport enthusiasts and as time marched on, more and more powerboats and jet skis began zooming around. The vibrations and the noise disturbed both the birds and the water, so the trio decided to head in for an early lunch.

As they sat on the verandah of the small bistro waiting for their food to arrive, Frank told Bethany about the incident with Officer Shepherd. As expected, she was upset.

"You're joking! He actually said he wanted you to pay him money?" His sister's eyes widened and her mouth gaped.

Frank shook his head. "Not in so many words, but he didn't have to. His meaning was clear." Frank sighed and ran a hand across his beard as he recounted the meeting in its entirety, leaving nothing out.

"I know how important the station is to you, but you seriously can't be considering giving into him," Bethany said, genuinely shocked.

"Of course I'm not. The station's near and dear to my heart and I'd do almost anything to keep it, but I wouldn't sink to that level. You know me better than that, Beth."

"I'm sorry. You're right. I do know you better than that. It just shocked me to hear that he'd suggest something like that to you. What are you going to do?"

Frank shrugged. "I'm not sure. I'd like to report him, but it'd be his word against mine. I've got no proof."

"But if he's done it to you, he's probably done it to others."

"Yes, but I'm not sure how we'd go about proving anything."

"Okay then, so what will you do?"

Frank released a heavy breath. "We have some emergency funds but not enough to cover the licenses and certifications. It would put us in the red for the year and most likely the next, and the next, and the next... And we wouldn't have any money left in reserve if there was a true emergency."

"How much do you need?" Graham asked quietly.

"I can't take your money, Graham, if that's what you're suggesting. You've worked long and hard to get where you are today. I'm not going to dip into your savings."

Seemingly unperturbed by Frank's protestation, Graham said, "Then consider it a loan. We can even draw up terms and interest if that will make you feel better about it." He looked at Bethany and she nodded in agreement. "We simply want to help, if you'll let us."

Accepting money from his sister and brother-in-law felt wrong. "I don't know, Graham. I'd like to see if there's another way first." He didn't know if it was his pride talking, but he wanted to weigh all his options before he considered borrowing money from them.

"No problem, but know the offer is there." Graham paused before adding, "And I can put you in touch with a private investigator if you want to investigate Shepherd. I did hear talk of there being a bad egg in the department."

Frank breathed in slowly. Did he want to go down that path? Having been a solicitor, Graham had the right connections, but Frank wasn't sure he had the energy to take on something like that. After a moment, he smiled gratefully. "Thank you. On both counts. Let me think about it."

"Sure."

"Have you considered Julian's suggestion?" Bethany asked tentatively. She was aware of his reluctance to open the station to tourism and was treading carefully.

He let out another heavy sigh and crossed his arms. "I've

been giving it some thought, but both my heart and gut tell me there's another way. I just haven't figured out what it is yet."

"Well, you have a bit of time. Why don't you visit some of the other stations that have opened to tourism, or at least call them and gather some information?" Graham suggested.

"I'm not sure how willing they'd be to talk to me, given that I'd potentially be in competition with them," Frank said.

"Could you ask Maggie to do some research on your behalf? From what you said, she's already seen several other stations," Bethany added.

"Hmmm...maybe, although I'm not keen to burden her with our problems."

"What if you came at it from a different angle? Put a bug in her ear about how stations are having to adapt and change because of the increasing cost of raising cattle, and see what she comes up with. A lot of stations have already had to consider tourism in order to continue their way of life. It could be a good article for her magazine, and it would be good information for you."

"I don't know, Beth. That feels a little deceitful."

"Well, be honest with her. I'm sure she'd be willing to help you out."

Frank scrunched his face, not really liking that suggestion.

"Well, pray on it. We'll pray as well. There *will* be a solution, Frank. God won't leave you high and dry, but it might be that this is a time of change for you, and you might need to be open to things you've never thought of or considered before."

Frank grimaced. "That's what worries me. But you're right. I'm not one for change, you know that, but I've slowly been coming to that conclusion myself."

. . .

THE NEXT MORNING Frank woke at six, despite no pressing urgency for him to get up. He'd called Maggie the previous evening when he arrived back at the hotel and told her he'd love to go to church with her. Bethany and Graham were heading out of town and wouldn't be going, but Maggie's service didn't start until ten.

After ten minutes of trying to lie in bed, he gave up and made himself a coffee which he took onto the balcony. He eased himself onto one of the rattan cane armchairs. Being a Sunday morning, the port was relatively quiet, although early morning joggers and bike riders were out in force. The sun sparkled across the blue waters of the harbour, but although it was peaceful and relaxing, it didn't completely quell the inner turmoil inside him. His mind kept turning to the meeting with Officer Shepherd, leaving a bitter taste in his mouth.

"For I know the plans I have for you," declares the Lord, "plans to prosper you and not to harm you, plans to give you hope and a future."

Frank drew a slow breath. *I'm so glad for that promise, Lord. I truly am. Thank You. Please help me remember that You're in this with me. With my family. I'm not alone.*

AT FIVE TO TEN, Frank arrived at Maggie's church in downtown Darwin. She was standing by the steps and looked as pretty as a picture in her Sunday dress. The colour reminded him of the national flower, the Golden Wattle, with its bright fluorescent yellow blooms. She'd done something different with her hair—it was swept back with a clip of some kind, exposing the elegant shape of her neck. The sight of her brought a smile to his face and immediately brightened his day.

"That colour is lovely on you," he said after greeting her with a kiss on the cheek. He hadn't intended to kiss her, but it had seemed so natural to do so.

She flushed and a shy smile lit her face. "Thank you."

"You're more than welcome." His heart swelled as he gazed into her eyes.

The church bells tolled, signalling the service was about to begin. "Shall we?" he asked, offering her his arm.

Nodding, she linked her arm through his and they headed inside together. It was a medium sized church with a large ornate sanctuary and traditional wooden pews. Light flowed into the chapel via a beautiful three-pane stained glass window depicting the last supper.

They chose a pew halfway down the main aisle. Maggie had told him that the later service was more traditional than the earlier contemporary service that catered to the younger families, and that suited him just fine. Not that he didn't like the more contemporary services, but right now, his spirit was in need of calm, and as the organist began to play 'A Mighty Fortress Is Our God', the words of the old hymn spoke to his heart.

A mighty fortress is our God, a bulwark never failing
Our Helper He, amid the flood of mortal ills prevailing
For still our ancient foe doth seek to work us woe
His craft and pow'r are great, and, armed with cruel hate
On earth is not his equal

And though this world, with devils filled, should threaten to undo us,
We will not fear, for God hath willed His truth to triumph through us;
The Prince of Darkness grim, we tremble not for him;
His rage we can endure, for lo, his doom is sure,
One little word shall fell him.
That word above all earthly pow'rs, no thanks to them, abideth;
The Spirit and the gifts are ours through Him Who with us sideth;
Let goods and kindred go, this mortal life also;
The body they may kill: God's truth abideth still,
His kingdom is forever.

It felt good to be in church. He hadn't lost his faith when Esther passed away, but over the years he hadn't attended church as regularly as he should, although being more than two hours' drive from the closest church didn't make it easy to attend. But being here was a reminder that he needed to refresh his spirit in more ways than just in prayer and Bible study. Corporate worship was important, too. He made a mental pact to attend service as often as he could when he returned to the station.

Today's sermon was entitled 'The Worthy Walk.' The pastor, an older man with greying hair and a kind face, began by reading a passage from Colossians chapter one.

"For this cause we also, since the day we heard it, do not cease to pray for you, and to desire that ye might be filled with the knowledge of His will in all wisdom and spiritual understanding; That ye might walk worthy of the Lord unto all pleasing, being fruitful in every good work, and increasing in the knowledge of God; Strengthened with all might, according to His glorious power, unto all patience and longsuffering with joyfulness."

He looked up from his Bible, removed his glasses, and cast his gaze around the congregation as he spoke. "The notion that people are intrinsically good and will usually do the right thing once they know what it is, is quite widespread in our day. It's easy to understand why people want to think that way. It's flattering to think of ourselves as good. But the Bible paints a totally different picture. Romans three verse twelve says, *They are all gone out of the way, they are together become unprofitable; there is none that doeth good, no, not one.* And Romans three twenty-three says, *For all have sinned, and come short of the glory of God.*

"Praise God that when we accept Jesus as our Lord and Saviour, we receive a new nature. Our sinful pasts are gone, our slates are wiped clean, and in Christ, all things are made new. But how many of us cling to our old nature and habits rather than purposely choosing to walk daily as a new creation of God?

"Beloved, because God is holy, He requires us to be holy. Because of Jesus' sacrifice, we're no longer in bondage to sin, without the ability to do what is right. Charles Spurgeon said, 'The liberty of the man of the world is liberty to commit evil without restraint; the liberty of a child of God is to walk in holiness without hindrance.'"

The Pastor's words rang clear and the sermon couldn't have been more fitting. It was as if God was speaking directly to Frank, and maybe He was.

"Although we don't work to earn our salvation or merit

with God, He has the right to demand that we live up to the new name He's given us. We have freedom in Christ, but it's freedom *from* sin, not freedom *to* sin. As believers saved by the blood of Jesus which was shed on the cross for us, we have the privilege and responsibility to walk in a manner worthy of being called a child of God. But praise God we have a helper. We're not left to do this alone. We have the Holy Spirit living in us, giving us strength to make the right choices.

"Every day we face temptations. And every day we must choose to live in a manner that is worthy of our calling. Will you pray with me?"

Frank bowed his head. He may not know his specific path yet, but he knew for sure it wasn't the one Officer Shepherd had suggested. He *would* walk in a manner worthy of his calling, and in reaffirming his faith, he felt renewed confidence that there was another way. A better way. He simply had to lift his eyes to Jesus and trust God's plan for him and his family.

CHAPTER 18

Following church, since Maggie and Frank still had some time to kill before the markets opened, she suggested they go to Berry Springs for a picnic. She was surprised to discover that Frank had never been there. When she mentioned it was also a nice place to swim, but maybe for another time, Frank said he had his swimming trunks at the hotel. He'd thrown them in because the hotel had a lap pool and he'd thought he might do some laps. "It seemed like a good idea at the time," he chuckled.

Without giving herself a chance to talk herself out of the idea, Maggie suggested that since he had his trunks they may as well go swimming, too. She could swing by her place and grab her suit and then pick Frank up at his hotel on the way to the springs. He agreed readily, and since the hotel was within walking distance, he set off at a clipped pace while Maggie got into her car and headed to her apartment.

When she pulled up, she dashed inside to grab one of her

swimsuits. As she laid them out on her bed, she fretted over which one to choose. What on earth had possessed her to invite him swimming!

It wasn't that she was super modest or hadn't been in a swimsuit recently. It was just that she hadn't been concerned about her appearance in a swimsuit in a very long time. She was turning sixty next year and had begun to feel a little self-conscious about her body, especially after Cliff had left her for a much younger, fitter woman.

She didn't have much time to agonise over the decision, so she chose the floral suit with the skirted bottom and a light cotton wrap to go over it. That would have to do. She grabbed her beach hat and a couple of towels in case Frank didn't have one and headed out the door. She made it to his hotel in record time, and still had a few minutes to spare. However, he was already out the front waiting for her. Her heart lurched at the sight of him.

They stopped at Famished to pick up a picnic basket for two, and then they were on their way. They chatted a bit about the sermon but rode most of the way in companionable silence. She enjoyed how easy it was to be with Frank. She didn't feel compelled to make small talk, and the silence between them was not awkward at all. It was as if they'd known each other all their lives and were simply happy to be in each other's company. It was vastly different from her time with Cliff.

She remembered feeling anxious around him when they'd first started dating. Always jumpy and a bundle of nerves, afraid of saying or doing the wrong thing. Although he wasn't in politics when they met, he was from a prominent family, and it was intimidating to be around him. He'd always been a bit aloof, and she usually felt a little out of place. Like she was one step behind him at all times and trying to play catchup. She wondered now why she'd married him and determined she'd been attracted by his charisma. But she didn't want to mar her time with Frank thinking about her relationship with Cliff. That was in the past, and that's where it needed to stay.

It was a little past twelve when they reached Berry Springs, and being a lovely day, the car park was almost full. It took Maggie a few times around to find a spot to park. She wasn't sure if she was pleased that it was crowded or not. Part of her thought it would be a good distraction to have other people around, then all eyes wouldn't be on her. But another part of her wished she and Frank could have the place to themselves.

~

FRANK WAS MORE RELAXED than he'd been in days, weeks, maybe even months. Maggie put his soul at ease. He didn't mind the silences between them. It wasn't that they didn't have anything to say to each other, they just didn't need to be constantly talking. It had been a long time since he'd been that comfortable with a person. Six years to be exact. That had to mean something.

It got him thinking that maybe he needed to slow down, take time to enjoy life more. Not that he didn't enjoy his life. He loved his family, and he loved the station and he didn't mind the hard work. It was all he'd ever known. But maybe there was a piece missing. And maybe, just maybe, that piece might be Maggie.

He glanced over at her. Waist-deep in the clear pool created by the spring, she trailed her hands in the water, completely carefree and lost in the beauty of her surroundings. It made him happy that she'd finally relaxed and could enjoy their swim together. She'd been self-conscious at first. There'd been a certain hesitancy in her movements as she removed her wrap and waded into the water to join him, but her simple floral-print bathing suit flattered her petite figure, which still had enough curves to make her look womanly. To him, she looked gorgeous.

She also wore a wide-brimmed floppy hat to protect her face. Her skin was more delicate than Esther's. Paler and dotted with freckles. He'd smiled when she'd layered on the sunscreen and offered the tube to him. He bashfully admitted that he never wore the stuff. Besides, he almost always had on long sleeves and a cowboy hat, so the only parts of him that got exposed were his forearms if he rolled up his sleeves. Not to mention, he was blessed with darker skin that tanned easily in the long days in the sun.

She chastised him and lectured him good-naturedly about the importance of sunscreen and the prevention of skin cancer, but then let him be. He liked that she cared enough to educate him. Or maybe she lectured everyone about sunscreen, but he liked to think it was because she cared for him. After a quick snack, they spent a lazy hour or so relaxing in the cool waters, swimming around and drifting down the stream under the shade of pandanus palms and ferns. But eventually he couldn't contain the loud growls of his stomach. He thoroughly enjoyed the sound of her unabashed laughter, even if it was at his expense. It was boisterous and infectious.

After one particularly loud grumble, he found himself joining in.

"I guess we should eat," she said, her eyes twinkling with amusement.

They grabbed their towels and dried off before finding a picnic table in the shade of some River Oak trees to enjoy their lunch.

∼

"A LOT SURE has changed here since I was a kid," Maggie commented as she looked around the picnic area. "It was never this…" she paused as she searched for the right word, "well kept."

"How long has it been since you were here?"

"Oh…" She frowned as she tried to remember. "Probably a good ten years or more."

"Really?" The shock was evident in Frank's expression. "Why so long? I thought this was one of your favourite spots?"

His question was innocent enough, but it was a painful reminder of the joys in life that she'd given up during her marriage. "It was. I mean, it is," she corrected. "Cliff was never one for the great outdoors unless it was on a fancy yacht or at a five-star resort. He didn't care for anything remotely rugged."

"That's unfortunate," Frank said. "Some of my best family memories were made on camping trips and outdoor adventures."

Maggie envied the nostalgia in his voice. "It sounds like you had a lot of fun."

"Yes, we still do. You'll have to come along sometime." He

gave a playful wink that made her chuckle. Oh, how she loved his warmth and his spirit. His optimism and 'glass half-full' outlook was so refreshing. It also didn't hurt that his playful nature gave her stomach a nice little flutter deep in her belly that tickled all the way to her toes. She couldn't remember the last time she'd felt the familiar stirrings of attraction, or how much fun flirting could be. It made her feel vibrant and desirable for the first time since Cliff had left her.

After eating, they took another swim before heading back to town. The markets bustled with people of all sorts, but now, holding Frank's hand, Maggie didn't mind. Amidst the hustle and bustle of the crowds, the live music and the aroma of exotic cuisines filling the air, there was an energy she couldn't describe, and it was infectious.

She and Frank took their time meandering from stall to stall. Maggie appreciated his willingness to explore and his ability to never seem in a hurry. Cliff had rarely done anything like this with her, mostly because he was either too busy or found the entire idea a complete bore. He would always rush her from store to store and would never have considered buying anything from a market stand. He was too good for 'peasant' things. Those were his exact words. She inwardly cringed just thinking about it. She hadn't realised how much of a snob her ex-husband had been until recently.

Maggie hadn't grown up in as prominent or wealthy a family as his, although they hadn't been poor, either. Her family had a modest home, and she'd still attended a private school. But that didn't mean she couldn't appreciate the simple craftsmanship of a homemade item. To Cliff, homemade was a dirty word, but to her it meant someone had spent extraordinary time and effort creating something beautiful.

There were some cheaply made items in some of the stalls, but they were few and far between. Most of the hand-crafted items were exquisite. The artisans took pride in their craft and it was obvious in the quality of their work. Maggie fell in love with a hand-woven scarf in a rainbow of colours. It was made from Merino wool and was incredibly soft. She bought one for herself and a dark blue one for Serena.

It appeared that Frank also enjoyed shopping, but he mostly shopped for others. He piled his arms full of bags of gifts for his children and their spouses and bought quite a few things for his grandkids. When she raised her brow at the number of bags in his arms, he grinned sheepishly and said, "I don't get to spoil them often."

Maggie laughed at his unabashed love for his family. "I think it's wonderful. I'm sure they'll love the gifts." She patted his arm. "Besides, it's our duty as parents and especially as grandparents to spoil our families with love."

"My sentiments exactly." He looked down at his overloaded arms. "Perhaps we should make a trip back to the car to unload these bags. That way, we can make room for some more spoils!" he said with a wink.

True to his word, after they dropped the first load of bags in the boot of her car, Frank attacked the remaining stalls with gusto. They left not one stall unseen. She laughed as he playfully put his head in a shark jaw from Crocodile Darwin. She loved this playful side of him. He seemed to lose himself in the moment and didn't care what anyone else thought. That was a novelty to her, having spent most of her marriage trying to be conscious of what everyone around her thought and having to placate each one of them. To have the freedom to be whatever she wanted, whenever she wanted, regardless of who saw her was incredibly liberating.

She even found herself joining in on his frivolity. They had a contest to see who could find the silliest, most outrageous hat. Maggie was delighted to be crowned the champion after she found a giant lobster hat from Funky Frog Imports, complete with claws that clapped when she pulled the chin strap. For a prize, Frank bought her the hat.

"Here, to commemorate your victory," he said as he placed it on her head.

"I shall wear it with pride—where no one will ever see me!"

"Where's the fun in that?" Frank asked as they laughed together.

"It will be our little secret," she replied.

He paused for a moment and tilted his head as he regarded her. "Okay." He nodded. "I can go with that. Our little secret." With an irresistible grin, he reached out his hand.

Maggie felt that all too familiar flutter in her belly, the one that sent warm tingles down her spine. She took his hand and that tingle sparked into a fully-fledged flame as awareness between them deepened. She blushed at the longing in his eyes, knowing it mirrored her own. Try as she might, she couldn't look away. It was as if an invisible rope tethered them together.

Finally, he blinked and she was able to break the intense gaze, but she didn't let go of his hand. He coughed under his breath. "I know we had a late lunch, but it's going on six. Would you like something to eat?"

Grateful for the distraction, Maggie replied, "Yes, after all that shopping, I'm actually hungry."

"Shall we find a sit-down restaurant, or would you like to try some food from one of the stalls? We could pick some things from a few different ones and make our own buffet," he said.

"I like that idea. Let's be adventurous and see what we can find."

Together they scoured the various international cuisine stalls and decided on an eclectic selection of foods ranging from Sri Lankan, to French, to good old-fashioned grilled corn on the cob. They found an empty picnic table near the edge of the market that offered some quiet from the din of the crowds but also had a great view across the bay. As the sun dipped lower in the sky, an orange glow spread across the water. It was simply beautiful.

They dined with gusto on their buffet of Beef Rendang, Pepper Beef Curry with Roti bread, and grilled corn on the cob. Maggie was pleased to find that Frank also enjoyed spicy food. Cliff had suffered from acid-reflux and couldn't even handle the heat of a pepper without complaint. On the other hand, she loved spicy foods, and the hotter the better. But during her marriage, she'd rarely had the opportunity to enjoy Thai or Indian cuisine, or cuisine from any other country known for its spices.

She forgot how much she'd missed the taste when she tried the curry. It had a slow heat that increased with each bite, but was tempered by the sweetness of the grilled corn and the Roti bread.

For dessert they had fluffy lemon and sugar crepes from La

French. The light and delicate pastries were the perfect complement to the heavier cream from the curry and had just the right amount of sweetness. After dinner, there was still a little daylight left as the sun, large and red, hovered above the horizon, so they decided to walk off their meal.

A stiff breeze was blowing in off the sea and Maggie shivered. Goosebumps appeared on her arms as the warmth of the day began to dissipate. Frank pulled her closer and she nestled under his arm. "I don't have a jacket to offer, but I can at least block some of the wind."

She liked the way she fit in the curve of his arm. Not only was she kept toasty by the heat of his body, but she felt safe and cosy tucked against his side. Not worrying if this was too soon for them to be acting so familiar, she nestled in closer and enjoyed the feel of him.

She stayed like that as they walked to the end of the boardwalk and stood and watched the sun set over the water. As dusk finally fell, Maggie knew the night had to end, and with it, their time together. Earlier at the springs, Frank had mentioned that he would be heading back home in the morning. As she drove him to his hotel, he kept his arm over the back of her seat, occasionally playing with her hair or touching her shoulder. Neither spoke. She used the quiet to reflect on their time together, and more importantly, what it meant to her.

With Cliff, she'd been more reserved about how she felt and had waited for him to make the first move. He initiated the first date, their first kiss, and he was the first to say I love you. And although she and Frank weren't there yet, she felt compelled to let him know how she felt. She didn't want this to be the last time they spent together. Despite the distance between them, she wanted to see him again.

She turned to face him after she pulled in front of his hotel and put the car in park. He looked at her intently, a wistful smile on his face as he continued to toy with a strand of her hair. She almost forgot her words. He had such an easy way about him, but sometimes, like now, it disarmed her. But she didn't want to lose sight of what was important.

Taking his hand, she took a deep breath. "I've had such a wonderful time, Frank. Spending the day together has been...incredible."

His smile broadened. "Yes, it has."

"I..." She paused as courage suddenly escaped her. All the self-doubt from her husband's betrayal suddenly crept into her mind. All the what-ifs came one after the other. *What if this was just a one-time thing for him? What if he doesn't feel the same way? What if she was making a fool of herself? What if...what if...what if!*

"What is it, Maggie? Whatever it is, you can tell me." He squeezed her hand reassuringly as he searched her eyes. "I'm going to take a chance and say that I'm probably thinking the same."

Bolstered by his admission, she ignored the doubts and went all in. "I really enjoyed our time together."

"I did too," he interrupted.

She held up her hand. "Please. Let me get this out, then I promise I'll let you have your say." She was afraid she'd lose her courage if she gave herself too much time to think. "I've only ever dated one man. I was with him for more than thirty years before he pulled the rug from under me and broke my heart. No, no, let me finish," she said as Frank started to interject.

"I've spent the last year and a half wallowing in anger and resentment. It never occurred to me to move on…that I would want to move on." She took a deep breath and looked Frank straight in the eyes for the last part. "But, these last few days have shown me that not only can I move on, but that I want to." She gulped. "With you."

"Yes," was all he said.

"Sorry...?" His response took her by surprise. It wasn't so much the reply itself, but the speed and absolute surety with which he said it.

He leaned forward and placed his hand gently on her cheek. "Maggie, I'm saying yes to moving on…with you."

"Really?" Her nerves quivered with awareness and excitement. This was new ground for her. It had been decades since she'd experienced a new romance and she wasn't sure there was a guidebook on how to date at sixty, but she was willing to muddle her way through if he was.

He looked deep into her eyes. "I don't want our time together to end after I go home. I'd never thought about moving on either, but since the day I met you, you're all I can think of. I don't know what God's plan is for me or for us, but I'm willing to find out."

Something new and exciting blossomed in her heart. She wasn't sure what God's plan for them was either, but she was more than eager to take a chance.

As Frank gently drew her face to his, her whole body filled with anticipation. His lips were soft, warm and inviting. She pressed into him, her arm curling around his neck. She didn't want the moment to end.

Later that evening as she lay in bed, Maggie thought about

the verse that had recently become her favourite, Jeremiah chapter twenty-nine verse eleven. Not because she'd been exiled like the Israelites, although in many ways she'd exiled herself from life, but she thought about how the Lord had told them not to despair.

"For I know the plans I have for you," declares the Lord, "plans to prosper you and not harm you, plans to give you hope and a future."

A hope and a future. That promise was for her. After Cliff left, she'd exiled herself from love and the possibility of building a life with someone new. The Lord had placed Frank in her life for a reason and she needed to trust His plans. As she felt the soft pulls of sleep, she prayed for the strength and courage to embrace new beginnings.

As it turned out, Frank wasn't the only new beginning that night. Only a few hours after she'd fallen asleep, Maggie was woken by her phone ringing. It was Jeremy. Emma's waters had broken and she'd gone into labour. He was taking her to the hospital for the baby to be delivered. Maggie jumped out of bed, quickly dressed and rushed to be by their side.

Chloe Renee Donovan was brought into the world at seven forty-three a.m. As Maggie got to hold her precious new granddaughter, she couldn't help but think about the coincidence that she'd been praying about new beginnings, and that the Lord had blessed her doubly with not only one, but two. What joy filled her heart.

CHAPTER 19

When Frank returned home after his trip to Darwin, instead of being able to revel in the joy of his budding relationship with Maggie, he had to deal with the breakdown of another. The tension he'd witnessed these past few months between Olivia and Nathan had boiled over into something far worse than miscommunication or petty arguments. Nathan was threatening to leave the station with the children, and Olivia was beside herself.

He'd walked straight into it the moment he'd arrived home. It wasn't a mere disagreement, but a full-blown argument that was close to becoming an altercation. He could hear the raised voices from the truck as soon as he pulled up.

Rushing inside, his voice boomed through the house. "What on earth is going on here?"

It wasn't his words alone that got their attention. His shouting caused Olivia and Nathan to stop instantly and turn and look at him.

Frank never shouted. Not ever. He hated to do it, but he'd felt the situation warranted it. Things were quickly escalating out of control and he needed to shock the pair back to reality. He would have to ask the Lord for forgiveness later. Right now, he had to figure out what in the world was going on between his daughter and son-in-law.

His gaze shifted from Olivia to Nathan, waiting for one of them to explain themselves, but he was met with stony silence. Neither would look him in the eye and that frustrated him more than anything. He hated to be ignored.

"Nathan, are you going to tell me why I could hear you yelling at my daughter all the way outside as I pulled up? And if I could hear you, don't you think the entire household could as well?"

But before Nathan could offer an excuse, Frank turned and gave his daughter a long hard glare as well. They were both adults and they were both at fault as far as he was concerned. "And you, Olivia, what must the children think of such behaviour?" He glanced up the stairs towards their bedrooms. "They must be worried sick about what's going on."

He started to head up the stairs to check on them, when Olivia's quiet voice cut through.

"They're not here."

With his hand on the railing, he stopped and looked at her. "What do you mean, they're not here?"

"Janella's minding them." It was Nathan's turn to speak. "While Olivia and I… work some things out."

That got Frank's attention. "*Work some things out?*" He tried to get Olivia to look at him, but she turned her head away in shame. He could have sworn he saw the beginnings of tears pooling in her eyes. "What exactly does that mean?"

"Look, Frank, this isn't how we wanted you to find out. Not this way."

"Find out what?"

"It's no secret that Olivia and I have been having problems," Nathan answered. "I know you've felt the tension between us these last few months, and don't pretend like you haven't." His gaze remained steady, challenging Frank to say otherwise, but the truth was, he couldn't.

"All right, yes, I have noticed things were a little tense between the two of you. But that's only natural in a marriage. Relationships go through ups and downs. The Lord knows, Esther and I went through our own fair share."

"But we aren't you and Mum, Dad." Olivia dabbed her eyes as she spoke quietly.

Frank longed to reach out to his daughter, but something held him in place. She needed to get this out on her own.

"You both loved the station. It was your whole life, both yours and Mum's."

Realisation dawned on Frank. He glanced over at Nathan whose shoulders were slumped as he leaned against the back of the couch. "But it's not your life." He spoke directly to Nathan now.

Nathan sighed heavily and shook his head. "No, it's not. At least not anymore."

Deep in his heart, although Frank knew Nathan's words to be true, they stung.

"It's not that I don't appreciate everything you've done for me and Olivia and the kids, but there isn't a place for me here."

"That's not true." Frank's immediate response was to argue with him, but even he understood where Nathan was coming from. Frank imagined he felt very much like the third wheel, and he was right.

"Yes, it is," Nathan replied. "You don't need me here. There isn't anything I can do that Julian and Joshua don't already do and do it better." He held up his hand before Frank could interrupt again. "This isn't the life I dreamed of. I came here to support Olivia when Esther died. I knew she needed to be here, that you needed her to be here. But that was six years ago."

"And you're ready to move on."

Frank's acceptance caught Nathan off guard. "Er…yes." Nathan looked from Frank to Olivia and back again. "Look, Frank, I'm sorry if that hurts you. But yes, I'm ready to move on."

"Then that's what you should do…what you both should do."

Olivia gasped. "Dad, you don't mean that."

Frank walked to her and took her hands in his. "Sweetheart, it's not that I want you to go, but I understand it's what you need to do. Nathan is right."

"I am?"

"He is?"

Under any other circumstances, Frank would have found their responses comical. But now was not the time to make jokes.

"Yes, he's right. You were never meant to be here forever. You had your own dreams before your mother died, and they had nothing to do with the station."

"But, Dad."

"No buts, Olivia. If it's the difference between saving your marriage or splitting up your family, then you need to go. You need to figure out what the two of you truly want for yourselves. And the only way to do that is to be away from the station for a while. It's what the Lord would want of you."

"I don't care what the Lord would want of me!" she yelled in frustration as she yanked her hands from his. Her eyes blazed with anger and something deeper.

But Frank couldn't see past his initial shock at her outburst. Stricken by her vehemence, he snapped back. "Olivia May! You don't mean that."

Both Nathan and Olivia gaped at him. His response was very uncharacteristic. He rarely ever raised his voice, and now he'd done it twice in a matter of minutes.

"I'm sorry, Dad. It's just…" Words escaped her as she raked her fingers through her hair in frustration. "I just don't want a biblical lecture right now."

Frank was still stung by her words. Faith had been the backbone of his family going generations back. It was what had gotten him through when he'd lost Esther. To hear his own daughter say she didn't want anything to do with faith, however temporary that stance might be, hurt him deeply.

Olivia winced. "I'm sorry. I didn't mean that, either. I just don't know how I'm supposed to feel or what I'm supposed to do."

"Then that's the best time to call upon the Lord. Ask Him to show you," Frank said gently. He knew he would have to tread carefully if he wanted Olivia to see reason.

"But I feel so conflicted. I don't want my family to break up, and that includes you, Joshua, and Julian, too."

Her voice quivered and her despair tore at Frank's heart. He could only imagine the internal struggle she was battling. But the Lord's guidance was clear, at least to him.

"You know the verses, Olivia. *Wives, submit to your own husbands, as to the Lord. For the husband is the head of the wife even as Christ is the head of the church, His body, and is Himself its Saviour. Now as the church submits to Christ, so also wives should submit in everything to their husbands.*"

That admonishment would be hard for his daughter to hear right now. He'd raised her to be strong and independent, just like her mother had been, but she needed to realise that she could be both strong and independent and submissive before her husband and the Lord.

Before she could make any further protest, Frank continued. "But, in the same sentiment," he looked directly at Nathan, "You Nathan, are to *love your wife, just as Christ loved the Church and gave Himself up for her.*"

Nathan folded his arms. "I've done that."

"Yes, you have, and admirably so. You gave up your life and your dreams for Olivia." Frank turned to his daughter. "And now it's your turn to do the same for Nathan. Your marriage needs it, your family needs it. Nathan wouldn't be asking you to do this lightly, honey, and you need to take heed."

He wrapped his arms around her, holding her close as she wept against his chest. When her sobs subsided, he spoke softly. "You'll always have a place here, if that's what you want." Frank raised his head to look at Nathan. "What you BOTH want."

CHAPTER 20

After breakfast the next morning, Frank called a family meeting to talk about a few important matters. Those being his meeting with the DPI officer, Olivia and Nathan's decision to leave the station and move to the city, and his new relationship with Maggie and the desire to slow down and enjoy life a little more. Things were changing at Goddard Downs and he wanted to ensure that everyone was not only aware of the changes but could also have a say in the station's future. His only regret was that Joshua still wasn't back from his latest adventure, but this couldn't wait.

"What's this about, Dad? Surely it can wait until the morning chores are done," Julian said, his expression one of pained tolerance.

"Jim and Dean can handle the morning chores just fine. What I have to say is important for you all to hear." Frank paused and blew out a heavy breath as he figured out the best way to start. It wasn't often they had such a serious meeting.

"As you all know, I went to Darwin last week to meet with our prospective buyer, Mr. Tamala, and also with the DPI officer about the station's certifications and licensing. The first meeting went well, but to say the second didn't go as planned would be an understatement."

Julian crossed his arms. "I told you I should have gone with you. I would have handled the situation."

"I handled the situation just fine, Julian. I was well prepared with all your notes and research, but it didn't make a difference in the end."

"You should have let me…"

Frank stared him down. It was enough to stop Julian in his tracks. He didn't often use his position in the family as a means of controlling a room, but he did so now. He didn't even have to get up from the table. All he had to do was fold his arms across his chest and wait. He didn't say a word, he simply pinned Julian with his gaze. Julian's tirade faded and the seconds ticked by. No one flinched or uttered a word.

Finally, Julian let out a breath and shook his head. He was still angry, but at least he had enough respect for his father not to open his mouth again.

"Now, as I was saying, the meeting didn't go as planned." He looked directly at his eldest son. "It didn't matter how thorough our research was, or that we did in fact, qualify for the exemption for this year."

"What do you mean?" Julian demanded.

"Money."

"Money? I don't understand. We have the money to cover the fees."

"Not that kind of money, son."

Julian's brows drew together. "I don't get it."

Frank rubbed his thumb and two fingers together.

Julian's eyes widened. "Bribery? You mean bribery, don't you? That's ridiculous!"

"He didn't exactly say that, but it's what he intimated."

"Are you sure?" Julian asked.

Frank shrugged. "Not entirely, but I'm not stupid."

"You didn't agree?" Olivia asked, sounding horrified.

"Of course not."

"And that's why you called this emergency family meeting," she said.

Frank nodded. "We need to figure out what to do for the station. Since we can't afford to make all the necessary license and certification changes in time for next year, we either pay the penalty or find another source of income."

They were all aware that if they couldn't export their beef, the station wouldn't survive. They could sell domestically, but with seventy-one percent of all their beef and veal production exported, there was little money in domestic sales. They'd have no choice but to look at alternatives, or worst-case scenario, sell the station. The last thing any of them wanted.

Julian leaned forward. "I've always said we should expand into tourism. Now is as good a time as any. Better to get in now while there's some buzz than be one of the last stations to enter the market."

Opening the station to tourism had never sat well with Frank. It still didn't. He'd not acted on Bethany's suggestion. It didn't seem right to burden Maggie with their worries. He drew a slow breath and folded his arms. "There are other things we need to consider before we start throwing out solutions, especially ones that would radically change our business."

"Like what?" Julian asked, his brows raised.

Frank glanced at Nathan and Olivia. They both gave a nod. "Well, things are going to be changing around here soon. Nathan and Olivia have decided to move back to the city. They'll be leaving in three months' time."

"What?! When was this decided?" Julian's brows drew together as he looked at his sister in disbelief. "You sure picked a fine time to leave."

"That's not fair!" Nathan's expression was tight with strain and the muscle in his jaw quivered. "We dropped everything to be here and support the family when your mum died. We've given everything to this place for six years!"

"Enough! Both of you!" Frank glared at Julian. "You have no right to judge your sister and Nathan's decision to move on with their life as a family. You knew this wasn't their lifelong dream, but they put everything on hold, including Olivia's university studies, to be here with us. To help us out. It's well past time they did something for themselves and their family."

Julian's face coloured. Contrite, he apologised to Nathan and his sister. "I'm sorry, my emotions got the best of me. It's hard to imagine this place without either of you or the kids."

Olivia nodded. "It wasn't an easy decision, and we're going to miss you all, but this is something we need to do as a family." She reached out and squeezed Nathan's hand.

"And we're all going to miss you," Janella said quietly, emotion thick in her voice.

Olivia brushed tears from her eyes and smiled wistfully at her sister-in-law.

"It's going to be an adjustment for everyone," Frank said, "but we'll get through this and whatever else might come, including changing how we run the station."

"I still think tourism is our best option," Julian said. "I've already looked up the licensing costs. It's negligible compared to the export fees."

"We'll put that idea on the list, but can we think of other options?" Frank asked.

"What about using some of the fields to grow soy or cotton?" Olivia suggested.

"Or even hemp," Janella added. "It's fast growing and doesn't damage the soil like some of the other crops. And the market for hemp is exploding since it's such a sustainable and eco-friendly resource." She was passionate about minimalistic processes and had helped to implement sustainable farming methods around the station, including the use of biodynamics to reduce the amount of fertiliser the station purchased by incorporating the cattle, swine, and sheep manure into their composting process. Not only had it saved them thousands of dollars, the fertiliser helped produce some of the finest crops and vegetables the station had ever seen.

Julian rolled his eyes. "That's a novel idea, hon, but crops can be high risk because they're dependent on the weather. One nasty drought or too much rain could kill our entire yield. Then where would we be? Tourism isn't as fickle."

Janella sat back in her chair and let out a heavy sigh. Frank silently prayed that troubles weren't ahead for these two as well. Janella had always acquiesced to Julian, but he sensed she was growing frustrated with his increasingly overbearing manner. They all were. "Whatever we do will carry some level of risk. Even tourism. The best thing we can do is pray for guidance."

There were nods all around.

"Let's do that now." Frank extended his hands and waited until the circle was complete before bowing his head.

"Lord, we come to You in prayer seeking wisdom and guidance. Help us to not lean on our own opinions, thoughts or dreams, or on what society, culture, and government regulators might have to say about what we should do. We need Godly, not earthly, wisdom. Things are uncertain and emotions are running high. Help us to be patient and kind with one another, and to consider each other's opinions with respect.

"You've commanded us not to be anxious about anything, but in everything by prayer and supplication with thanksgiving to let our requests be made known to You, and by doing so, Your peace, which surpasses all understanding, will guard our hearts and our minds. We humbly bring these requests to You now and will wait on You for a solution.

"In Your Son's precious name, we pray. Amen."

CHAPTER 21

Breaking news: Another terrorist attack in Paris results in mass casualties with dozens dead and hundreds more injured. We're bringing you an update from our correspondent Serena Donovan who is live at the scene.

At the mention of her daughter's name, Maggie jerked to attention. Putting her laptop to the side, she grabbed the remote and turned up the volume to listen to the news report as her daughter appeared on the screen. Behind Serena, smoke billowed from a building that was barely visible, while emergency personnel scurried all around.

"Serena, what can you tell us about the attack and the current situation?"

"Michael, the police and the gendarme are still gathering evidence on the attacks and emergency personnel are still tending to the wounded, as you can see behind me. What we do know is that there were three separate blasts outside this stadium, the Stade de France.

The first one happened at approximately nine twenty pm. A second blast followed ten minutes later. It's speculated that this second blast caused the greatest casualties as hordes of spectators rushed out of the stadium to evacuate from the first blast. Twenty-three minutes later, a third blast was set off on another side of the stadium.

"We can confirm that the President, Emmanuel Macron, was, in fact, inside the stadium at the time of the first blast but was safely evacuated by his security detail and is unharmed. The same can't be said for hundreds of others."

"Serena—do we know who was behind these attacks?"

"Nothing has been confirmed yet, Michael, however, rumours have already begun to circulate that ISIS is claiming responsibility. Again, though, nothing official has been confirmed."

The news cut back to the main anchor who recapped what Serena had detailed. Maggie's heart pounded in her chest so hard she could hear her own heartbeat pulsing in her eardrums. Serena was safe, but the fact that she was even there in the city where the attacks took place filled Maggie with fear for her daughter's safety. Grabbing her phone, she quickly sent a text asking if she was okay.

She stared at the phone for several minutes, willing Serena to reply, but nothing. Maggie tried not to be disheartened by the lack of response as she was sure her daughter was fine, but it would have been nice to have that familiar beep back for reassurance. She knew it could be hours, or even days before she might hear from Serena. The mobile phone networks in France were probably overloaded and inundated with family members trying to reach their loved ones. At least Maggie took comfort in knowing that Serena was not among those injured or missing.

Even so, she bowed her head and prayed for her daughter.

Dear Lord, precious Father, I come to You this morning with a heavy and concerned heart, asking for protection for Serena. Let Your angels guard and keep her safe. Surround her and her colleagues with Your divine protection as they travel around the afflicted areas.

I also pray for those who've been affected. Those who've lost loved ones. Those who've been injured. Comfort them all in their time of grief.

I ask all these things in Your precious name. Amen.

Maggie kept her eyes glued to the television all day. She called Frank and asked him to pray. She spoke to Jeremy. He hadn't heard the news but was just as concerned as her when he flicked it on. That night, sleep came fitfully, her dreams tormented by images of bomb blasts and unspeakable injuries. At one point, she dreamt she was there during the blast and that she and Serena had been separated. She was terrified as she fled barefoot down a long, dark corridor. Smoke and debris clouded her sight and choked her breath as she screamed for her daughter, but her cries went unanswered. Sirens blasted in the distance, growing louder and louder until it was all she could hear.

She jerked awake as the sound of her alarm broke through her dream. It took three tries to swipe the screen to shut it off, her hands were shaking so badly. She flopped back against the pillows as she let the last remnants of her dream wash over her. Sweat matted her hair against her neck and her pulse was thready.

It was only a dream. It was only a dream.

She repeated the words over and over until she could finally control her breathing. She glanced at her phone. Still no response. She wouldn't panic, although it had been twenty-four hours since she sent the text. Sometimes it took Serena longer than that to reply. If she didn't hear anything by the following morning, then she'd panic. Until then, she'd go about her day as normal.

Determined to be productive, Maggie locked her phone in her desk drawer. Out of sight, out of mind, or so she hoped. She read what she'd already written and tweaked bits here and there, and then pulled out all her notes and journals from her trips and interviews and spent the better part of an hour sifting through them.

She'd considered downloading some journaling software to help her put her thoughts in order, but she'd dismissed the idea. She was an old school journalist and preferred pen to paper and sticky notes to technology.

She purposely put her notes on Goddard Downs at the bottom of the stack. She didn't want to be distracted by thoughts of Frank right now. However, they kept creeping into her mind, alongside thoughts of Serena. Tired of fighting the pull, she finally opened the drawer and took out her phone. Still no message. The waiting was driving her crazy, so much so that when her phone rang, she almost dropped it on the floor in her hurry to answer it.

But it wasn't Serena. It was her boss, Suzanne. She was checking on her to see how the article was coming along. Maggie gave her a brief summary of where she was at with it and a quick rundown of how she would like to extend it.

"I love what you have here, Maggie. You've got such a variety of information."

"I hear a but coming."

Suzanne chuckled. "You know me too well. It's a good but. I promise."

"Okay, let's hear it."

"I feel like something's missing."

Despite herself, Maggie felt a little deflated. She'd put so much effort into collecting as much information as she could. She thought she'd covered everything. "Like what? Are you thinking I need to visit a few more stations?"

"No, I don't think you need more of the same perspective." Suzanne grew quiet and Maggie could imagine the cogs turning in her brain. She'd known Suzanne long enough to know when to give her a few minutes to work out whatever it was she was trying to say. Eventually, Suzanne spoke her thoughts out loud. "Maybe that's it. We need a different perspective."

"But whose? This is supposed to be from the women's point of view. I don't think we should include the men's perspective of station life. Not much has changed in that regard in over a century." They worked for a women's magazine and the whole point of the story was to shed light on how women faired with station life, not how the men fared.

"That's it!"

Maggie must have missed something because she had no clue what Suzanne was excited about. "What is?"

"A generational perspective. That's what's missing."

"I'm still not following. I spoke with a number of the older children on most of the stations."

"I don't mean the younger generation. I mean the older one.

Were there any older women on any of the stations who might remember a time, perhaps fifty years ago or longer?"

The lightbulb finally came on in Maggie's head. She'd been so focused on the next generation of women coming up that she'd completely excluded the older one. Not intentionally, but there weren't any matriarchs still living on any of the stations she'd visited, and she told Suzanne as much.

"Do you think you could find out if there are any still alive but living elsewhere? I think that having at least one perspective from that age group would help round out the article, especially since we know there was a time when women weren't allowed to do physical work on the station. I'd like to hear firsthand what that time was like."

The idea held merit. Showing how far women had come would definitely round out the article. Maggie thought about it for a minute as she tried to remember if anyone she'd interviewed had mentioned a parent or grandparent who'd been a part of the station and was still alive. Then she had an aha moment. Frank had mentioned that his mother, Mary, was still alive. She'd have to be in her eighties or nineties. It was worth a shot.

"Frank Goddard mentioned that his mother was still alive and lives in Kununurra now."

"Was she an integral part of station life?"

"Yes, I believe she and her late husband worked together for many years."

"She sounds like a good fit. Do you mind taking another trip out there to see her if she's amenable? I think a personal visit and some snapshots would be much more poignant than a telephone interview. But I know it's quite a long way."

Would I mind having an excuse to see Frank again? Maggie's heart leapt with joy at the prospect, but she quickly repressed her excitement before she responded. "Of course, I don't mind, especially if it adds something more to the story. Besides, Frank's family is quite welcoming." *Most of them, anyway.* "And I don't mind the long drive. I found it quite relaxing last time."

"Perfect."

They finished finalising the details of the article, and discussed what questions Maggie should ask Mary, and then Suzanne left her to make the plans.

Maggie was giddy with excitement as she dialled Frank's number. She wasn't sure why she was nervous. She'd spoken to him almost every night since he'd returned to Goddard Downs, but this time it was different. If it worked out, she'd be seeing him again soon and not just talking to him on the phone.

She felt the familiar flutters in her belly as she waited for him to pick up. She didn't have long to wait because he answered on the third ring. After a few moments of greeting, she quickly gave him the rundown of her conversation with Suzanne and asked if it would be possible to come to the station again and interview his mother there.

"She lives in Kununurra with my older sister, Sarah, but I'm sure she'd be happy to talk with you. I can have her call you, or I can give you her number."

Maggie's heart dropped. "I was actually hoping I could come out there and interview her in person." That part was true enough. Face to face meetings often revealed more inciteful details and information that wouldn't normally be discussed over the phone. Plus, Suzanne wanted her to get some shots of Mary on the station if possible. She took a deep breath. "My boss would like some photos of her on the station. Do you think that might be possible?" She held her breath.

"Sarah was planning on coming out to the station to visit this weekend. I'm sure she could bring Mum with her and that she'd be happy to meet with you then. Is that too soon? I know it doesn't give you much time. I can ask them to delay the trip a week if that doesn't work for your schedule."

"No, no, I wouldn't want them to do that just for me. It so happens that this weekend works for me too." Truth be told, she would have made it work even if it hadn't been convenient. But she already had the okay from Suzanne to make another trip, so she was good to go.

"Would you like to stay in the cabin again?"

The gentleness of his voice enveloped her, and she momentarily closed her eyes, remembering the taste of his lips on hers before she replied, "Won't you need that for your mum and sister?"

"Mum prefers to stay at the main house with Julian and Janella and me so we can be there if she needs anything. She and Sarah will share one of the guest rooms. It's perfectly fine if you want to stay at the cabin, Maggie."

"Well, then yes. I'd love to. Thank you."

"That's settled, then. I'll look forward to seeing you on Friday."

"Until Friday." Warmth spread through her as she imagined being in his arms again. Then her phone beeped. A text from Serena. Shorter than she would have liked but at least she knew her daughter was safe. Serena said that the connection was spotty but promised to call her as soon as she could on a more secure landline. Knowing that her prayers had been answered and that her daughter was safe put Maggie's mind at ease. It made it easier for her to focus on her upcoming interview with Mary. And seeing Frank again. She quickly packed and got ready for the long drive to Goddard Downs.

CHAPTER 22

Mrs. Mary, as everyone affectionately referred to Frank's mother, was a spitfire even at ninety-four years young. She was a tiny thing, and bent over, she barely reached Maggie's chin, but she was as full of vim and vigour as someone half her age, putting Maggie to shame. Despite her advanced age, she got around well and was active in her church and local charities, volunteering her time each week to help those in need. In the two days Maggie had been at Goddard Downs, she'd quickly come to admire the spritely matriarch.

On Maggie's first night, Mary regaled everyone with stories from when she'd first come to the station as a young bride. Maggie had asked if she minded the conversation being recorded, and she didn't, so Maggie was able to sit and listen without the need to take notes. That night, she gained new respect for the pioneer generation. The struggles and challenges they faced every day and night were amazing.

"I don't know if I would have survived," Maggie said after Mrs. Mary finished the story about the night a herd of wild buffalo stampeded through the property, destroying most of the outbuildings. William had been camped out with a few of the hands and she was at home with two young children. Since the buffalo destroyed the radio tower, she was unable to call anyone for help. She thought they would all die that night, but they didn't. And when William returned, they went about rebuilding.

"I think you're made of sterner stuff than you think," she said to Maggie. "People often surprise themselves when they're faced with adversity."

"But I've never had to face the kind of adversity you have. I'm not just talking about that night, but in general. It's so remote out here, but I'm sure it was even more so in the '50's. It couldn't have been easy for you, especially being a young mother."

"Station life is never easy, no matter who you are, or what time period you're from." Mrs. Mary rocked in her chair for a moment before elaborating. "But it's true, being a woman on a cattle station, especially, one who worked alongside the men, was much harder sixty to seventy years ago. Although that doesn't mean it's easy now."

"Amen to that!" Both Oliva and Janella said in unison.

"Ha, you two are more pampered than you think," Mary said, her eyes twinkling.

"But you just said..." Olivia interjected.

Mrs. Mary cut her off. "I know what I said, child. I'm not saying your work is easy, but you have it easier than I did sixty years ago. It was post World War II and though the economy was thriving, out here in the outback we didn't enjoy the same benefits as those in the city. Drives were still done totally on horseback. We didn't have any of the fancy machinery or tools you have now that do in hours what took us days. We didn't have mobile phones or satellite phones to keep in contact with our men when they were out for days or weeks on drives. For a long time, we didn't even have landlines. We couldn't call anyone for help in times of trouble. We were on our own."

The two younger women looked well and truly admonished.

Maggie continued with her questions. "Can you tell me more about how you handled the times when William was away for weeks on end?"

"I had no choice but to do what had to be done. Station chores still needed doing, kids and animals needed tending. Life didn't stop just because he wasn't there."

Maggie was surprised by Mrs. Mary's nonchalance about such a huge undertaking. "True, but didn't you find it more difficult by yourself?"

"Yes. And more so at night. But the work got done, it always got done. William never left me short-handed when he went on drives. Those who were left behind stepped up and worked a little harder, that's all."

"But when the work was done…" Maggie prompted.

"That's when I missed him the most. Especially after I'd put the kids to bed. Life on the station can be lonely, and even though we worked side by side every day, the quiet times at night were always special. That was our time together, so when he wasn't there, I felt lonely." Her eyes moistened as she spoke. "William was my best friend. Even though he's been gone almost twenty years, I miss him now as much as I did then."

Maggie dabbed at her own tears. To hear Frank's mother speak of such love touched her immensely and made her long to experience the same. She glanced at Frank and wondered if he was thinking along similar lines.

SHORTLY AFTER THEY all bid each other good night, Frank walked Maggie back to the cabin. His arm was draped over her shoulders and she nestled against him. She felt as if she was wrapped in a warm cocoon she didn't want to leave. But her time at the station was quickly coming to a close.

When he asked if she'd like to go on a proper date before she left, she readily agreed. They hadn't spent much time together since she'd mostly been with Mrs. Mary and he'd had things to attend to on the station. He suggested a sunset cruise on Lake Argyle, and Maggie thought it sounded wonderful.

Reaching the cabin, neither was in a hurry to part. "Would you like to sit awhile?" he asked, rubbing her arms as he faced her.

"Sure." As she joined him on the bench seat outside the cabin, he slipped his arm around her shoulders again and pulled her close. She snuggled against him as she sank into his embrace.

The frogs were already creating a cacophony, but somehow, despite their noise, it was peaceful. Natural. So different to the traffic noise of the city. But could she live here? She was probably thinking too far ahead, but if her and Frank's relationship continued to develop, that was the most likely scenario. She would have to live here, because she couldn't see Frank giving up the station to live in Darwin. This was his life. And maybe this was what God had in mind for her. Hadn't she asked Him for something new?

She raised her head and studied his profile. His jaw was firm, but his face was kindly. He was a good man. And she was falling for him. No. She needed to rephrase that. She had fallen for him, hook, line and sinker.

He glanced down at her and their gazes met and held. As he lifted his hand to her cheek and let his finger slowly trail down her hairline, a dizzying current raced through her. When he lowered his head and brushed his lips gently across hers, she knew she was in love.

After he bid her good night with a lingering kiss and a promise to see her soon, Maggie went to sleep with joy and contentment filling her heart.

CHAPTER 23

Maggie spent the next day and a half with Mrs. Mary, Olivia, and Janella while Frank, along with Julian, Nathan and a few of the hands, moved some of the cattle from the north side to the south side of the station. They were camping out overnight, so she barely saw him until he returned late on Sunday morning.

With the men away, she heard more of Mrs. Mary's recollections, which she found fascinating. Mrs. Mary gave her some old black and white photos of her and William and their family on the station to use for the article. Touched, Maggie promised to take exceptional care of the family heirlooms and return them to her in the same condition as they were lent.

Mrs. Mary took several rests throughout the day, leaving Maggie to her own devices. Some of the time she spent with Olivia and Janella, but she also spent time on her own, sitting by the lagoon. Olivia had set her up with a rocking chair and a lap tray so she could work on her articles. The sound of bullfrogs and cockatoos provided a great backdrop and in their own way were soothing.

By Sunday morning she found she needed that soothing. Today was the day of her date with Frank and time was going by ever so slowly. For some reason, Maggie was anxious and jittery. Being near the water calmed her some, and she tried to force herself to focus on her article, but it wasn't as easy to get lost in her story as it normally was.

She rubbed her eyes with the back of her hand. She'd been staring at the small screen for well over an hour and her eyes were tired from the glare. She closed the computer and set it to the side before leaning back in her chair. She hadn't meant to doze. She'd only planned to rest her eyes for a few moments, but her body had obviously thought otherwise. When she finally stirred from her impromptu nap, she felt rested and more at ease.

Glancing at her watch, she realised she had less than an hour to get ready for her date. She quickly gathered her belongings and headed into the cabin. After taking the world's quickest shower, she was putting on her second earring when his truck rolled up. He was early.

She quickly clipped the earing and met him at the door. He looked dapper in his pressed cream trousers and button-up white shirt. In his hand, he held a beautiful bouquet of wildflowers. She smiled and thanked him when he leaned in and kissed her cheek and handed the bouquet to her.

So far, their dates had been fairly casual, but something about this afternoon felt different. When he took her hand and kissed it gently as they walked to the truck together, she sensed a deeper closeness between them. Her heart filled with anticipation while she tried to ignore the fact that come morning, she'd be leaving.

It was a little over an hour's drive to Lake Argyle, but the time passed quickly as he told her about the last day and half with the cattle. Before she knew it, he was pulling into the dock area. The sun was low in the sky and cast a brilliant shine across the huge expanse of water. Frank had booked the new sunset couples tour which was a three-hour lake tour with a complimentary glass of champagne and plates of canapés. It was a smaller cruiser than the main one, and there were only four other couples besides Frank and Maggie. She liked that it was a more intimate setting. There was plenty of room for each couple to spread out and have their own space on the boat.

As the captain piloted them away from the dock, the first mate gave a brief history of the lake. Interestingly enough, Lake Argyle was the home of one of the first cattle stations in the East Kimberley. One of the founding families, the Duracks, later built one of the largest cattle empires in all of the Kimberley. Maggie found it ironic that even on their special date, she was still able to obtain facts for her story.

They spent the first hour standing at one of the high-top tables sipping their champagne and sampling the array of cheeses and meats arranged beautifully on the silver platters. She normally wouldn't have indulged in champagne, but for this one date, she decided to let her hair down like Serena had encouraged her to do. Mostly, they talked about his mother. Frank laughed as Maggie recalled their conversations.

"Yes, my mother is quite the spitfire, even now. She gave my dad a run for his money, but I know he wouldn't have had it any other way. He always looked at her as if the sun rose and set by her."

"And your mother had the same look in her eye when she spoke of him." Maggie leaned against the railing and gazed out across the expanse of water, her voice tinged with longing. "A love like that doesn't come around often. It sounds like a one of a kind romance. A fairy tale that most people don't get to experience." Surprised at her boldness, she figured it must have been the champagne that had allowed her to speak her heart.

When Frank remained silent so long that Maggie finally turned around, his gaze was fixed on her, his brow slightly furrowed, and his expression was one of grim determination. Concerned, she reached for his hand. "Frank…is everything okay?"

"What if it's not?"

She frowned. "What if what's not?" He wasn't making any sense.

"What if that kind of love isn't one of a kind?" His expression softened and he covered her hand with his. Now he spoke with excitement and fervour, his blue eyes brimming with tenderness and passion. "What if that kind of love, the kind that my parents had, isn't a once in a lifetime kind of love. Do you believe in second chances?"

Maggie sucked in a breath. Time stood still as his words sunk in. He was talking about them. In that moment, no one else on the boat existed but her and Frank. Her ears began to thrum, kind of like the feeling when you sat next to the engine on an airplane right before take-off.

Frank's expression eased further. "I don't mean to scare you, Maggie. I know this might seem sudden, but I don't think it is. I think we were meant to meet. I feel strongly that it was God who brought you into my life."

He smiled and the softness in his eyes was nearly her undoing. "I've been alone for a long time, and I didn't even know that I was missing something. Not until you came along. You changed my life, my perspective. At the end of each day, I find myself wanting to tell you about it, and I wonder how your day was. I'm falling in love with you, Maggie."

These were words she'd longed to hear, but now that Frank had uttered them, she found she was speechless as panic and self-doubt crept its way into her mind. There was no way a man like Frank could think she could be his fairy-tale ending. Cliff had left her because she wasn't enough. Frank needed a woman who was stronger than her. Plus, things like this didn't happen to her.

She tried to pull her hand away, but Frank held on.

"Maggie, look at me."

She couldn't.

"Please."

Slowly, she lifted her gaze to his. She didn't see anger or disappointment. Instead, she saw understanding and love.

"I know this is scary. It is for me, too."

Maggie drew a breath. "It doesn't seem like it. You seem so sure of yourself."

"I'm not. If you felt my chest, you'd know my heart was beating a mile a minute. And I'm pretty sure I would have sweated through my shirt if we didn't have the breeze from the lake."

His poor attempt at a joke made Maggie smile. She'd been so concerned with her feelings, she hadn't even stopped to consider his. What it must have taken for him to reveal how he felt. And here she was, acting like a scared rabbit instead of a grown woman. She could do better than that. He deserved better than that. He deserved the truth.

"I don't know what to say, Frank. I want to believe it can be true. But I thought I had my fairy tale with Cliff and it turned out to be anything but. It scares me…no, it terrifies me, to believe in love."

"I can't pretend to understand what you went through, that much is true. Esther and I had a wonderful marriage. We had our share of troubles and at times we didn't like each other very much, but we had a happy life together. Yours wasn't the same. But this is different. And I'm not Cliff."

"I know that, Frank. I would never compare the two of you."

"But you are."

Those three words stopped Maggie in her tracks. It was true. She was comparing him to Cliff and that wasn't fair. *Judge not, that you be not judged.* She felt the sharp sting of her subconscious reprimanding her with that verse. She needed to heed the words of her inner voice right now because she was at risk of losing something, no someone, very precious to her.

"You're right. I was. And I'm truly sorry for that. I've been angry for so long. I guess it was easier to think the worst than consider other possibilities."

"And can you? Can you think of other possibilities with me?"

Could she? Isn't that exactly what she'd been hoping for?

She looked at those kind blue eyes that were fixed on hers. She didn't see deception or false platitudes. Instead, she saw honesty, compassion, and an earnestness that calmed her spirit. If Frank could be so willing to try again after losing the love of his life, so could she.

"Yes. Yes, I can."

He smiled and pulled her close. "You don't know how happy that makes me." He kissed the side of her hair.

As she rested her head against his chest, she placed her hand over his heart. Just like he'd said, it was pounding. She could feel the steady thrum beneath her palm. She liked that she had that effect on him, because the feeling was mutual. She raised her head and looked into his eyes. "So, what does this mean? Where do we go from here?"

He brushed her hair with his hand. "I'm not sure yet, Maggie. Our lives are complicated at the moment. It's not like either one of us can simply pick up and move halfway across the country tomorrow, but we'll work it out. One thing I know for sure, I want to see as much of you as I can."

He gazed over her shoulder and she could all but see the gears working in his mind. Then he slipped his arms lower and put them around her waist as he gazed into her eyes. "I'd have to rearrange some things at the station, but I'm sure I can visit you at least one week a month. And maybe you could arrange with your boss to do the same."

"That's a lot of driving, Frank. For both of us." At his crestfallen face, she quickly added, "But I'm willing to do it, if that's our only option." As she spoke, her mind was already whirling.

Why couldn't she pack up and move to Kununurra? They'd be just over an hour from each other then. It wasn't like her job required her to be in the office every day, or even every week. She hadn't physically been to her office in over three weeks.

She could work anywhere, as long as she had access to the internet.

"Are you going to enlighten me as to what's going on in that lovely head of yours?"

Frank's question roused her from her thoughts. His eyes twinkled as he raised his brows. Apparently, she'd been lost in thought for longer than she knew.

"Well, I don't want to get your hopes up prematurely, but…"

"But…what?"

"Well, my job doesn't require me to be in an office every day, or even every week. As long as I have internet, I can communicate with my boss and deliver my articles."

Frank's face lit up. "Goddard Downs has internet." He said it with such a mischievous gleam in his eye, she couldn't help but laugh.

"Yes, I know. But I wasn't thinking of moving to the station. I don't think that would be appropriate. But I could move to Kununurra." She held up her hands before they both got carried away. "I'd have to run it past Suzanne, but I don't see it being an issue. I can base myself anywhere. I can rent a little place in town and still be closer to you."

"Or, you could live in the cabin on the station until…" His voice trailed off and he bit his lip.

He snapped his mouth shut and Maggie knew he'd said more than he meant to. She cocked her head to the side and regarded him closely. "Until what?"

He shifted his weight to his other foot under her scrutiny. "Well, I'd meant to wait and let you get used to the idea of me loving you first." He wouldn't look her straight in the eye.

"First? Before what?" When he didn't answer right away, she pressed him. "Frank?"

He stared at his feet for a moment as if to find his courage and then looked her straight in the eyes. "Marriage."

There it was happening again. The scenery fading around her until all she saw was him.

Marriage.

If he'd wanted to shock her, he'd succeeded. Never in her wildest dreams had she imagined that he'd propose so soon. *Marriage?* The word sounded foreign in her mind. It sounded even more strange when she said it out loud. "Marriage?"

"Yes, marriage." He tucked her under his arm and guided her to the back of the boat away from the other couples. "I'd wanted to do this more formally, and actually get on one knee, but given the circumstances of our current conversation, I think it's important you know my intentions." He paused as he reached into his trouser pocket and pulled out a tiny black jewellery box.

"I'm a traditional man, with traditional values. I wouldn't invite you to stay on my property indefinitely without giving you the promise of a future together."

Maggie gasped and her hand went to her throat as he opened the box. In it was a solitaire diamond set on a thin white gold band. It was modest, but to her, it was perfect.

"Maggie Donovan, I've loved you since the moment we met. I believe God brought you into my life for a reason and that reason was to be my life partner. Will you do me the great honour of becoming my wife? Will you marry me, Maggie?"

So many thoughts ran through her mind. Mostly reasons why not to accept. It was too soon. She barely knew him. It was inappropriate. But when she looked into those kind eyes, she knew he was right. God had put them in each other's lives for a reason. She felt that with every cell in her body. So, for once in her life, she didn't second guess herself. She simply took a leap of faith. "Yes. Frank Goddard, I love you with all my heart and I would love to marry you."

She'd barely finished before he pulled her into his arms and kissed her passionately. She could feel the wealth of emotion behind his kiss and answered it in kind. This kiss held more than want and desire, it held the promise of a love that was brought upon them by the grace of God and would stand the test of time. In her heart, Maggie knew that Frank would never leave her of his own volition. There was an unwavering conviction in him that made her feel safe. Safe in that no matter what life threw at them, he would remain steadfast in his devotion to her and to Christ.

She had no idea that his devotion would be tested so soon.

They'd barely had time to bask in the glow of their newfound commitment to each other before life crashed down around them. As he pulled up to the main house, ready to announce their engagement to the family, Maggie received a phone call. There'd been another terrorist attack, and Serena was missing.

Maggie tried to listen as Danny, Serena's station manager, relayed as much detail as he could, which wasn't much. There'd been an attack at the hotel Serena was staying at. A suicide bomber had targeted the restaurant on the first level and the blast caused part of the building to collapse. Dozens of patrons and guests of the hotel were still unaccounted for, including Serena.

Maggie's knees gave way and she collapsed right there on the porch steps and sobbed uncontrollably. Her daughter was missing half a world away. It was a mother's worst nightmare. She wanted to rail at God. Scream and curse Him for being so cruel. How could He make all her dreams come true in one moment and then dash them the next? Logically, she knew it wasn't His wish for her, but she was blinded by her pain.

Frank did his best to console her, but the only thing that would assuage her fear was to have her daughter in her arms. And the only way she could do that was to go to Paris and find her. Nothing else mattered. Not even Frank.

She couldn't think about moving forward with her life until she found Serena.

Their announcement would have to wait.

∽

CHAPTER 24

The twenty-seven-hour flight from Kununurra to Paris was the longest Maggie had ever taken. Or at least it seemed that way. Unable to fully rest because of worry over her daughter, Serena, she'd dozed on and off the entire trip. Each time she woke, there was a heavy lump in her stomach. A dull ache of foreboding pervaded her entire body despite her attempts to trust God that Serena would be found alive under the rubble.

During the two-hour transit in Singapore, the first thing she did was check her phone. There were no messages from Serena. She hadn't expected any. But there was one from Danny, Serena's television station manager. He simply said that Serena was still listed as missing, but the search was continuing and there was still hope she would be found alive.

There was another message from Frank saying he loved her and was praying for her. Frank… Maggie had been on cloud nine before she received the phone call from Danny. She and

Frank had just returned to Goddard Downs, the cattle station in northern Australia that Frank owned, bursting with joy and excitement over the future following his proposal during a sunset boat trip on Lake Argyle. But the evening, filled with wonder and new beginnings, quickly became a mother's worst nightmare.

Danny had called, panic-stricken. There'd been another terrorist attack in Paris, this time, at the hotel where Serena was staying. She, along with many others, was missing. Maggie had dropped everything and caught the first flight to Paris. Frank had driven her to Kununurra, the nearest town to Goddard Downs, and waited with her at the small airport until she boarded the plane. He'd wanted to go with her, but he had his own problems to deal with on the station, so she'd convinced him that she'd be okay. They'd promised to stay in touch as often as possible, and for the time they were together before she boarded, he'd comforted her as best he could.

Even after her arrival, it had taken another twenty-four hours before Serena was found. She'd been buried underneath the rubble of the hotel and was found in the south stairwell. That's what saved her. The heavy concrete of the stairwell had deflected most of the blast, but the weight of the upper floors crashing down on each other had crumbled part of it. Serena had dived under a landing but had been caught in the debris.

She suffered numerous injuries, including a collapsed lung, a perforated spleen, a broken ankle, and a concussion. But that wasn't the worst of it. The weight of the rubble had trapped her as fires raged all around. Unable to move, she couldn't escape the inferno and had sustained significant burns across sixty percent of her body. The burns were the greatest concern because of the risk of infection. The doctors weren't optimistic about her survival. They weren't even sure she'd make it through that first night, and at one point, they almost lost her. The memory still gave Maggie a chill...

Code Blue!

Those two words had sent a rush of fear through her. It was a phrase no one wanted to hear, especially with a loved one in the ICU. Panic rose in her chest and bile built in the back of her throat as she waited for what seemed an eternity for the call to come again.

Code Blue! Room 314. Code Blue!

Serena's room...

Pure, unadulterated fear paralysed her. A flurry of activity swarmed around her, doctors and nurses frantically rushing to answer the emergency call. Maggie was rooted to the floor. She couldn't think, couldn't breathe, let alone get her feet to move in Serena's direction. It was as if her feet had grown roots and were planted firmly into the tiled floor of the hospital waiting room. The dismal cup of watered-down coffee she'd just poured herself was all but forgotten.

"Maggie!"

Snapped out of her shock at the sound of the familiar voice, she turned and came face to face with Cliff, her ex-husband.

"Maggie. What's happening?" His eyes were glassy and wide.

"I...I don't know." She pointed down the long corridor. "Serena's room... emergency."

Not waiting, he sprinted down the corridor.

Adrenaline pushed through Maggie's fear and she was

finally able to move. She tossed the coffee cup in the vicinity of the rubbish bin and took off after him.

Serena's room was towards the end of the wing. By the time Maggie got there, Cliff was standing at the door, arguing with a nurse.

"Sir, I have to ask you step back. You can't come in." The nurse, although shorter than Cliff, stood firm.

"That's my daughter in there! I need to see her."

"I'm sorry, sir. Calm down or I'll have to call security."

Maggie grabbed his arm but snuck a peek around the nurse. Her stomach lurched. Serena was surrounded by a team of medicos and she could tell by their intensity that Serena was in dire straits. She swallowed hard, and although she wanted to be with her daughter, she said to Cliff, "Let them do their job, Cliff. Come away. We have to trust them."

He shrugged her arm off but stepped back.

They returned to the waiting room and sat on the plastic chairs. Cliff was the last person Maggie wanted to be with, but he was Serena's father and he had as much right to be there as she did.

"When did you arrive?" she asked. She wasn't interested, but she had to say something.

"An hour ago. I got a taxi from the airport. How about you?"

"Yesterday."

"How…how is she?"

Maggie blinked back tears. "Not good."

"She's a fighter."

Maggie nodded.

They waited for news. Maggie prayed silently. It was all she could do. Finally, a doctor emerged and said she'd pulled through. "But she's not out of the woods yet." His English was good, but his accent was thick.

"Can we see her?" Maggie asked.

"Yes. But she's heavily sedated."

They stood and walked together down the corridor. Maggie told Cliff what to expect. "You'll barely recognise her."

"It doesn't matter. She's my daughter."

She bit her lip. Now wasn't the time to allow her indignation with Cliff to take precedence over their joint concern for their daughter.

Although she'd warned him, he wasn't prepared, and when he entered the room, he gasped. Maggie didn't blame him. There was little, other than the name on the board, that suggested this was Serena.

Cliff sat on the chair beside the bed. He went to pick up her bandaged hand but stopped himself. "I…I had no idea she was this bad."

"She's lucky to be alive."

"I don't know why she was here."

"It's her job. You know that."

"It was too dangerous. The NABC should have known that."

Maggie agreed, but even now, almost two years after their divorce, he would see it as a victory if he knew she sided with him. The terrorist attacks had been rocking Paris for weeks, and Serena had been sent there to cover the unrest since she was the European correspondent for the Northern Australia Broadcasting Commission. "She didn't have a choice, Cliff."

"Of course she did. I could have stepped in."

Maggie exhaled loudly and narrowed her gaze. Who did he think he was? Seriously? Yes, being the federal member for Stuart in the Legislative Assembly, he held some sway, but Serena would never have condoned him stepping in on her behalf. She was ambitious, and she knew the risks. "You haven't changed a bit, Cliff. I don't know why you came."

His shoulders drooped. "Maggie! Don't be like that. Can't we let bygones be bygones? For Serena's sake, at least." He quirked a brow and gave her a look she knew so well. But she wasn't going to fall for it. He was still the arrogant, selfish man she'd come to loathe, of that she was sure.

But I say to you, love your enemies and pray for those who persecute you, so that you may be sons of your Father who is in heaven.

Maggie grimaced. *Lord, You're going to have to help me with this one.*

Cliff was right. For Serena's sake, she needed to let bygones be bygones and at least be civil. She wasn't sure how she could love him after his infidelity, though. She'd forgiven him. That much she'd done. And she'd moved on. With Frank. She reached for the ring hanging around her neck. She'd taken it off her finger when she realised that the announcement they'd intended to make to his family would be delayed. Nobody other than the two of them knew about their engagement. For that reason, it sometimes didn't seem real, but the diamond ring was a constant reminder of his love and their commitment to each other. It was real, and she drew comfort from it as she spoke to her ex-husband. "You're right, Cliff. I'm sorry. Of course you should be here. Serena is your daughter, too."

"Thank you, Maggie. I'm glad you see it that way. It will be good for my constituency to see us presenting a united front."

"Is that all you think about?" She couldn't help it. He made her ill. "I'm sorry. I've got to go. I'll come back later."

"Maggie…" he said in a condescending tone. "Don't act so immaturely. It doesn't suit you."

A shudder ran down her spine. How would she survive spending time with him? Her only hope was that he wouldn't stay long. She gritted her teeth and stayed put. Memories of Cliff controlling, humiliating, and putting her down nibbled around the edges of her mind. But he couldn't hurt her any longer, she needed to remember that. They were divorced. He had no control over her. She drew a slow breath. "Where are you staying?" She asked the question more to be civil than because she cared.

"At La Parisienne. What about you? Where are you staying?"

"At a guest house not far from here."

"We should grab a bite to eat. I'm guessing you've barely eaten."

"Thanks, but I'm not hungry."

"Maggie. I'm not here to cause trouble. I'm here for Serena, just like you are. Okay?"

She wanted to scream. How did he always turn things around so she looked like the one in the wrong? It was a true talent he had. But she needed to act maturely. She also needed to behave in a manner pleasing to God. She'd been studying the 'fruits of the spirit' in her quiet times lately. *Love, joy, peace, patience, kindness, goodness, faithfulness, gentleness and self-control.* She needed a good helping of each right now. She inhaled slowly and gave a nod. "Okay."

"So… shall we grab something to eat?"

She clenched her hands. Dining with Cliff was the last thing she wanted to do, but there was probably no way out of it. "Sure. But I don't want to leave Serena for long. Why don't we take it in turns to have a break?"

"That's not a bad idea, but she seems stable at the moment. And it doesn't look like she'll wake for a while."

She drew a slow breath to calm herself. There was no use arguing since he always won. "All right, but after that, we take it in turns to stay with her." She didn't wait for a response. Instead, she moved closer to Serena and placed a gentle kiss on her daughter's bandaged forehead. "I love you, sweetheart. I'll be back soon."

They passed a nurse on their way out. Maggie stopped her and asked to be called if there was any change while she took a short break. She'd been at the hospital since she'd arrived in Paris, taking only enough time to check into the guest house and drop her bag off. The bed had looked inviting, but she needed to be with Serena. There'd be time for sleep later.

As Cliff followed her out the door, he placed his hand on the small of her back. An involuntary shudder raced down her spine. She assumed his action was done out of habit, nothing else, but still, she couldn't help thinking he'd done it to control her. To show he was still in charge. Her thoughts immediately flew to Frank and how different he was to Cliff. Frank was never overbearing or arrogant. He was such a kind, caring man, and right now she wished she'd agreed to let him come with her. She would much rather be with him than Cliff.

"Shall we go to the hospital cafeteria so we're close by in case something happens?" Maggie asked as they stood waiting for the lift.

"I'd rather go to a restaurant. I don't fancy cafeteria food."

She bit her lip. *Of course you don't.* "The food is fine. Anyway, that's where I'm going. Suit yourself." She suddenly felt stronger. She wouldn't allow him to dictate to her. She was here for Serena, not to dine with Cliff at some fancy French restaurant when their daughter was in such dire straits.

"You win. The cafeteria it is."

The lift arrived and they took it to the ground floor where the main hospital reception area was. Although it was late afternoon, the area was a hive of activity. Maggie knew where the cafeteria was, so she led the way. She'd grabbed a baguette soon after she'd arrived but had only nibbled it. Seeing Serena had stolen her appetite.

They grabbed a tray each and joined the line. Her appetite was still lacking, so she chose a small Caesar salad and a strong coffee. Cliff chose a large serving of Steak-Frites and a Coke. They sat at a booth opposite each other. Maggie tried to avoid eye contact as she toyed with her salad, but he wanted to talk, so it was next to impossible.

"So, I hear you're dating a cowboy."

Maggie's head shot up. "How…how do you know that?"

He tapped his nose. "I have my ways and means."

Her brow creased. "Are you spying on me, Cliff?"

"Now, why would I do that?"

She shrugged. Goodness he was annoying. "I don't know. It's just something you'd do."

"Maggie… come on. Do you really think I care that much?"

There it was again. Cliff turning it around. She groaned. "I guess not."

"No, Jeremy told me. That's how I know. Goddard. Is that his name?"

Maggie pursed her lips. She had no desire to discuss her relationship with Frank with her ex-husband. It was none of his business and she told him so.

"I see you've got some fire in you. It must be serious." He speared a chip with his fork and waggled it in the air while his gaze penetrated her like a laser.

"It really is none of your business, Cliff. But yes, it *is* serious. In fact, we're getting married." She blinked. She hadn't meant to tell him that.

An annoying grin spread across his face. "I knew it. I knew there was something different about you. Well, congratulations are in order." Placing the chip into his mouth, he leaned back against the seat and studied her while he chewed it slowly.

She swallowed her pride and thanked him. "And how is Mandy? And the baby? Ruby, is that her name?" Maggie knew all too well that it was. She didn't spy on Cliff, but Jeremy, their twenty-nine-year old son, always seemed eager to talk about what his father was up to, even if she didn't want to hear. Maggie guessed he spoke to his father about her in the same way. He was the opposite of Serena who wanted to distance herself from her father. She'd hated that he'd been unfaithful and resented that he'd started a new family, whereas Jeremy just wanted everyone to be happy and get along.

"They're both fine. And yes, we called her Ruby. She's just started walking."

All of a sudden, Maggie felt pity for Cliff's much younger wife. She didn't know her personally, although she knew of her and had seen her around, but if Cliff treated this wife the same way he'd treated her when their children were young, she knew that Mandy would most likely be raising the child pretty much on her own. It had always irked her that Cliff had managed to present an image of a doting father when that was far from the truth. He knew how to work the media, to be present when it mattered. Not for her, but for the public.

"It must be strange to be starting again. To have a daughter younger than your granddaughter." Jeremy had two children with Emma, his wife. A son, Sebastian, who'd just turned three, and a new little daughter, Chloe.

He chuckled. "Yes, it is a little strange. But Mandy's a good mother."

Maggie simply smiled. She ate half her salad and then pushed it aside. "I think I'll get back. I don't like leaving Serena for long."

"I might check into my hotel. I'll come back later and stay for a bit so you can get some sleep."

"That would be nice. Thank you."

"You're welcome. Call if anything changes. Do you have my number?"

"No. You'd better give it to me."

And so it began.

CHAPTER 25

After Cliff left to check into his hotel, Maggie returned to sit with Serena. He arrived much later with alcohol on his breath. He wasn't drunk, but he'd certainly been drinking. She was reluctant to leave, but she was dead tired. It had been four whole days since she'd slept in a bed. She promised to return in a few hours' time, but when her head hit the pillow, she fell into a deep sleep and slept longer than she'd expected.

When she woke, the sun was streaming in through the window. She quickly grabbed her phone and checked the time. *Nine a.m.* How had that happened? She quickly threw the bed covers off and headed down the hallway to the shared bathroom. Fortunately, the shower was empty, and as the warm water flowed over her body, the fog slowly cleared from her brain and all the thoughts that had lain dormant while she slept came to the fore. *Serena.* How was she doing? Did Cliff stay with her all night? Unlikely. She needed to get to the hospital as quickly as possible. She hadn't seen any messages on her phone, so no news was good news, she supposed. But there weren't any messages from Frank, either. That worried her. Maybe something had happened to him. She should call. It would be late afternoon at Goddard Downs so he could be near the house and have phone reception. After quickly drying herself, she slipped on her robe and headed back to her room.

Rummaging through her suitcase, she found a fresh pair of trousers and a lightweight knitted top. She'd only brought a few outfits with her since she'd been at Goddard Downs when she received the call and hadn't returned to her apartment in Darwin to pack properly. Fortunately, she'd thrown in a few warmer items, just in case. Now they were coming in handy. Autumn in Paris could be cool.

Before heading downstairs, Maggie rechecked her phone. No messages. She speed-dialled Frank's number. While waiting for him to answer, she stood by the window. The guest house overlooked a small park filled with a pretty display of flowers. An elderly man, with an equally elderly dog lying beside him on the gravel path, occupied one of the bench seats. A young woman rocking a pram sat on another. To the left of the park, a row of shops lined the busy road. A *boulangerie*, a *boucher*, a *pattiserie*, a small grocery shop, a florist, and several cafés.

If she'd been here for any other reason, she would have loved to stroll along the strip, stop for coffee and perhaps a croissant or baguette. She loved Paris. It was such a vibrant city. So much history, art, and atmosphere. She'd spent many weeks here in her younger days before she was married, when, like Serena, she'd been sent here for work. It was the city of love and romance, and she'd love to bring Frank here, although right now, it was the last place anybody wanted to be. She couldn't understand the mind of the terrorists. What had started out as peaceful political protests regarding the increase in fuel taxes had quickly escalated into riots. The 'Yellow Vest Movement' had spurned zealots and fanatics who were now wreaking havoc and devastation across Paris and other major cities in France. And now it seemed that ISIS was involved.

The phone rang out and went to Frank's voicemail. His familiar tone warmed her heart and made her long to be wrapped in his safe arms. She left a message. "Frank, it's me, Maggie. Nothing wrong, I just wanted to talk with you, that's all. I miss you. Hope all is well back home. No change with Serena yet. Call me when you can. Love you. Goodbye."

She exhaled slowly and slipped her phone into her bag. Before heading out, she flicked the brush over her hair and tied it in a bun, and applied a light coat of foundation to help cover the dark circles under her eyes. At the last moment, she decided to apply some mascara and blusher, simply to make her feel better.

It was just before nine-thirty when she headed downstairs. Madame Guillard, the owner of the guest house, greeted her with a cheerful smile. "*Bonjour*, Madame Donovan. I hope you slept well."

Maggie smiled. "Yes, thank you. I did."

"Would you like some *petit déjeuner*? The other guests have finished, but I haven't cleared it away yet." Although her English was very good, her accent was heavy.

"Maybe a quick coffee and a croissant? I need to get to the hospital. I overslept."

"Of course. How is your daughter?"

The genuine concern on the woman's face made Maggie tear up. She'd been so strong, but now, for some reason, tears streamed down her cheeks and she found she was unable to speak.

Madame Guillard stepped around her desk and gently rubbed Maggie's back. "There, there, *ma chère. C'est bon*. I will make you coffee." She bustled away and quickly returned with a steaming mug. "Here you are. This will help."

Maggie took the mug gratefully and sipped the strong brew.

"Would you like to drink it in the dining room, or would you prefer to take it with you? I can pack some croissants if you like."

"That would be lovely. *Merci*. I haven't heard how Serena is this morning, and I'm eager to get there."

"I understand. *C'est bon*. I'll be right back."

Moments later, she handed Maggie a paper sack containing several croissants. "And here's an apple for later."

Maggie smiled at the woman's thoughtfulness. "Thank you. You're too kind."

"You're more than welcome. Let me know if you need anything else."

"I will. *Merci beaucoup*." Maggie slipped the apple into her bag and headed out the door.

WHEN SHE REACHED THE HOSPITAL, she wasn't surprised that Cliff wasn't there. The duty nurse hadn't seen him, so Maggie guessed he'd left in the early hours of the morning.

Who knew when he'd be back? When it suited him, she guessed.

Serena had been moved into a different room. A bigger, airier one with a view. Maggie figured that was Cliff's doing. She was in a public hospital because they had the equipment to handle emergencies and burns better than the fancier but less equipped private hospitals. But she guessed that even here, money talked, and he was able to get special treatment for Serena.

Maggie sat beside her and very gently lifted her bandaged hand. "Hey, sweetie. I'm here. How are you doing today?" Maggie didn't expect her to answer, but Serena's eyes flickered open.

"Serena! You're awake! Oh, my goodness. Are you okay? Do you need anything?"

"Where am I?" Her voice was not much more than a whisper as her gaze darted around the room.

"You're in the hospital, sweetheart. There was another attack. Let me call the nurse." Maggie pressed the buzzer and then leaned closer to Serena. "I'm so glad you're awake. I was so worried."

"What's wrong with me?"

Maggie groaned inwardly. How much should she tell her? Serena was strong, but was she strong enough to handle knowing the extent of her injuries? Maybe she should let the doctor tell her. "How about we wait for the doctor?"

"That bad, huh?"

Maggie blew out a slow breath. "You're alive, darling. You survived. Many weren't so lucky."

Serena's eyes fluttered and closed before the nurse arrived.

It was going to be a slow journey to recovery. Maggie prayed that Serena would be able to deal with her injuries, particularly her burns once she knew the extent of them. She also prayed for strength for herself, because she secretly feared what lay beneath the dressings.

When the nurse arrived, Maggie stood and moved away from Serena and quietly told the nurse that Serena had woken but had now drifted back to sleep.

"That's normal, Mrs. Donovan. It could be days, even weeks, before she fully wakes. It's better if she sleeps for now because of the pain, but I'll check on her regularly. We'll need to redress her burns shortly."

"How bad are they?" Maggie knew they covered sixty percent of Serena's body, but didn't know what degree they were. She'd assumed third degree but prayed for first or second. She had no idea how Serena would cope if she had permanent scarring, especially on her face.

"You need to talk to the doctor about that, I'm sorry. He should be along shortly."

Maggie gave a nod. "No problem. Thank you anyway." She stepped aside and let the nurse attend to Serena. She checked her vitals and spoke to her, but Serena didn't answer. She'd obviously slipped back into oblivion for now. Maggie was pleased, because she knew as soon as Serena was conscious, the real challenge would begin.

She spoke to the doctor a little later and was told that half of Serena's burns were third degree and that she would need skin grafts and ongoing treatment for a long time to come. She would most likely have permanent scarring on one cheek, even after plastic surgery. "I'm sorry the news isn't any better, Mrs. Donovan, but it's no use sugar coating the truth."

"It's okay. It's better to know than not know." She didn't correct the man, either. She very much disliked being called Mrs. Donovan, but what did it matter when her daughter was in such a terrible state?

Cliff arrived in the early afternoon. Maggie told him what the doctor had said. He vowed he would get Serena the best treatment available. "I'll pull whatever strings are needed."

Without thinking, Maggie stepped into his arms and sobbed against his chest.

CHAPTER 26

The days following Maggie's hasty departure to Paris to be with Serena passed slowly for Frank. Their sunset boat cruise and his proposal seemed so long ago, although less than a week had passed. It was doubly hard since none of his family knew about his and Maggie's engagement. His heart was heavy as he went about his daily chores and only his time in the Word helped lift his spirits.

He looked forward to his daily chats with Maggie, but sometimes they missed each other because of the time difference and the fact that he was so often out of range. She said she didn't mind if he called her in the middle of the night, she just wanted to hear his voice, but she sounded dreadfully tired, so he avoided doing that. Mostly. From what she'd told him, he guessed it could be months before she returned to Australia with Serena. He'd wanted to go with her, but she'd told him it would be better if she went on her own, and that had hurt him. Especially when he heard that her ex-husband was there. He had every right to be, of course. Frank knew that. But it still rankled that Maggie was spending time with her ex instead of him.

Two other issues weighed heavily on his heart. The issue with the licensing for the station, and the anniversary of Esther's death. It was seven years tomorrow since that fateful day. Sitting on the steps, he pulled his boots off and gazed around. Little had changed in those years. Olivia and Janella had ensured that Esther's vegetable patch had remained productive and the chooks were well cared for. Esther had been passionate about both. She'd kept her favoured 'girls' close to the house in a separate coop away from those raised for commercial purposes. She'd given the favoured ones scraps of food and extra attention, and in return, they produced the largest eggs he'd ever seen. While those hens were long gone, others had taken their place, and now Olivia's three-year-old daughter, Isobel, helped look after them. But that would soon be changing when Olivia and Nathan left Goddard Downs and moved back to Darwin. Things were certainly going to be different around here without them. He was sure going to miss them.

He let out a heavy sigh and checked his phone. A missed call from Maggie. She'd left a message that he listened to as he walked inside. Just hearing her voice lifted his spirits. He'd call her back a little later, after dinner when he could talk without interruption.

The aroma of beef stew wafted down the hallway. Janella, his eldest son Julian's wife, was a good cook and had willingly taken over the role of providing the majority of the meals for the family after Esther's passing. And Sasha, Janella and Julian's ten year-old-daughter, was following in her mother's and grandmother's footsteps, so it seemed. In between her 'School of the Air' classes when she logged on and did her lessons remotely with other isolated students and a teacher who taught them over the internet, she was often in the kitchen baking something or other.

Little Isobel raced down the hallway and hugged his legs. "Grandpa."

"Hello, Issie." He swung her into his arms and hugged her. "What have you done today?"

"I helped Mummy in the garden, and I collected six eggs."

"Six eggs? Wow! That's a lot. Did you carry them carefully?"

"Of course I did. I'm always careful."

He smiled. "Yes, I know you are, sweetheart. Is Mummy around?"

"Yes, she's in the kitchen with William and Aunt Janella. William's been crying a lot. It's hurting my ears."

"Maybe he's teething. He's at that age."

"That's what Mummy says. I sure wish those teeth would hurry up."

Frank chuckled. "I guess they'll come when they're ready and not a minute before." When they reached the kitchen, he set her on the floor and ruffled her hair as she ran off. "Something smells good," he said, peering into the pot to see what Janella was stirring.

She looked up from the gas range and smiled. "It's just stew."

"But Nellie, your stews are the best."

She flashed him a smile. "And you're too kind."

He laughed. "How long until dinner?"

"Ten minutes, tops."

"Anything I can do to help?"

She shrugged. "Help Issie set the table?"

"Yes, Grandpa. Help me set the table."

"Okay, sweetheart. Let me wash my hands first."

"All right."

He turned the tap on and peered out the window as he lathered his hands with soap. "Looks like Joshua's back. Did we know he was coming today?" Joshua, Frank's youngest son, had driven to Alice Springs, almost two thousand kilometres south, for a rodeo three weeks earlier. He was only meant to be gone a week.

"No, but it's not before time." Olivia stood, and positioning William on her hip, walked to the window. "Looks like he's brought trouble with him."

"Olivia. That's no way to talk about your cousin," Frank said.

"No, but it's true. Sean Goddard is bad news."

He let out a sigh. "He might have changed."

"And we might get snow this Christmas." She lifted a brow.

Frank shook his head and chuckled. There was absolutely no chance of them getting snow in the Kimberley, at Christmas or any time of the year. The rainy season was coming, and with it came higher humidity, not snow. In fact, the rainy season was late this year. Seven years ago, the Ord River had flooded. He drew a slow breath. "You know what tomorrow is, girls?"

"Yes," Olivia replied, slipping her spare arm around his waist and resting her head against his shoulder. "I still miss Mum so much."

"We all do," Janella added as she poured the stew into a serving dish. "We should do something special."

"I agree," Olivia said. "Perhaps we could do a special dinner. Barbecue some ribs. Mum always loved barbecues."

"That's a good idea, sweetheart," Frank said. "Let's do it."

"Okay, but right now, dinner's ready and the table's not set. I'm about to ring the bell," Janella said, reaching for it.

"Onto it." Frank saluted his daughter-in-law and chuckled. "Come on, Issie, let's get this table set."

"I've already done it, Grandpa. I did it while you were talking."

He smiled and ruffled her hair again. He was certainly going to miss her. "You're a good girl, Issie."

The bell sounded, and within minutes, Julian, Nathan, Caleb, Sasha, Joshua and Sean arrived at the door and filed inside after removing their work boots. Other than Sean, they each had set places at the large wooden table. Joshua grabbed a chair and squeezed it in between his and Nathan's.

Frank smiled at how Issie had set the table with knives and forks back to front and upside down. He saw the puzzled looks on several faces, including Julian's, but he spoke before anybody could say anything. "Issie set the table tonight. Didn't she do a wonderful job?" Without waiting for a reply, he extended his hands. "Shall we give thanks?"

When they all nodded and joined hands, he bowed his head and prayed. "Lord, we thank You for this day and for Your many blessings. Thank You for returning Joshua to us safely and for bringing Sean to our table. We thank You for the food spread before us and we ask that You bless the hands of those who prepared it. In Jesus' precious name, we pray. Amen."

A chorus of Amens sounded around the table. "So, Joshua, welcome home, son. How was the track?" Frank asked. Joshua had driven home via the Tanami Track, a thousand-kilometre dirt track traversing the desert of the same name. It was the shortest route between the Kimberley and Alice Springs and was often used by off-road enthusiasts to test their driving skills.

"It was pretty chopped up. Too many city slickers on it these days with their fancy campers. They don't know how to drive it."

"At least you got through before it closed for the season."

"Yep. I'd have hated the highway. More grey-nomads on that stretch of tar than you can shake a stick at."

"Tourism brings big money to the area. You know that, Joshua, so don't knock them," Julian said, glaring at his younger brother.

"Yeah, but they hog the roads. The truckies hate them, don't they, Seano?" Joshua heaped a pile of stew onto his plate and passed the bowl to Nathan.

"Yeah," Sean said. "I've been doing a bit of driving lately. The vans are a…" Frank gave him the eye and Sean, his younger brother Steve's only son, stopped himself just in time. The family had owned a cattle station not far from the Alice, but Steve and his wife Jillian had sold it several years earlier when Jillian was diagnosed with MS and they now lived in town. Sean had been doing odd jobs ever since and had picked up a colourful language Frank didn't allow around his table. At least Sean knew that and had enough respect for his uncle to stop himself. He finished the sentence with "pain in the neck."

"Yes, well, they're here to stay," Julian said. "And we might soon be appreciating them even more, mightn't we, Dad?"

Frank narrowed his eyes. He wasn't sure what had stirred his oldest son quite so much. It seemed he was itching for a fight. They'd agreed not to discuss the issues regarding the station at the dinner table with the children present. There was no need to concern them at this stage while they were still working through their options.

"What do you mean?" Joshua asked.

"We'll talk about it later, son. Tell us about the rodeo. Good to see you came back without any broken bones."

"Yeah. It was cool, wasn't it, Seano?"

Sean nodded as he chewed on his stew. "Yeah, it was wicked all right."

For the next ten minutes, the two young men shared stories of their time at the rodeo. Frank knew they left out bits they didn't feel comfortable sharing with the family. That in itself was good, but he worried about them. They both seemed to have a complete disregard for safety and had a need to push the limits. One day they'd go too far, of that Frank was sure.

When they finished, Frank cleared his throat. Everyone grew quiet and turned their attention to him. "Tomorrow, as you all know, is a special day for our family. It will have been seven years since we lost your mum." His gaze travelled around his adult children and their spouses, then shifted to his grandchildren. "And your grandma." He blew out a breath. "I'll be going to the graveyard first thing in the morning if anyone would like to come with me. And then, I think the girls are putting on a barbecue tomorrow night for dinner."

"I'll come with you, Grandpa," Isobel said quietly.

The gesture was so sweet, an ache tore through his heart. "That's wonderful, sweetheart. Grandma would be so pleased you want to visit her grave."

"I'll come too," Sasha said. "I really miss Grandma."

"I know you do, sweetie. We all do." He reached out and squeezed her hand. He wondered how much Sasha remembered about that day. Only four at the time, it had been essentially her who'd triggered the sad chain of events that led to Esther's death, although Frank knew that Caleb, Sasha's older brother, bore the weight of responsibility because it had been him who'd agreed to let her out of the car.

He looked at Caleb, who'd slunk down in his seat and folded his arms. It grieved Frank that Julian wouldn't allow him to have counselling. Julian simply told him to man up and move on. Frank didn't understand his oldest son and wondered how Janella put up with him. Right now, Esther would have been disappointed with him, but she'd always looked for the good in people, so she would have found something to be positive about.

Nobody blamed Caleb, but it seemed he still blamed himself. They tried not to talk too much about Esther and what happened in front of him, but they couldn't treat the boy with kid gloves forever. At some stage he needed to face what had happened and deal with the guilt he carried. Although Frank knew he'd be feeling it more because of the anniversary, it was also important they remember her properly and show their respect. If it caused Caleb to talk about his feelings, that would be a good thing. "How about you, Caleb? Will you come, too?"

The whole table seemed to hold its breath. Moments passed

and the clock ticking was the only sound. Finally, he said, almost under his breath, "Maybe next year."

"Okay, son. That's fine. Nobody's pushing you. But if you change your mind, I'll be going at six before we start chores." Frank lifted his gaze. "And the rest of you are welcome, too." He expected Olivia would go on her own to pay her respects. Julian, he wasn't sure about. His oldest son confused him at the moment. Joshua? Maybe. And then there were the two in-laws, Janella and Nathan. He expected they'd pay their respects in their own way. "Thanks for dinner, Janella. Will you excuse me a moment? I've got a call to make."

"Sure. But Sasha's made apple pie for dessert, so don't be long."

"Apple pie?" He looked at Sasha and quirked a brow.

His granddaughter nodded eagerly.

"Well, I can't miss that. The phone call can wait. I wouldn't miss your apple pie for anything."

She giggled and the look on her face warmed his heart.

The pie was as scrumptious as he'd expected, and he told her so. "Great pie, Sash. You're a wonderful cook."

The ten-year-old beamed. "Thank you, Grandpa. It was Grandma's recipe."

"I thought I recognised it." He winked at her and then concentrated on eating, all the while keeping one eye on Caleb who'd winced again at the mention of his grandmother.

CHAPTER 27

After dinner, Frank excused himself and spoke on the phone with Maggie for about fifteen minutes. She told him that Serena had woken briefly but was now sleeping again. She also told him what the doctor had said. "I'm worried about her, Frank. She's always been concerned about her appearance, and I'm not sure how she's going to cope with permanent scarring."

"She's probably stronger than you think, Maggie. I think we all carry scars of some kind—. Not many of us get through life unscathed in some way, only some wear them on the inside where nobody can see them. They hide them away and let them fester. This will be her journey, Maggie, and she'll grow as a result of it. Don't shield her from it too much, although I understand why you'd want to. I feel the same way about Caleb sometimes. I wish he'd talk about Esther and what happened, but whenever she's mentioned, he withdraws into his shell." He didn't tell Maggie it was the anniversary tomorrow. On top of everything else, she didn't need to know that. "I'll be praying for you all," he said.

"And I for you. I miss you, Frank."

"And I miss you, Maggie. I love you more than anything and I can't wait until you come back."

"I'm not sure how long that will be."

"It doesn't matter. I'll be here waiting for you."

"I know you will be. Oh, I've got to go. A nurse has come in and wants to see me. I love you."

"Love you, too." He ended the call and drew a long breath before releasing it slowly. The concern in Maggie's voice was real and it grieved him to hear her anguish. She was worried about her daughter, and rightly so, but God was bigger than any problem any of them could ever face, including permanent scarring, so he bowed his head and prayed for them as he promised he would.

Look after Maggie, Lord. Be her strength and portion. Give her wisdom and compassion. And Lord, help Serena deal with her injuries when she wakes. May she turn to You in her time of need, when she faces the reality of her injuries. May she grow through this experience and become a better person. And Lord, I pray for Caleb. My heart grieves for that boy. Let there be a breakthrough soon, and if I can be of any use, I offer myself to You to be used in whatever way You deem fit. In Your precious Son's name, I pray. Amen.

Frank didn't return to the central living area of the house until after he'd taken a shower, but when he did, no one was about. It seemed they'd all gone their various ways, as they often did. They lived close together, but his children and their families all had their own lives to live. He could understand why Olivia and Nathan wanted to move back to the city, but he was going to miss them. And Joshua? Well, he lived in the bunkhouse away from the family. He and Julian didn't get on too well. But then, Julian didn't seem to be getting on well with anyone these days. Maybe it wasn't only Caleb who needed counselling.

Frank grabbed an apple and headed outside. The moon had recently risen and loomed large against the horizon. He sat on the steps and while he munched away, he stared at it. He'd shared moon rises with two very special women, Esther and Maggie, and both were on his mind.

THE FOLLOWING MORNING, Frank rose as dawn was breaking and spent time in the Word before his planned visit to Esther's grave. He'd been reading through Second Corinthians, and this morning he mulled over chapter four, verses sixteen to eighteen: *So we do not lose heart. Though our outer self is wasting away, our inner self is being renewed day by day. For this light momentary affliction is preparing for us an eternal weight of glory beyond all comparison, as we look not to the things that are seen but to the things that are unseen. For the things that are seen are transient, but the things that are unseen are eternal.*

It was so easy to focus on all the issues that pressed in on him and his family daily, but these would eventually pass. He was on a journey that led to eternity, where these transient problems would no longer weigh him down. That didn't negate the fact that these concerns were real and needed to be worked through, but along the way there was opportunity for growth. Life was a journey, and he was sure glad God was his tour guide. Frank's greatest wish was for all his children and grandchildren to open their hearts to God, for He was the great comforter, the creator of all things. He knew that would be Esther's wish as well, if she were still alive.

After a short prayer time, he closed his Bible and headed out. Issie, Sasha, Janella and Olivia stood at the foot of the front steps, each holding a small bunch of wildflowers. A lump settled in his throat as he approached them. He opened his arms and gave them a group hug. "Good morning, ladies." His voice hitched and came out ragged.

"Good morning," they all greeted solemnly.

"Shall we go?"

They nodded, and together set off for the Goddard family cemetery. It was only a short walk, less than a kilometre. They could have driven, but the walk was cathartic. The air was crisp and clean, and early morning sunlight warmed them as they slowly climbed the hill. Talk was subdued, with only Issie chatting. She held Frank's hand and asked if he was sad.

"Yes and no, sweetheart. I know God is looking after Grandma, and that she'd be happy we're remembering her. But I do miss her."

"But you have Maggie now to make you happy."

He smiled at that. "I do indeed."

"Are you going to marry her?"

"Isobel!" Olivia glared at her daughter. "You don't ask questions like that."

The little girl frowned. "Why not?"

"It's okay, Liv," Frank said. "Let me handle it."

His daughter raised a brow. "Okay."

"Well, little Issie. Sometimes you should wait for people to announce things like that rather than asking, because it can make them feel a little awkward. And sometimes they might want to surprise their family and friends, so asking can spoil that surprise."

"I think I get it. So, are you going to surprise us?"

He chuckled. "Maybe. You'll have to wait and see. But today we're remembering Grandma, so let's think about her for now."

"Okay. Do you think she'd like these flowers?"

"She'd love them. They were her favourites."

Issie dropped his hand and skipped ahead.

Olivia faced him, tilting her head. "So, are you going to surprise us, Dad?"

"Liv... you know you shouldn't be asking."

She grinned. "I know, but I want you to know that if you are, I approve. And I think Mum would, too." She shifted closer and linked her arm through his. "We all want you to be happy, Dad, and Maggie makes you smile. Plus, she's a lovely person."

"She is. But today is about your mum. Let's focus on her, shall we?"

She nodded. "Okay."

Frank glanced over to Janella and Sasha. Janella had her arm around Sasha's shoulder and they were talking quietly as they walked. Frank had so much respect for Janella. She had such a mature, caring way about her, and her faith in God was as strong as anyone's he knew. Being partly indigenous, she'd had her share of issues when she was younger. Prejudice ran rife in the area. Always had. Frank struggled to understand why people couldn't see beyond the colour of skin to what lay beneath. It's what was inside that was important, and Janella was beautiful, inside and out. Her skin was a lovely olive and her face always held a smile. She was the most cheerful person he knew. He prayed that his son appreciated what a special wife he had and gave her the love she deserved. Somehow, he doubted that was the case right now. Julian seemed to have an aura about him that put him at arm's length from everyone. It was probably because he was the eldest and took his role too seriously, but that didn't mean he had to distance himself from everybody. Frank sighed. He'd pray for his son and ask God to soften his heart. And maybe one day he'd get the opportunity to have a heart to heart with him.

The group finally crested the hill, and the cemetery, surrounded by an old timber fence in need of repair, lay before them. The fence wasn't on the maintenance schedule, but somehow, it didn't matter. They entered through the gate which Frank had to lift over the tufted grass to open, and headed to Esther's grave where they took turns laying their flowers. They stood and paid their respects silently for a few moments with arms around each other before Frank suggested they pray.

He prayed first, thanking God for Esther's life and legacy. Olivia prayed next, thanking God for her mother and for all she'd taught her. Janella finished by thanking God for the gracious woman who'd welcomed her into her family with open arms and an open heart.

Olivia handed out tissues and then they hugged each other and dried their tears.

"Thank you all for coming." Frank said. "It means a lot to me."

"We'll never forget her, Dad. She was a special woman."

"She was indeed. As were those who went before her." He

cast his gaze around the small cemetery. His father was buried there, as were his grandparents and great grandparents. "They all helped make this place what it is today and gave this family its heritage. We're indebted to each and every one of them. But now, there are chores to be done. Life goes on."

"It sure does," Janella said. "I'm making pancakes for breakfast so I need to get started or else the boys will be complaining."

Frank laughed. "Let them complain. See how far that will get them!"

"You're right. Probably not far," she said with a chuckle.

They headed back down the hill and went about their chores while Janella and Sasha prepared breakfast. At eight o'clock, when the bell rang, everybody made a beeline for the dining room. Everybody except Caleb.

CHAPTER 28

"Does anyone know where Caleb is?" Frank sat at the table and gazed around at his family.

"I haven't seen him this morning," Janella replied as she delivered a huge plate of freshly made pancakes to the table. "Maybe he's still mucking out."

"He wasn't in the shed when I passed by," Julian said. "It's unusual he's not here for breakfast, especially when it's pancakes. I'll check his room." He released an annoyed sigh as he pushed his chair back and left the table.

Frank glanced at Janella. Her dark eyes were heavy with concern. No doubt she was thinking the same... Caleb had gone off somewhere on his own. Again. Like he'd done last year on the anniversary of Esther's death. Janella had finally found him at the lagoon near the cabin and brought him back. Julian had given him a good talking to and told him never to do that again. But what the boy needed wasn't a good talking to. He needed to talk. To speak about how he felt regarding his grandmother's death. Frank knew Janella walked a fine line between respecting her husband and caring for their son. If only Julian could see that it wasn't weakness to show emotion.

Everyone else at the table carried on and enjoyed the pancakes, seemingly oblivious to the drama playing out around them. Frank prayed silently that should Julian find Caleb, he would go easy on the boy. He also prayed that should Caleb not be in his room, that he was safe, wherever he was.

Julian returned after a few minutes, his jaw rigid. He walked over to Janella, bent down and spoke quietly, but Frank could still hear enough... "He's not in his room. I'll go look for him. He could be anywhere."

A flicker of apprehension crossed her face. "Are you sure? I can go."

"No, I'll go. I warned him not to do this."

She grabbed his arm. "Go easy on him, hon. He's really struggling."

"You're too soft on him, Janella. He's got to man up."

A shiver ran down Frank's spine. He couldn't let this happen. Pushing his chair back, he stood and followed Julian outside.

Julian stopped and faced him. "Why are you following me, Dad?"

"Because I want to go, that's why."

"I said I'd do it."

"I know you did, son, but I'm worried about the boy. Janella's right...he hasn't dealt with his guilt."

"I know you mean well, Dad, but it's been seven years and he's not a kid anymore. He's got to build a bridge and get over it."

"And how do you expect him to do that?"

Julian shrugged. "How anybody does. Just get on with it."

"And that's how you deal with everything, isn't it?" Frank stepped closer. "Just get on with it. But what about feelings? I don't know what's happened to you, Julian. You've changed. You've grown hard. What's going on with you, son?"

"Nothing's going on, Dad. Now let me be so I can find Caleb."

"Julian, stop. I'll go." Frank pinned his son with his gaze and spoke in a manner that allowed no room for argument. He was overstepping the mark. Caleb was, after all, Julian's son, but he had to do this. Maybe it was wrong, and he'd apologise later, but right now, he felt strongly that his grandson needed him, not his father.

"I don't know where you get off, Dad. You think you can control everyone. Fine. Go find him. But tell him he'll still have me to answer to."

Frank gritted his teeth. "Let's talk later, son. It's about time we had a good chat."

Julian's eyes narrowed but Frank could see he was conflicted. "Yeah, well, a chat solves everything, doesn't it?"

Frank frowned. *What was his son talking about? What was he dealing with that he wasn't aware of?* "Okay, son, whatever's going on, you know I'm here for you. Right?"

"Whatever. Go and find Caleb if that's what you want to do."

"I will. And Julian, I really am here for you. You can talk to me." He clapped his son on the shoulder and headed for the shed. He had an idea of where Caleb might be, but he'd need a horse to get there. Funny enough, Caleb's horse was missing. It was strange that no one had seen him ride out. That in itself concerned Frank. It was possible Caleb had been missing longer than anyone thought.

He quickly saddled his horse, a large black stallion called Midnight, and headed down the road until he reached a fork. He took the track on the left and picked up the pace. By the time he reached the river, the sun was almost overhead. He slowed the horse to a walking pace as he scoured the bank. Seven years ago, this area was covered in raging flood water. The Ord River had broken its banks and spread across several hundred metres. Now, this arm of the river spanned less than twenty and flowed at a gentle pace. That would change soon, once the rains came.

He looked for the roughly made cross he'd erected on the first anniversary of Esther's death. He'd attached it to a boab tree, but it wasn't that easy to find, and on several occasions, it had fallen off in wild weather and he'd erected another. He didn't come here often. He didn't need to, but he guessed this was where Caleb had come. And he was right. Up ahead, on a bend in the river, he spotted Caleb's horse.

Climbing off his own, he tethered it to a tree and approached slowly, not wanting to frighten the boy or the horse. Caleb was sitting on the ground with his knees drawn to his chin, his arms wrapped around them. He looked asleep, but lifted his head as Frank approached, his eyes widening.

"It's okay, Caleb. I thought I'd find you here." Frank eased himself onto the ground beside the boy and said nothing for a few moments. Finally, he said, "It still gets to you, doesn't it?"

Caleb nodded. "I can't get it out of my head."

Frank could imagine that. It must have been such a horrific

experience for a young boy to see his grandmother swept away in the raging waters. To know that if he hadn't weakened and allowed Sasha out of the car, she would probably still be alive. "You can't change what happened, son. There's nothing you or I or God can do to bring her back. But you know what? Grandma wouldn't want you wallowing in guilt for the rest of your life. She sacrificed her life for yours and Sasha's, and I'm sure she'd want you to live yours to the fullest. To cherish it."

Caleb looked up. "I get that, but I don't know how to change how I think. It's always there, in my head."

"Well, the first step is forgiving yourself. No one blames you, Caleb. You shouldn't blame yourself."

"How can you not blame me? She was your wife." Tears flooded his eyes.

"And I loved her very much. I still do. But you know what? Things happen all the time that are out of our control. I could have been angry with both you and Sasha for disobeying your grandma. But you were kids, and you'd already suffered enough. Blaming you wouldn't have made it any better for anyone, me included."

"Dad blames me."

"Well, your dad has stuff he needs to work on, too." The penny was slowly dropping. Maybe Julian had never truly dealt with his mother's death, either, and was taking his anger out on everyone, his son included. "Caleb, we're each responsible for our own attitudes and thoughts. Letting go of blame and guilt will change your life. I can see how hanging on to it has affected you already, and I don't want you to go through your whole life carrying it. The only real way of finding freedom from guilt is to give it to God. You know that, don't you?"

Caleb shrugged. "I've never really understood how that works."

"Would you like me to explain?"

He shrugged again and made a hole in the dirt with his finger. "Guess so."

"We're all guilty of sinning before a just and holy God. His standard is perfection, and we all fall short of that, no matter how good or perfect we think we might be. Without Jesus, there's no way we can be acceptable to God. Jesus is the bridge between a perfect God and an imperfect people. He offers a hand up, so to speak. And in that nail-scarred hand, we find not only freedom from sin, but freedom from guilt. There's no blame for those who have confessed their sin and have accepted Jesus as their Lord and Saviour."

Frank paused a moment, giving time for his words to sink in before continuing. It was a lot to absorb, although Caleb had heard the gospel message before. But sometimes it didn't make any sense until you were ready to hear it. "Don't dwell on the past, Caleb. Instead, dwell on God's love for you. Dwell on His grace. He knows you're sorry, so fix your eyes on Jesus, because He doesn't condemn you." Frank paused and drew a slow breath. "Have you ever invited Him into your heart?"

Caleb shook his head.

Frank waited another moment before asking quietly, "Would you like to?"

Caleb looked up and stared at the water. Frank guessed that all sorts of thoughts were warring in the boy's head and heart at that moment. He prayed silently that the Holy Spirit would draw Caleb to Himself. That he would see that surrendering his life to God wasn't a sign of weakness, but an acknowledgement of God's immense love for him.

Caleb finally turned his head and nodded, his eyes glistening. "Yes, I would."

Frank smiled as gratitude and joy swept through him. "That's wonderful, son. Grandma would be so pleased." He brushed the tears from his own eyes. "So, you understand what you're about to do? That by confessing your sin to God and inviting Jesus into your life as Lord and Saviour, you'll be a new person inside?"

Caleb nodded.

"And in that moment, your sin will be wiped away and you'll have a clean slate? You won't need to blame yourself anymore?"

"Yes. I want that. I really do."

"It's only the start of the journey, but it's the most important part. Afterwards, you'll need to get to know God better by reading His word and praying, and that way, you'll learn to live the way He wants you to. You'll still have choices on how you live, but You'll never be alone. If you're ready, all you have to do is pray this simple prayer after me."

He nodded again. "Okay."

Frank placed his hand gently on Caleb's back and closed his eyes. His heart soared as he led his grandson into the kingdom, into a life free of guilt and condemnation. It was a privilege he would always cherish.

After Caleb finished praying, Frank gave him a bear hug. "God bless you, Caleb. I believe God has good things planned for your life. You're a special young man and I look forward to seeing what's ahead for you."

"Thank you, Grandpa. I feel better already."

"That's wonderful. I'm so very pleased."

"Do...do you think we could go to Grandma's grave now?"

Fresh tears pricked Frank's eyes. "Sure, son. I'd like that very much."

They stood and walked over to their horses. "I don't think I want to tell Dad about what I just did. Not yet, anyway. I'll tell Mum. She'll understand."

"That's fine. You can tell your dad when you're ready."

They climbed onto their horses, and after letting them drink from the river, walked slowly to the cemetery. They chatted more about living as God wanted, and Frank offered to spend time reading the Bible with Caleb every day. He was so pleased to have this time with the boy and prayed silently for him whenever there was a lull in their conversation. He would still face challenges. His dad, for a start. Frank had warned Caleb about what Julian had said, but told him simply to apologise and not get angry or upset if he could help it. Frank was tempted to step in on Caleb's behalf, but that *would* be going too far. He'd have his own time with Julian sometime soon, but for now, he'd have to leave Caleb to face his father on his own.

When Frank's phone came into mobile range, it beeped with ten messages. Nine were from Janella. One from Maggie. He sent a message to Janella telling her he'd found Caleb and they were on their way home. He quickly read Maggie's message. It simply said she loved him and was praying for him. Even though they were half a world from each other, he felt so connected to her. He loved her so much and couldn't wait to see her again.

The time he spent with Caleb at the cemetery was also

special. The boy shed tears as he told his grandma he was sorry for carrying blame for so long, and he promised to live a life that would make her proud.

When they arrived back at the homestead, Caleb went straight to his father and apologised. Frank didn't know what they said to each other, but at the barbecue that night he detected a slight change in Julian. Frank even caught him giving Janella a hug, something he hadn't seen for a long time.

At the end of the evening, when he was in his room alone, he got down on his knees and thanked God for His goodness and mercy. He made the mistake of quickly checking his emails before he climbed into bed. At one p.m. that day, almost at the exact time Caleb had given his heart to the Lord, an email had come in from Officer Shepherd confirming that his application for a stay on the licensing requirements had officially been denied. Although Frank had already guessed that would be the outcome, seeing it in black and white made it real.

He drew a slow breath and closed his eyes again. *Lord, once more I come to You and ask that You lead us through these troubled times. Let my heart be open to Your leading, Lord, and not be resistant to change. You know how stubborn I can be. Help me look forward to the future, whatever that might look like, with eagerness and complete trust in You. In Your precious Son's name, I pray. Amen.*

CHAPTER 29

David Kramer, Serena's long-time on and off again partner, arrived in Paris six hours after she woke up and learned the extent of her injuries. Maggie had called to warn him what to expect, but he was already mid-air, so she simply left a message. Serena had told her she didn't want to see him, now or ever. Maggie felt sorry for the man. She knew he would readily marry her daughter if she ever agreed. He was a long-suffering, patient man who loved Serena dearly. It was a pity she couldn't see his good qualities enough to commit. And now, with her injuries, especially her burns, Maggie feared she would push everyone, including David, away.

Maggie's phone rang as she was holding Serena's least burnt hand while the nurse redressed her face. Maggie could barely look at her charred, disfigured right cheek. She didn't blame her for not wanting to see anyone, but David wasn't anyone. He was her partner, and he truly loved her and would stand by her and help her through her recovery. But Serena didn't see it that way.

The phone rang out and went to her voicemail. Moments later, it beeped. She assumed it was David calling since his plane would have just landed. She'd check the message and call him back as soon as the nurse finished with Serena. She had no real idea what she would say to him. If only Frank were here to help her handle the situation instead of Cliff. Cliff wouldn't be sensitive to either Serena or David's feelings and would simply tell Serena to get over it. Maybe that's what it would come to in the end, but Maggie knew it was important to try to work things out in a less confrontational manner. Serena had only recently learned of her injuries, after all, and was still in shock.

She winced as the nurse used a long tweezer-like instrument to apply some kind of ointment to Serena's cheek. Maggie had a weak stomach when it came to things like this but forced herself not to look away. She needed to be strong for her daughter. Bile rose in her throat and she thought she was about to be sick. Until now, when the nurse had changed Serena's dressings, Serena had been asleep because of the high dose of pain medication she was on, and Maggie had been able to leave the room. Now that Serena was awake, she wanted her mother to hold her hand. *Lord, help me cope. Please. For Serena's sake.*

When the nurse finished and left the room, Serena said she needed to rest and closed her eyes.

Maggie stepped outside the room and checked her phone. As expected, the call had been from David so she quickly called him back.

He answered almost before it rang. "Maggie, how is she?"

"Not great, I'm afraid. I was there when the nurse changed her dressings and her burns are worse than I thought. She's in a really bad way." Maggie's voice caught.

"But she's alive."

"Yes. You're right. It'll be a long road, but at least she's alive." She ran a hand over her hair. "Where are you, David?"

"Waiting for a taxi."

"You must be tired."

"A little. I slept a bit on the plane, but you know how it is."

"Yes. I barely slept on the way over."

"I'll come straight to the hospital. I should be there within half an hour."

"Okay. She's not in a great frame of mind."

"I can imagine. I feel so bad I couldn't get here earlier." He'd been walking the Kokoda Track in Papua New Guinea with a mate when the blast happened, and it had taken days for him to get the message and return to civilisation before he could even think about getting a flight to Paris.

"Call me when you get here and I'll come down and meet you."

"Okay. I appreciate that. See you soon."

Maggie took the opportunity to grab a coffee and a small baguette. She'd been at the hospital since early morning and it was now mid-afternoon, and she was fading. Madame Guillard had left a pre-prepared breakfast for her, but that was hours ago. Serena's waking had been unexpected and Maggie had been reluctant to leave her side since she'd been so upset when she discovered what had happened. And Cliff. *Cliff.* He'd promised to be there, but she hadn't seen him. Maggie assumed he had other important matters to deal with. Nothing had changed.

By the time she'd eaten her baguette and drained her coffee, David had arrived. She met him in the main reception area and gave him a hug. He was a tall, strong, fit man. A firefighter who loved the outdoors. Dressed in knee-length khaki shorts and a white T-shirt, he looked a little out of place amongst the well-dressed Parisian crowd, but it didn't matter. He'd flown to Paris from Papua New Guinea with only the clothing he had with him. Much like she had.

"Where is she?" he asked, straightening after bending down to hug her.

"Upstairs. In the ICU ward."

"Can I see her?"

"Let's have a coffee first."

He ran his hand across his short, sandy hair. "That sounds ominous."

Maggie drew a slow breath and prayed silently for the young man. He was going to need all the patience and love he had to win Serena over. Maybe it would be too much for him. "Well, like I said on the phone, she's in a terrible state."

"I'm a firefighter. I've seen burn victims."

"I know." They reached the cafeteria and she asked what he'd like.

"Just a coffee. However it comes."

She ordered two long blacks with milk on the side and grabbed several sachets of sugar. She normally drank her coffee without sweetener, but right now, she needed a boost.

They carried the cups to a table and sat. "I'm not sure how

to say this after you've come all this way, but Serena said she doesn't want to see you."

He was silent a moment and then said, "It's a knee-jerk reaction. That often happens after someone suffers a major trauma. They want to hide from everyone. Especially when they're disfigured."

Wow. She knew he was well-grounded, but she hadn't quite expected him to be quite so rational and calm. "Well, she's resting at the moment. What would you like to do?"

"I'd like to go and sit with her, if that's okay. If she throws me out, I'll leave quietly and try again tomorrow. I won't cause a scene."

Maggie smiled. She couldn't imagine David Kramer ever making a scene. He was much like Frank in that way. "I didn't think you would. Okay, let me take you up once you've finished your coffee. Did you want to freshen up first?"

"I had a quick wash at the airport. I think I'm fine. I don't smell, do I?"

She laughed. "No. Not at all. So, how much of the track did you do?"

"We were on day four, so almost halfway."

"Wow. You couldn't have been more remote."

"Nope. We were about as far from civilisation as you can get."

"I was at Goddard Downs. That was a bit of a mission, too. Not as much as yours, obviously." She looked up as a familiar figure approached their table. "Cliff!"

"I thought I'd grab a drink before I headed up. I didn't expect to see you two here."

"I just arrived. Maggie was filling me in." David stood and shook Cliff's hand. "Sad state of affairs."

"Yes, you could say that. I'm trying to pull some strings and get her transported home as soon as possible. I'm not sure I trust these French doctors."

"Oh, I'm not sure I agree," David said. "I've heard good things about the French medical system."

"Yes, well, maybe. But I'd still like her to be home, as I'm sure we all would. We can't take months off work to be here with her."

"I can," Maggie said. "I've already squared it away with Suzanne. But I guess it's different for you, Cliff. Your constituents need you."

"Don't be like that, Maggie. You know how politics works."

She sure did.

David cleared his throat. "I think I'd like to head up now, if that's okay."

"Sorry, David. We shouldn't have carried on like that in front of you," Maggie said.

"It's okay. Seems like not much has changed." He let out a small chuckle. He'd been on the scene when Maggie and Cliff's marriage fell apart and had witnessed their ugly divorce. There wasn't much he hadn't seen.

"But still. It was wrong, and I'm sorry."

"Apology accepted." He stood and tossed his paper cup in the bin. "Will they let us all in at the same time?"

"That's a good point. Why don't you go on your own? Cliff and I can wait down here."

"Are you sure?"

"Yes, that's fine." Maggie momentarily swung her gaze to Cliff, daring him to disagree. He simply shrugged.

"Thank you," David replied. "I might be back in a few minutes if she throws me out."

"Let's hope she doesn't. She's in Room 9 of the ICU on the third floor."

"Thanks. I'll let you know how it goes." He nodded and then walked out of the cafeteria, leaving Maggie alone with Cliff. Again.

"You may as well join me," she said.

"I thought you'd never ask." His eyebrows waggled.

"Don't play with me, Cliff. I agreed to be civil, but that's all."

"And I guess that's all I deserve. I did treat you rottenly, didn't I?" he said as he sat opposite her.

Maggie's brows lifted. That was the closest thing to an apology he'd ever given. "Yes…you did." She could easily have said a lot more, but there was no point. It was in the past, and she'd finally dealt with it. "Anyway, we're not here to talk about us. Where were you today? I expected you ages ago."

"I had some business to attend to. I'm sorry."

"Serena's worse than we thought. Her cheek's a mess. I can't see that it'll ever look normal again." Maggie took a deep breath and swallowed the lump in her throat. She didn't want to break down in front of Cliff, but the image of her daughter's injuries plagued her mind. They were horrid.

"It's amazing what plastic surgeons can do these days."

"Yes, well I guess we'll see. She was in shock when she woke up and saw some of her burns. She hasn't seen her cheek yet. The doctor thought it best to wait."

Cliff nodded. "He's probably right if it's that bad. I've

contacted a few of my friends in high places to see who they recommend. I should hear back soon."

Maggie sighed. "I doubt she'll be fit to travel for weeks, if not months."

"I'm sure I can get a sooner time frame arranged."

"Really? How?"

"Oh, for me to know and you to find out, Maggie, my dear."

She gritted her teeth. How she hated him talking to her like that. *Lord, give me patience.*

∼

DAVID FOUND THE ICU EASILY. The nurse at the desk was a little hesitant at first to let him in, but finally, agreed. He didn't get upset or angry, he simply explained who he was and how long he'd been travelling to be with Serena. He also thought it wise to tell her that Serena might react adversely to him being there because of her burns. "If she does, I'll leave without a fuss and try again tomorrow."

"That's a good attitude to have, Mr...?"

"Kramer. But you can call me David if you like."

"Okay, David. That's a good attitude you have."

"Getting angry won't achieve anything."

"You're right. Anyway, come with me. I think she's still resting."

He followed the nurse to Serena's room. He knew what to expect, but the sight of her brought tears to his eyes. He quickly blinked them away.

"Buzz if you need me, otherwise, you're welcome to stay as long as you like," the nurse whispered.

"Thank you." He sat on the chair closest to Serena. He wanted to hold her and tell her he loved her, that he would be there for her, but all he could do was stare at her. He hadn't wanted her to come to Paris, but he understood that it was her job. Much like she didn't want him fighting raging bush fires, laying his life on the line. Life wasn't risk free, but he also knew that facing whatever challenges those risks brought made a person stronger. Hiding from them did nothing for a person's character. But Serena's journey to recovery would be long and fraught with many ups and downs. "I'm here for you, darling. Whatever you need, I'm here. Don't push me away."

He'd met Serena five years earlier when she was covering the bush fires that raged through the Kakadu, destroying thousands of hectares of precious bushland. Something about her had attracted him. She was a beautiful woman, but it was more than that. She had spunk, and he liked that. He'd grown bored with his previous girlfriend, Kelly. In fact, he wasn't sure why they'd started dating in the first place. She wasn't overly fond of anything he enjoyed, but for some reason, she'd pursued him and for a while they'd enjoyed each other's company. But when she'd chosen to sip cocktails by a pool instead of joining him on his hikes, he'd called it quits.

But Serena. *Serena.* She was a risk taker. A thrill seeker. And this time, it was him pursuing her. He'd tried to tell himself he didn't mind their loose relationship. He could understand why she was reluctant to commit after her parents' ugly divorce, but no matter how many times he'd told her he'd never hurt her, she said she preferred to keep their relationship as it was. He hoped that one day she'd change her mind and would be prepared to make a long-term commitment. That she might consider marriage. But the 'M' word was a definite no go as far as Serena was concerned. But maybe now she'd see things differently.

Her eyes fluttered and then opened. "David…" Her voice was barely a whisper. Her throat would still be raw from inhaling the smoke. He knew what that was like.

"Serena." He swallowed hard and picked up the tumbler off her tray and held the straw to her mouth.

She took a sip and then another before she pushed it away. "I didn't want you to see me like this."

"I don't care what you look like. I want to be here with you. Don't push me away."

Her eyes blinked but stayed open. "Don't waste your life on me. I'm a mess."

"But you're alive, Serena. You'll get through this. I'll help you."

"So much pain…" She groaned as she shifted in the bed.

"Do you want the nurse?"

She nodded.

"I'll call for her. It'll be okay, darling. It'll get better."

She turned her head and closed her eyes.

As he buzzed for the nurse, anguish washed over him. He hated seeing Serena in so much pain, but her reaction was normal. It would take a while for her to start fighting. Right now, she simply wanted to give up. Given the extent of her injuries, her pain level would be high and the medication wouldn't allow her to think rationally. He knew that, so he'd do the fighting for her until she was able to do it herself.

The nurse arrived and gave Serena some more pain relief. "She'll sleep for a while now."

David nodded. "I'll stay with her."

"Call if you need me."

When she left, he called Maggie and gave her an update.

"Are you sure you don't want us to sit with her? You must need a sleep."

"I'm okay. I can sleep in the chair."

"All right. As long as you're sure. I'll come and see her a little later."

"No problem. Come whenever you want."

"Thank you."

He ended the call and took Serena's hand, stroking the small piece of unburned skin. "I love you, Serena. You'll get through this. I know you will."

CHAPTER 30

Maggie slipped her phone into her pocket and relayed to Cliff what David had told her.

"I guess we're redundant now that he's here," Cliff said.

Maggie drew a breath. That's how she felt. Deflated. The whole time since arriving in Paris, the need to be with Serena had consumed her. Now that David was here and Serena hadn't pushed him away, she and Cliff weren't needed. That was her initial reaction, although she knew they would each have a role to play eventually. "Not totally, but yes," she said.

"Well, I think we should use the time to explore Paris."

Maggie's brows shot up. "Together?"

"I don't see why not. We're adults, Maggie. Surely we can put our differences aside for a short while."

"I'm not sure."

"How about we try?"

"It seems wrong to be enjoying ourselves while Serena's in such a state. And what if another blast goes off?"

"Paris is a big city. We'll take care."

"I'm not sure how we do that."

He shrugged. "Keep our wits about us. Look for anything unusual."

Maggie had to admit that the idea appealed a little. It would be a pity not to see any of Paris while she was there, but exploring the city on her own when the danger level was high was a little daunting. She would have much preferred to explore with Frank, but Cliff was here, so he would have to do. "Okay. I guess we can."

"Good. You know, I always wanted to bring you here. I'm not sure why it never happened."

Maggie gave him a pointed look. "Because you were always too busy. That's why."

"Yes, I guess you're right. Well, we're here now, so let's make a start." He drained his coffee and tossed the cup in the bin. "After you." He stepped aside to allow her to go ahead. "Where do you suggest we go first?"

Maggie let out a sigh, hardly believing she was doing this. Somehow, she felt disloyal to Frank. She'd do it once, and then no more. She'd already explored Paris. It might have been years ago, but she'd seen all the sights. Cliff could explore on his own. "How about the Eiffel Tower? That's always a good place to start."

"Sounds good to me. Lead the way."

Maggie paused. Should they grab a taxi or take the Metro? She glanced at Cliff. She couldn't see him catching a train, even though that was the cheapest and possibly the fastest way to get around the city. "I think we should catch a taxi," she said.

"Whatever you think, Maggs."

She shuddered. She intensely disliked being called that. How did he not know after all these years? She turned around and told him.

"Why didn't you tell me before now?" His eyebrows furrowed. He looked crushed. Shocked.

"I did. Countless times. You never listened."

"I'm sorry."

Maggie blinked. Cliff said he was sorry. *Amazing.* Miracles really did happen.

When they walked out the main doors, she shivered and grabbed her thin jacket from her bag. If she stayed much longer, she'd need to go shopping. Not that that was a problem. Who ever had a problem shopping in Paris?

A number of taxis were lined up in the rank. They climbed in the first one and Maggie gave the driver instructions in French. Her French wasn't perfect, but it was mostly understood and helped her get around easily. The French seemed to like it when she at least tried to speak their language. That was fair enough. It was arrogant to think that everyone should speak English.

The drive to the tower took a little over fifteen minutes. Seated in the back of the cab with Cliff was strange, like she was in some kind of time warp. It didn't seem real. "I can't believe you've never been here," she said, more for something to say than anything else.

The taxi skirted past *Notre Dame* and Maggie couldn't help but crane her neck and stare. The spires that had stood proud and tall for hundreds of years above the famous Gothic cathedral on the *Île de la Cité* in the middle of the River Seine, were no longer there. They'd burned in the recent fire that destroyed a good part of the cathedral. "It's so sad, and it's hard to believe it happened."

"I would have liked to have seen the cathedral," Cliff said. "I've heard it was quite unique."

"Yes, it was. *Is.* I'm sure it will be rebuilt. It's one of the finest examples of French Gothic architecture anywhere, and the stained-glass windows were amazing. I guess they're all gone." She grew sadder.

"At least it wasn't a terrorist attack."

"No, I guess it could have been worse. It makes you wonder what place they'll target next."

"Hopefully not the tower."

"Yes, hopefully not the tower." She gulped. The terrorists could target anywhere, but they seemed to favour places with high traffic. *Lord, please keep us safe.* Suddenly, she was having second thoughts. But the taxi had pulled up and the driver had turned around and was waiting to be paid. Cliff handed over some bills and thanked him in terrible French. At least he'd tried.

Maggie drew her jacket closer again. Cliff noticed. "Are you cold?"

"A bit. I'll be fine."

"I can lend you my jacket."

Memories of Frank lending her his as they strolled along the jetty in Darwin not that long ago flashed through her mind. His jacket had floated on her but she hadn't minded. As he'd rolled up the sleeves, his light blue eyes had twinkled and she'd laughed. A pang of longing to be near him stabbed her. But he wasn't here and she needed to answer Cliff. She gave him a grateful smile. "Thanks, but I really am okay."

"As long as you're sure."

"Yes, I am." She looked around, taking in the area. It wasn't as busy as she'd expected. People were probably staying away because of the attacks. That was beneficial for them because it meant the line to get tickets wasn't as long as usual. But it also wasn't good. People were staying away for a reason. "Are you sure you want to do this?" she asked.

"Yes. The terrorists don't intimidate me."

"But you might not even know they're here. *If* they are. I'm not saying they are."

"I'm not going to let them dictate what I do."

She let out a sigh. "Fair enough. Let's get our tickets."

They lined up, and within ten minutes were whizzing to the second level in the lift.

"Wow, this is awesome." Cliff said as they stepped out and leaned against the railing. The city spread out before them in all directions and Maggie began pointing out the main places of interest as they slowly walked around. The *Champs Élysées* leading to the *Arc de Triomphe, Sacré-Cœur* and *Montmatre,* the *Champs de Mars,* the *Louvre. Notre Dame,* or what remained of it. *Pont Neuf.*

As the sun lowered in the sky, the lights of the city began to twinkle. They gazed down at the River Seine, a thin ribbon of dark blue that wove through the city and contained so much history. Maggie was a history buff and could regale Cliff all night with her knowledge, but she knew he'd grow quickly bored. Already he was eager to go to the top level. "Although you can see further from up there, you can't see the places of interest as clearly," she said, "but we may as well go up since we've got tickets."

They headed back to the lifts and caught the one going to the very top. When they stepped out, Maggie tried to hide her shiver as a blast of cold wind almost knocked her off her feet.

"Hey, Maggs." He winced. "Sorry. Maggie, are you okay?" Cliff asked with something akin to concern in his voice, surprising her.

"Yes, I'm fine. The wind caught me off guard, that's all."

"Have my jacket. You're shivering."

Against her better judgment, she gratefully accepted his offer and slipped the jacket over her shoulders. The familiar smell of his cologne tickled her nose and immediately roused memories, memories she didn't want rekindled. It was true, she had once loved him, but that was long ago, when she had blinders on and hadn't seen him for what he was. She had to admit as she stood next to him that he seemed to have changed a little. In fact, there was something she couldn't quite put her finger on that was different. He seemed kinder than she remembered, but it wasn't only that. She quickly tore her thoughts from him. She didn't want to spend her time thinking about Cliff. She rubbed her arms and followed him around the perimeter. When they reached the lift again, she asked if he was ready to go.

"Yes. Where to next?"

Maggie grimaced. "I'd really like to go back to the hospital. Do you mind?"

He shrugged. "I guess not. But let's get something to eat first."

"Okay. But just a quick bite. Nothing fancy."

"All right. As long as it's not the cafeteria."

"Deal." She knew the very place to take him. She'd passed a

small restaurant when she'd walked from the guest house to the hospital and had thought it would be a convenient place to eat. They hailed a taxi, and within fifteen minutes were seated at a table on the pavement surrounded by potted plants and hanging baskets overflowing with cheerful annuals. There was also a gas heater, so Maggie returned Cliff's jacket before she began perusing the menu.

"Can you translate for me?" Cliff asked, pointing to an item halfway down the menu. "What's this?"

"Ah, *Aiguillettes de Poulet Marsala*," Maggie said in almost perfect French. "I think you'd like that one. It's sautéed chicken breast and mushrooms in a Marsala sauce."

"Sounds good. I'll have it."

"And I'll have the *Poulet Cordon Bleu*."

"I know what that is." He chuckled and called the waiter over and placed the orders using terrible French. The amused grin on the waiter's face made Maggie laugh, but she was impressed that at least Cliff had tried.

"How long do you think you'll stay?" she asked as she sipped the sparkling mineral water the waiter had poured.

Cliff's shoulders dropped. "I wondered when you'd ask that."

Maggie's eyes narrowed. "Is something wrong?"

"You could say that." He toyed with his drink and then looked up and met her gaze. "Mandy's left me."

Maggie's eyes popped open. "No. When did that happen?"

"Two weeks ago."

"So…so what happened?"

He shrugged. "We'd been fighting a bit, but I thought we

were okay. But then one day, she simply told me she was leaving. With Ruby. And she did."

"Didn't you try to stop her?"

"Yes, but she'd made up her mind."

Maggie studied him, and for the first time in her life, she saw below his façade. He was hurting and almost seemed like a lost little boy who didn't know what had happened to him. He'd always been the one in charge, but it seemed that he'd met his match in Mandy. "Do you love her, Cliff?"

"Yes. But seeing you again has also made me realise what a fool I was to walk out on you. Do you think we could try again, Maggie?" His eyes implored, but she couldn't believe what he was saying. Try again? He had to be joking.

"I think it's too late for that, Cliff. Mandy's your wife, and if you love her, you should fight for her. And for Ruby."

"I've been a fool, haven't I?"

She nodded. "Yes." There was little more she could add to that.

He drew a slow breath. "The truth is, I don't know what I want. It seems that nobody apart from Jeremy wants anything to do with me. Not even Serena."

"Do you blame her? You married someone younger than her. How do you think she feels?"

"I got carried away, didn't I?"

Maggie nodded again. "But you have another daughter now to think of as well. It's never too late to make amends and become a better person. If Mandy's leaving makes you wake up, it could be a good thing."

The waiter arrived with their meals. They paused their conversation while he topped up their glasses and asked if he could get them anything else. When they said no, they were fine, he left and Cliff leaned forward, letting out a heavy sigh. "What should I do, Maggie?"

"Go home and try to make amends with Mandy. Offer to go to counselling." She pinned him pointedly with her gaze. How many times in the year before he took up with Mandy had she pleaded with him to go to counselling with her? Each time he'd told her he'd never be seen dead or alive in a counsellor's office. "If you really love her and want her back, that's what you have to do. And you need to apologise and mean it. And become a nicer person."

"Ouch. All the things you wanted me to do…"

She nodded again. "Yes."

He drew a slow breath and picked up his silverware. "Maybe you're right. Maybe I should go home and try. It's not like Serena needs me. Not with you and David here."

"I think that's a good idea, Cliff. You don't want two failed marriages under your belt, do you? That wouldn't be a good look for your constituents."

"No need to be nasty. But you're right. I worked hard to win back their confidence after our divorce. They mightn't like a second one." He sliced a piece of chicken and popped it in his mouth. After swallowing it he said, quietly, seriously, with his gaze fixed on hers, "unless of course you'd reconsider my previous offer. I mean it, Maggie. I should never have left you. We were good together, and I loved you. I might not have shown it enough, but I did. I…I do."

Maggie swallowed hard as she struggled with the array of emotions and memories that flooded back. Cliff was right. In the early years, they *had* been good together. She'd been young and in love and hadn't minded his charismatic personality. Until he began to use her to gain approval and votes. Then she'd started to see through him. She breathed in deeply. "No, Cliff. I've moved on. And I'm happy. I really am. Frank is a wonderful man and I'm looking forward to marrying him."

"Do you really think you'll be happy living on a remote cattle station? You're a city girl, Maggie. I can't see you roughing it."

Maggie chuckled as she recalled Frank's arms around her as he showed her how to use the staple gun. "Yes, I do. It will be different for sure, but I'm looking forward to living a simpler life. I don't need the city, Cliff."

"And what about Serena? She'll need you, and she lives in the city."

Maggie gulped. She hadn't really thought that through. No doubt, when Serena was able to return to Australia, she *would* need her. "I'm sure we'll work something out."

"So, when's the big day?"

"We haven't decided yet."

"I noticed you're not wearing a ring..." He raised a brow. "Do you think you might have acted too hastily?"

Indignation rose within her as she reached for the ring hanging under her blouse and fingered it. "Absolutely not. We were going to announce it to his family when I got the phone call."

"So, you could change your mind." He quirked a brow.

All the old emotions rose within her. Frustration. Annoyance. Exasperation. She clenched her other fist in her lap. She wouldn't allow him to do this to her. She leaned forward and glared at him. "No. I am *not* going to change my mind. I love

Frank and I'm going to marry him. End of story. Go home and get your own house in order and forget about me." She folded her napkin and placed it on her plate. "I've lost my appetite. I'm going to the hospital to see Serena." She stood and tossed a twenty Euro note on his plate. "That should cover my meal."

He began to stand, his mouth agape.

"Don't bother, Cliff. Finish your meal. Goodbye." Striding off, she held her head high, but her heart thumped and her hands shook. She hadn't intended to grow angry and she felt bad that she had, but it also felt good. He hadn't changed. Not really. He was still looking out for number one.

She asked for forgiveness as she hurried to the hospital, and she also prayed for Mandy and Ruby. Her heart went out to them. Perhaps Cliff might change over time and Mandy might decide to take him back, but somehow, she doubted it. He had to get past his over-inflated ego first, and the only true way of doing that was to allow God into his life for real. To humble himself and allow God to change his heart. It wasn't impossible, and she would pray for him, just like she prayed for Serena. Perhaps this was the wake-up call he needed. And perhaps Serena's injuries were the wake-up call *she* needed to draw her back to God. Maggie prayed they wouldn't cause her daughter to push Him further away.

CHAPTER 31

Frank's confrontation with Julian came sooner than expected. The rains came the day after the anniversary of Esther's death and although they were prepared, there were always last-minute jobs. Julian had taken one of the quad bikes out early that morning to check on the herd on the western boundary but had gotten into trouble. The quad had slipped in the mud, hit an embankment and rolled. He was lucky not to be badly injured, but the quad was damaged and would need to be fixed. Julian radioed in for help, and Frank offered to go. He was only doing odd jobs around the property. Nothing that couldn't wait.

He headed out in the truck, taking with him some emergency supplies and medical equipment in case Julian was in a worse state than he'd indicated. It took over an hour to reach him. The tracks had already turned into raging torrents and deep culverts had appeared. The rain was so heavy at times he had to slow way down in order to see where he was going. He wasn't sure why Julian had chosen to take the quad instead of the truck when he knew rain was coming.

He prayed for his son as he drove, and asked God to give him wisdom with what to say when they rode back together. The breakthrough with Caleb yesterday had encouraged him greatly and he knew God could do great things. And it wasn't as if Julian didn't believe. It was just that, somehow, he'd lost his way and allowed his heart to harden.

The quad was wedged on its side in a deep culvert. Frank was glad to see that Julian hadn't been sheltering under it, but instead had hunkered down under his rain jacket away from the fast-flowing water. He stood and waved a hand as Frank approached. He was limping, but thankfully the quad had roll bars, otherwise he could have been a lot worse.

Frank pulled up and jumped out, quickly zipping his jacket up and slipping on his hood. "Hi son, let me help." He placed his arm around Julian's shoulder before helping him climb into the passenger side of the truck. He quickly assessed his son's injuries before climbing in beside him. "Looks like Someone was looking after you." He helped Julian out of his saturated jacket and covered him with a blanket.

"Yeah. Maybe. The rain came out of nowhere."

"Just like it always does…"

"I should have known better. You don't need to say anything." He hunkered down in his seat.

Frank lifted a brow and bit his tongue. That would have been his next question…*Why did you take the quad?* Instead, he asked if he'd like a mug of hot tea.

Julian nodded. "Yes, please."

Frank opened the flask and poured him a cup. "Get that into you. It should help." It wasn't cold outside. Far from it. With the rains came high humidity, but Julian was shivering and Frank was a little concerned about him. Shock, perhaps? "Are you all right, son? Is it just your knee or is there another injury?"

"Not one you can see."

"Ah... that's it. Your pride's wounded."

"Maybe."

"No one's going to make fun of you."

Julian lifted a brow. "Really?"

"I'll make sure of it."

"Just like you do with everything," Julian muttered under his breath.

"Sorry, what did you say?"

"Nothing."

"I think you did. Spill the beans, Julian. Let's have it out, once and for all."

"You won't want to hear it."

"Try me."

Julian studied Frank as if weighing up the situation, making Frank wonder what was on his son's heart. A number of possibilities floated through his mind... Was he sick? Had he been hiding an illness from them all? Or were he and Janella splitting up? Did he want to leave Goddard Downs like Nathan and Olivia? Frank's thoughts raced, but then, one of his favourite Bible passages popped into his mind... Philippians chapter four, verses six and seven... *Do not be anxious about anything, but in everything by prayer and supplication with thanksgiving let your requests be made known to God. And the peace of God, which surpasses all understanding, will guard your hearts and your minds in Christ Jesus.*

He let out a deep sigh. *Lord, I'm so sorry for worrying. I hand this to You. Whatever Julian is about to say to me, I'll handle it with Your grace and Your strength.*

"It's not what you think. Or maybe it is," Julian said.

"Well, I won't know that until you tell me." Frank sipped his tea, and leaning against the truck door, faced his son and waited.

Julian kicked his uninjured leg against the seat. Whatever it was seemed to be causing his son a whole lot of grief.

"Just say it, Julian. You've never been backward in being forward before."

"No." He lifted his head and met Frank's gaze. "But I've also never had to tell you that, unless you back off, I'm going to leave the station."

"Wha…what? What do you mean?"

"I'm thirty-eight years old and I'm tired of living under your control."

"You want to be in charge?"

He nodded.

"Well. What do I say to that?" Frank scratched his head. "Has that been your problem all along? If so, I don't understand why that would make you short with everyone else. Surely your grievance is with me alone. No one else."

"You're right, but it's been eating away at me and affecting all my relationships."

"Bitterness does that, you know."

"I'm not bitter."

"Oh, I think you are. You're bitter that you're not getting your way. That you have to acquiesce to me."

"I work harder than anyone else, but I don't get any credit."

"Come on now, Julian. That's not true. The research you did for the meeting was way more than I'd ever expected, and I told you so."

"But you didn't let me go. It might have turned out differently if you had."

"Are you saying you would have bribed the man?"

"I'm not saying that at all. I'm just saying I might have been able to talk him around."

Frank was about to say he didn't think so but stopped himself. Perhaps he hadn't allowed Julian enough rope. He'd given him what he thought was enough, but perhaps it wasn't. Perhaps he did need to give him more responsibility. After all, he'd eventually be taking over the reins.

But not yet... I'm not ready to hand them over...

He jolted with shock. He'd never seriously considered what it would be like to step back and let someone else shoulder the responsibility for the station. As he contemplated his life with Maggie, he'd also contemplated the idea of slowing down a little, but letting someone else make the decisions? No, he hadn't considered that. What would it be like to hand over control to someone else? To Julian... His son was right; he did like being in charge. It was his station, after all. No doubt his own father had experienced the same misgivings. It was a pity he wasn't here. If he was, they could have had a chat about it.

"Well, son, I'm thinking we both have some soul searching to do. I don't know that it's as easy as me saying 'you're in charge now'. It has to be a process, and I'm not sure I'm ready for that amount of change just yet."

"When do you think you will be? Because I don't know that I can stay like this forever."

Frank let out a slow breath and drummed the dash with his fingers. He'd alluded to Olivia yesterday that he and Maggie might have an announcement to make but hadn't stated definitively that they were engaged. Maybe he should tell Julian now. Maybe that would help. Frank looked at him. Could he entrust his son with that news? Would Maggie mind? They'd agreed to wait until she returned and tell the family together, but he sensed that the news might help ease Julian's frustration a little. To know that things *were* happening. Things *were* changing. And that one day, in the not too distant future, he *would* take over the reins. He just needed to exercise a little patience in the meantime. Yes, he'd tell him and pray that Maggie wouldn't mind.

"I have some news that might help…"

CHAPTER 32

Over the following weeks, Maggie split her time between sitting in a café writing articles and sitting with Serena, trying to cheer her daughter. Not only did she finish the articles, she ended up writing an entire piece on Mrs. Mary alone, and she also began writing Clara Goddard's biography.

Cliff returned to Australia the day after she'd walked out on him and she hadn't heard whether he'd been successful in reconciling with Mandy or not. She continued to pray for them every day. Not so much for Cliff, although she'd be over the moon if he truly did change his ways, but more so for Mandy and the baby. Having been through a marriage breakup herself, she knew the gamut of emotions the young woman would be feeling. She had no idea if Mandy had any knowledge of God and the hope and peace that could be hers in Christ, but that wasn't a reason not to pray for her.

She also prayed for Serena and David. She'd come to

appreciate what a special young man he was and how much he loved her daughter. He'd told Serena again and again that he didn't care what she looked like, but she kept pushing him away, saying he deserved better. He didn't go away. He went every day to sit with her and encourage her through the countless surgeries and skin grafts. The doctors were pleased with her progress, but her skin, especially her right cheek, was a mess. In fact, a lot of her body would be scarred for life. She still wanted to hide herself away, but it was early days and she was still heavily medicated. But, she'd been given the all clear to travel home to Australia, and Maggie and David had started to make the arrangements. Cliff had left sufficient money to hire a nurse to accompany Serena on the trip, and the flight was scheduled to leave Paris on the last Thursday in November.

Maggie stood back while the nurse settled Serena into the wheelchair and prayed once again for her daughter. While her physical scars were beginning to heal, her emotional scars were still raw and deep. "Are you ready, sweetheart?" she asked after the nurse finished settling her.

Serena looked up from the wheelchair, her face almost completely masked by the over-sized sunglasses and head scarf she'd wrapped to cover the unsightly bandages she'd still have to wear for a few more weeks. She answered Maggie with her lips pursed. "Yes, but I don't see why I have to be wheeled out. I'm perfectly capable of walking out of here on my own."

Maggie glanced at David and shrugged. They both knew that was far from the truth. Although the plaster cast was off her ankle, Serena still struggled to walk the five metres from her hospital bed to the bathroom. There was no way she could walk to the car. Plus, it was hospital policy to be wheeled out, and Maggie told her so.

Serena didn't bother responding. Instead, she pulled the scarf tighter around her shoulders and hunkered down in the chair as the hired nurse, a young Australian woman by the name of Helen, wheeled her out of the hospital to the taxi waiting to take them to the airport.

Although Maggie was excited to be going home, her heart was heavy. Her daughter was well enough to leave the hospital and make the long trek to Australia, but she was far from healed. Both the physical and emotional scars from the terrorist attack would be with her long after she left this place. Serena faced months of physical therapy, but at least they would be in the comfort of their own homes rather than a foreign city.

Later, as Maggie sat in the plane waiting for take-off, her thoughts shifted to Frank. He'd told her he'd be waiting at the airport in Darwin when they arrived. She'd told him it might be best to wait a few days to give her time to settle in. She didn't have the heart to tell him over the phone that she was having second thoughts, but the thought of telling him face to face made her feel sick in her stomach.

Cliff's question had made her rethink her decision to marry Frank. Had she acted in haste like he'd suggested? Did she know Frank well enough to commit to spending the rest of her life with him on a remote cattle station, especially when she wasn't sure how welcome she'd be? She'd prayed a lot but had no peace either way. She needed time. Time she prayed Frank would give her.

Arriving at Darwin Airport almost twenty-four hours later,

she was relieved, although a little disappointed, that Frank wasn't there. She really did care about him. But did she love him enough to marry him? Did she even know what love looked like? Yes. David loved Serena, and Jeremy loved Emma. What she'd had with Cliff wasn't the true, abiding, deep love that conquered everything and would last through the good times and the bad.

Frank had told her he believed their love was like that. Was it simply that she'd had too much time to think and spent too much time with Cliff? As she recalled the way her heart had pounded when Frank looked into her eyes and asked her to marry him, she'd had no doubt then.

But he wasn't here and she felt empty. She followed the others through the arrival hall and out to the taxi stand. As they exited the air-conditioned terminal, she walked into a wall of heat. She'd almost forgotten how suffocating summer in Darwin was. She shrugged off the jacket she'd draped over her shoulders and laid it on her suitcase.

They waited for a taxi and when one came, David and Helen helped Serena into the vehicle. Maggie felt like a third wheel. The cab took them to David and Serena's apartment at Coconut Grove. Their apartment was on the third floor and had a great view across the sea. Maggie offered to make coffee for everyone. Serena said she wanted to go to bed. Helen washed and dressed her and redressed her burns, and then, with David's assistance, settled her in her bed.

They'd arranged for the apartment to be cleaned prior to their arrival, and Maggie had ordered some basic groceries online. After Helen left, she made coffee for her and David. They needed to talk.

The afternoon rain had just started and provided a welcome reprieve from the overbearing heat. They sat outside on the balcony in silence, watching the rain fall on the sea. Finally, Maggie broke the silence. "I think you're doing an amazing job with her, David. Not many men would have stood by when she's so been so short-tempered and rude."

"She'll come out of it eventually."

"For your sake, I hope so." Maggie sipped her coffee. "I'm not sure what you'd like me to do now that we're back, but I'm willing to help in whatever way you want. I'm sure you'll need a break every now and then."

"Thanks. I appreciate that. Let's see how things go over the next few days. I'm hoping now that she's out of the hospital her attitude might change. I'm also hoping she'll get some counselling. I think she needs it."

"She sure does." Maggie knew she needed more than counselling. She needed a heart transformation that could only be performed by the Master Surgeon Himself. Anything less would only scratch the surface. She needed to see herself as He saw her, precious and loved despite her external scarring. But that might take time, although Maggie prayed daily for opportunities to share God's unconditional love with her daughter.

"I'm looking forward to meeting Frank. Have you heard from him?"

"Not since we left Paris. I'm guessing he'll call tonight." Maggie had half expected a text from Frank to pop up on her phone when she landed, but there hadn't been one. Usually he either called or sent a text every day, and it concerned her just a little that he hadn't done either. But there was nothing stopping her from sending him one... other than her conflicted emotions. She hadn't told David and Serena about the engagement. They only knew they were seeing each other.

Maggie finished her coffee and said she'd head back to her place. "I'll call in the morning and see how Serena is."

David stood and walked with her to the door where she'd left her bags. "Are you sure you won't let me drive you?"

"No, it's fine. I'm happy to get a cab." She stepped forward and gave him a hug. "Remember to call if you need me."

"I will. Thank you for everything."

"I'll be praying for you both."

She felt him flinch a little, but guessed it was because it was the first time she'd said anything like that to him. She didn't normally talk about her faith, but since meeting Frank, she'd become bolder, and it felt good. There was no need to be ashamed. Even if David wasn't aware of his and Serena's need for God, Maggie knew that only He could truly heal her daughter's wounds.

Arriving at her apartment, Maggie unpacked and took a shower. It was late afternoon, but she suddenly felt very weary. She made herself a toasted sandwich and a cup of tea, but before she finished either, her eyes had closed and she quickly fell into a deep sleep.

Sometime later, she woke to the sound of her phone ringing. Glancing at the time, she realised with a start that she'd been asleep for a good number of hours. It was Frank, and when she answered, she knew she still sounded groggy.

"I'm sorry if I woke you, Maggie." His voice was familiar and sent warmth coursing through her.

She stifled a yawn. "It's fine. I shouldn't have been asleep… now I probably won't sleep tonight."

"Jet lag?"

"I think so. It wasn't the best of flights." That was an understatement. Although they had Business Class seats, Serena had found it hard to get comfortable and had been demanding and short-tempered for most of the flight. Maggie could understand, but her manner had made the long flight uncomfortable for them all and they'd only been able to snatch the odd hour of sleep here and there. If it hadn't been for Helen, Maggie was sure that neither she nor David would have gotten any at all.

"I'm glad you're back."

"So am I." Maggie turned the lamp on and rubbed the back of her neck. Her half-eaten sandwich looked very unappetising.

"I won't hold you for long. I just wanted to hear your voice. If it's not too soon, I was thinking of driving up this weekend. Julian said he can manage for a few days without me."

Maggie swallowed hard. Crunch time was coming. "That would be lovely, Frank. I don't have any plans at the moment. Not until we know how Serena is coping with being back."

"Okay. I'll stay with Bethany and Graham this time. They'd like to meet you."

"And I'd like to meet them." That was true. She'd enjoyed her time with Frank's older sister, Sarah, when she and their mother had come to Goddard Downs for the weekend and Maggie had interviewed Mrs. Mary, so she assumed she'd also like his younger sister, Bethany. But what if she decided to slow things down with Frank? What if he'd already told his family about their engagement, just like she'd told Cliff? He hadn't mentioned that he had, but she also hadn't told him that she'd told Cliff. No, she couldn't think like that. They were all adults and she wouldn't allow herself to be pressured. If she needed time, she needed time, and they would all simply have to understand that.

They talked for a bit, but Maggie had to apologise because try as she might, she couldn't chat on as if everything was as it had been before she left. "I need to go to bed, Frank. I'm sorry. Call me when you get to town?"

"I sure will. If the roads are okay, I should be there by Saturday afternoon, but I'll let you know. I love you, Maggie, and I can't wait to see you."

"I love you, too, Frank." Maggie swallowed hard. She wasn't telling an untruth, but she wasn't totally sure if she'd only said she loved him because she should, or if she truly meant it.

When she hung up, she bowed her head in prayer. *Lord, please guide and lead me, and give me peace. I feel so conflicted. I don't want to hurt Frank, but I don't want to marry him unless I'm completely sure it's what You want and that I'm sure of my love. Please help me.*

∼

FRANK COULDN'T BE MORE excited. He was about to see Maggie! The last two months had gone by incredibly slowly without her. Since it was the wet season and the roads were more dangerous, he'd taken two days to make the long drive to Darwin, and now, after stopping at Bethany and Graham's to freshen up and have a bite to eat and give his truck a quick clean, he was on his way to meet her. His whole being seemed to be filled with anticipation, and as he pulled up outside her place, his palms were sweating, and it wasn't just because of the humidity.

She'd invited him to have afternoon tea at her apartment rather than meeting at a café or restaurant. For dinner, he'd planned on taking her back to Pearls, the restaurant where they'd shared their first meal together, and had made a booking in the hope she'd be agreeable.

The complex where she lived consisted of six modern apartments, and although it was set back from the water, the bay wasn't a long stroll away. He pressed the buzzer for Number Three and waited like an eager schoolboy for her to answer. He even checked his breath and popped a mint just in case. She buzzed him through the security gate and told him her apartment was up one floor on the left. He found it easily and before he could knock, she'd opened the door.

He studied her for a moment, mesmerised by the sight of her. She was wearing yoga pants and a light floral shirt, and her hair smelled freshly washed. He took her hand and stepped towards her. "Maggie." His heart beat a crescendo as he lowered his face and gently brushed her lips with his. "I've missed you so much." He let go of her hand and slipped his arm around her waist, pulling her close. The feel of her skin against his made his pulse skitter. He breathed in her scent, and after kissing the top of her hair, reluctantly released her. He'd bought a bunch of wildflowers which he presented to her.

Smiling, she took them from him. "Frank. They're lovely." She gestured for him to follow her inside. "How was your trip?"

"Long."

She chuckled. "I already knew that."

"Yes, of course you did. It was fine. No major dramas, although I came through some heavy showers."

"It's not a great time to be on the road."

"No, but it was worth it just to see you." She was placing the flowers in a vase and had her back to him. He came up behind her, wrapped his arms around her waist, and nuzzled her neck.

"Frank!" Spinning around, they shared a moment of intense physical awareness. At that moment, the love he felt for her was so overwhelming. He lifted his hand and stroked her cheek before lowering his face, but just as his lips were about to find hers, she turned her head away. He frowned. "Maggie? What's wrong?"

She shrugged. "I'm sorry, Frank. I didn't mean to do that, it's just…it's just…"

"Just what, my love?"

She nibbled her lower lip. "Let me fix us a drink and we can talk."

"That doesn't sound good." A wave of apprehension flowed through him. He looked at her left hand. She wasn't wearing her ring. Not that it meant anything. They'd agreed she wouldn't wear it until they announced their engagement to their families, but he'd secretly hoped she might have put it on while they were alone.

She poured two tall glasses of lime soda and inserted ice cubes into each. "Come and sit down." She gestured to the cane lounge suite in her living area. She sat on one of the single chairs and he perched on the other. His heart beat in his throat. *Was she about to call off their engagement?*

"I don't know how to say this, Frank, so I'll just say it. I don't like beating around the bush."

He was right. She was about to call it off. Now he felt ill. "What is it, Maggie?"

"I think we were too hasty in moving forward with our plans. Perhaps we should give it a bit more time before telling our families of our engagement."

Relief flooded through him. That was all right. He could deal with that. "You can have all the time in the world. I'm not going to push you. I'm sorry if I did. I didn't mean to, it just seemed opportune."

"Really? You won't be upset if we don't announce it yet?"

He grimaced. "Well, it's kind of too late. I told Julian, but I don't think he's told the others."

Her lips tipped in a grin and she laughed. "Do you really think he wouldn't have told Janella?"

"No, you're right. I'm sorry, Maggie. We were having a bit of a showdown and I thought if I told him, it might appease him."

"Is everything all right between you two?"

"I think so, but let me tell you about that later. Right now, I want to talk about us." He shifted closer and took her hand. "Maggie, I meant it when I said you can take as long as you need. I didn't propose lightly. I love you with all my heart and I'll wait for as long as you need. The only thing I couldn't handle is if you were to call it off completely. Since I've met you, my life has been brighter. Happier. You've given me a new perspective on everything, and I can't imagine growing old without you."

Her eyes moistened. "Oh Frank, you're such a softie."

He chuckled. "Some would say otherwise, but you make me as soft as a marshmallow."

"I love marshmallows."

"Does that mean you love me?"

"I do. Very much. But I think we need more time to get to know each other. It hasn't been very long."

"It seems like it has."

"Maybe, but we need to be completely sure. I'd like to do more things together before we commit."

"Like what?"

She shrugged. "Maybe go on that camping trip you mentioned?"

"Really?"

She nodded.

"It's not great weather for camping."

"We could go glamping."

His brows knitted together. "Glamping? What's that?"

"You've never heard of it?"

"Nope. Enlighten me." He sat back in his chair and swirled his drink, making the ice clink the glass.

"It's camping with all the frills. The tents are already set up, so it doesn't matter if it rains. They're almost like a hotel room, just a little more basic."

"And how do you know that? I thought you never went camping."

"I did an article for the magazine a while back on glamping in the Kakadu."

"I've not been there."

"Really? You've not been to the Kakadu and you call yourself an Aussie?"

"I work too hard."

"I guess you do. So, what do you think? Could we spend

more time doing things like that? But maybe save camping for another time."

"And how do you propose we do that when you live here and have an injured daughter, and I live a thousand kilometres away?"

She blew out a heavy breath, her shoulders sagging. "That's the problem, isn't it? I'm not sure what Serena's recovery will look like yet. She's so bitter and depressed."

"And you want to be here for her, which is perfectly understandable."

She nodded again. "Yes. David's great with her, but I don't want to leave everything to him. Plus, he'll need to return to work at some stage."

Frank remained silent, pondering the situation. Could he leave the station under Julian's management for extended periods so he could spend more time with Maggie? He was sure Julian would jump at the chance, but was he ready to relinquish full control just yet? He wasn't sure. But if it meant that he and Maggie could marry sooner than later, perhaps he could. "Maybe I could spend half of each month here in Darwin."

Maggie's eyes widened. "Would you do that? I didn't think you wanted to leave the station so much."

"I don't, but if it means seeing more of you, I might be able to manage it." He leaned forward and massaged her hand with his thumb as he gazed at her.

Her eyes welled. "I really do love you, Frank. I can't believe you'd make such a sacrifice for me."

"It wouldn't be a sacrifice, Maggie. As long as you're here, it would be a pleasure."

"Where would you stay?"

"At Bethany and Graham's. They have a spare room."

"They wouldn't mind?" She dabbed her eyes with a tissue.

"Not if it results in us getting married."

"Do they know?"

"No, but Bethany was over the moon when I told her about you."

"What did you say?"

He chuckled. "That's for me to know and you to find out."

She slapped his arm playfully. "Frank!"

"I told her you were delightful and that I was falling for you. That was before I proposed." He grew serious. "Now I've fallen, well and truly. Nothing else but true love would make me consider handing over the reins of the station."

"I feel truly honoured, but also guilty. It's like I've blackmailed you, and I'm sorry."

"I don't look at it that way, Maggie. I understand where you're coming from, I really do. But I agree that it won't work if we don't see each other. This is the only way. I'll organise it with Julian when I go back."

"How long have you got this time?"

"I said a couple of days. He told me to take a week, so I guess I've got a week."

She smiled. "That's wonderful, Frank. We should be able to do lots of things in that time."

"What about your work?"

"I've finished that article I was working on and Suzanne has it. The first part will be in next month's edition. I don't have any new assignments right now. Suzanne has given me as much time off as I need."

"Well, that's good to hear. So, perhaps as well as me introducing you to my family, I could meet yours while I'm here?"

"Yes, I'd love them to meet you."

"Well, that settles it. Do you want me to take the ring back and repropose at some stage, or do you want to keep it?"

She reached for the ring hanging around her neck. "Let me keep it? When I put it on, you'll know I'm ready."

"I was hoping you'd say that." He finished his drink and set the glass on the table before taking her hands. "Maggie, I'd like to pray and ask God to bless our relationship. Is that okay?"

She nodded. "It's more than okay, Frank." She smiled and squeezed his hands. "I'd love to seek God's blessing."

"Let's pray, then." He smiled and bowed his head, clearing his throat before he began. "Dear Lord, thank You for bringing Maggie back home safely and for her love for her daughter. Lord, I pray for Serena's healing, but Lord, we both know she needs more than just physical healing. She needs spiritual and emotional healing. But You, Lord, are the great Healer, and You love her with Your whole being. Work in her heart, Lord, and may she come to know how precious she is in Your sight.

"I also pray for Maggie and for our relationship. Thank You that she was honest with me. I truly appreciate that, and Lord, I ask for Your blessing as we seek to get to know each other better. You know how much I love her, but Lord, we both have to feel right about it. I pray that You'll give us both peace over the coming days, weeks and months. And Lord, please help me to happily relinquish control of the station to Julian. You know how I've struggled with that, but I feel that it's time. Bless both our families, dear Lord, and may each of our children and grandchildren come to know Your saving grace. In Jesus' precious name I pray. Amen."

Maggie continued. "And Lord, I thank You for Frank and for his understanding manner. You've blessed me abundantly by bringing him into my life, but dear Lord, I simply ask for peace before we fully commit to each other. Bless our relationship as we seek to put You first in everything we do. In Your precious Son's name. Amen."

"Amen." Frank opened his eyes and smiled. "Maggie, you're the most beautiful woman I know and I love you with all my heart. I just want you to know that."

She chuckled. "You've already said that a few times today."

"I know. You'd better get used to it."

"I don't think that will be too hard."

He held her gaze and had a real desire to embrace her, but instead, he told her about the booking he'd made.

Her face lit up. "Pearls again?"

"Yes. I have fond memories of the place."

"So do I. Give me a few moments and I'll get ready. Would you like another drink while you're waiting?"

"No, I'll be fine, thanks. I'm happy just sitting here."

"Okay. I won't be long."

"No hurry, take your time."

As she stood and walked down the hallway, his gaze followed her. There was nothing about Maggie Donovan he disliked. Nothing.

CHAPTER 33

After Maggie left Frank, she walked down the hallway to the bathroom, closed the door, and allowed relieved tears to fall. She couldn't help it. She'd been so anxious about telling him she wanted to delay their engagement she'd almost made herself ill, but he'd been so understanding. It would have been a totally different story if it had been Cliff. Frank's reaction made her love him more. In fact, despite her resolve to wait and get to know each other better, she was almost tempted to say she was ready to commit. Right now. But that would be impetuous, and she didn't want to be impetuous. She wanted to be one hundred percent sure.

No, she would do what she'd suggested and spend more time with him. Get to know him better. Starting with their dinner date at Pearls. She splashed her face with cool water and applied the tiniest bit of makeup. It was useless putting much on because it would only slide off in the humidity. She then brushed her hair and clipped it up to get it off her neck.

Frank was dressed casually in chinos and a white polo shirt, so she chose a simple pale blue summer dress and her row of pearls. Quite fitting since that was where they were going. She then slipped on her low heels, grabbed her purse, and headed down the hall. Her heart skipped a beat when Frank looked up at her admiringly and smiled. She really did love him, of that she was sure.

They took his truck although she offered the Jeep. "I cleaned it at Bethany's before I came," he said, his eyes twinkling. "I guess I'm a bit old fashioned and want to drive my lady."

"I'd let you drive the Jeep," she said.

"Don't you like my truck?" His shoulders sagged a little and his forehead creased.

She squeezed his arm while stifling a chuckle. "Your truck is fine. I don't mind, really. And you didn't have to clean it."

"Oh, I did. It was covered in a thick layer of red mud."

"Well, I guess it's best you did."

He placed his hand against the small of her back as they headed to the door, reminding her of when Cliff did that in Paris. She'd felt that Cliff was trying to exert control over her. With Frank, all she felt was love.

He opened the truck door and helped her in before he drove them downtown. The afternoon storm had come and gone, and the sky was a clear blue as they walked hand in hand along the wharf to the restaurant. Frank was so easy to be with. They chatted about everything, from her time in Paris to what had been happening on the station. She was eager to hear how Caleb was doing after making his commitment. They sat at their table and ordered drinks and a prawn appetiser before he told her that Caleb was doing well. "We have a short Bible study together most days and he has a real thirst to know more. It's like for the first time in his life everything makes sense, although I do feel he still needs to talk with a professional counsellor."

"Just like Serena does. I hope she agrees soon."

"I've learned it's no use pushing. Prayer and patience are what's needed."

"I think you're right."

They continued chatting throughout the meal. Occasionally their fingers touched and each time a tingle went through her body. Later, they strolled along the wharf, pausing to watch the sun set. The colours were magnificent. They always were at this time of year. Deep orange and crimson splashed across the horizon. God's canvas. It was simply breathtaking.

Frank slipped his arm around her shoulders and kissed the top of her head. "I'll never tire of this."

She snuggled closer. "Nor will I."

THE FOLLOWING MORNING, Frank picked her up for church. She'd offered to go with him to his sister and brother-in-law's church in downtown Darwin. He said he'd like that and told her they'd invited them for lunch after church.

Maggie had deliberated over what to wear, but in the end decided on a knee-length floral dress. It was too hot to wear trousers, although Frank was wearing them. In Darwin, most men wore shorts everywhere, even to church, but Frank was true to his word. He was old school and preferred wearing trousers when worshipping, regardless of how hot and uncomfortable they were.

He embraced her at the door and said she looked lovely.

"You look pretty good yourself," she replied. And he did. For a man who lived on a remote cattle station, he scrubbed up well.

"Shall we go?" He offered his arm and she took it, and together they walked to his truck. "Have you heard how Serena is today?" he asked as they drove the short distance.

"Yes, I called David this morning. She's up and eating breakfast on their balcony."

"That's an improvement, isn't it?"

She nodded. "Yes, she hasn't wanted to get up since we've been back."

"Is it too soon for me to meet her?"

Maggie grimaced. "Probably. She hasn't even wanted to see Jeremy and Emma yet. Perhaps we could meet up with them a little later today? They'd love to meet you."

"I'd like that."

When they arrived at the church, Maggie wished she'd quizzed Frank as to which church his sister and brother-in-law attended, because she realised too late it was the church she used to attend with Cliff. While she had no expectation that he would be there—she assumed he'd stopped going after their divorce, although she didn't know that for a fact, she would know most of the congregation, and they would know about the divorce and Cliff's infidelity. Not that it mattered. It was in the past. But, she realised with a jolt that she probably knew, or at least would recognise, Frank's sister and brother-in-law, unless they'd started attending recently.

She said nothing to start with, but Frank must have noticed something was afoot because he asked if anything was wrong. She had to tell him, so she did.

"We can go elsewhere if you feel uncomfortable," he said, looking at her with understanding in his eyes.

"No. I'll be fine. It was just a shock. I should have asked. How…how long have Bethany and Graham been coming here?" She tucked a piece of hair behind her ear.

"Hmmm. Just under two years, I think. They were at another church further out of town before this one."

"So they probably started going not long after I left."

"I think they would have said if they'd met you before."

"Do…do they know who I am?"

"Cliff Donovan's ex-wife?"

She nodded.

"No. I didn't mention your last name."

"Well, they're about to find out. I don't think I can stay incognito for long. I know too many people here."

"Are you sure you'll be okay?"

She breathed deeply. "Yes. But be prepared for a lot of looks."

Frank frowned. "What do you mean?"

"Everyone is going to wonder where I found such a good-looking man."

"Oh. Maybe we should go somewhere else after all," he said with a small amount of mirth in his voice.

"Now who's nervous?"

He chuckled. "Come on. I'm sure we'll be fine as long as we stick together."

"Yes, I'm sure we will."

After they climbed out of the truck, Maggie slipped her arm into the crook of Frank's elbow. The church was so familiar. It had been built after Cyclone Tracy almost wiped the whole city of Darwin out in 1974 when it hit unexpectedly on Christmas Eve. It wasn't a traditional sort. More of a modern building with a sloping roofline and a cross on the top.

They'd arrived early and a group of worshippers was gathered on the front lawn under the shade of a sprawling poinciana tree in full bloom. Maggie recognised a few…Larry and Belinda O'Gorman, Suellen and Steve Davidson, Carmen Hicks. She dipped her head and wished she'd worn a hat. Not that she didn't want to talk with them, but they were mainly Cliff's friends. Well, not friends really, more like contacts. Cliff didn't have friends, only people he leaned on to get what he wanted. And these were some of the more prominent members of the Darwin community. People who could help fund his campaigns. Influencers. She wondered if he still saw them.

Frank steered her towards a smaller group chatting under the awning. They were in the shade and Maggie couldn't see them properly, but she gathered that his sister and brother-in-law were amongst them.

She was right. A woman whom Maggie assumed was Bethany looked up as they approached. Her face lit and Maggie noticed she had the same pale blue eyes as Frank. She waved them over, and smiling, placed her hand on Maggie's arm. "You must be Maggie. It's lovely to meet you. I'm Bethany and this is

Graham." She turned to the man standing beside her, a fit looking man with tanned skin. He gave a friendly smile and said hello. Bethany then introduced her and Frank to the other couple who turned to face them. Maggie's jaw dropped. There was no need for introductions. She knew them. It was Cliff and Mandy.

For a moment she was lost for words. She thought they were still separated... Jeremy obviously hadn't gotten the most up to date news. Cliff saved the day when he simply said, "Maggie and I already know each other." He smiled and shook her hand. "Nice to see you again, Maggie." He turned to Frank and extended his hand. "And it's nice to meet you, Frank." Frank took his hand and shook it. Cliff then turned to the young woman beside him holding a squirming baby. "This is my wife, Mandy, and our daughter, Ruby."

Maggie forced herself to smile at the woman. It was the first time they'd come face to face. She was very attractive with long blonde hair and a slim figure, but she also had dark circles under her eyes that she'd tried to cover with make-up. Maggie wondered how she was really doing. Was she simply putting on a happy face for church? Maggie remembered how she used to do that. It had almost killed her.

"Oh, I didn't know you two knew each other," Bethany said.

Frank gave his sister a pointed look. It seemed the penny dropped because her face grew pink. "Oh, this is awkward."

"Not really," Cliff said. "Maggie and I spent time together in Paris recently. Didn't we, Maggie?"

She could feel herself starting to boil inside. It wasn't what he said; it was the tone in which he said it. He was stirring up trouble and enjoying it. "Yes, we did. But we were only there for our daughter. Have you seen her since she's been back, Cliff?" Two could play this game.

"Ah... no, but I'm planning to visit this week."

"Good. I'm sure she's looking forward to seeing you." Maggie couldn't keep the sarcasm from her voice.

Graham cleared his throat. "I think it's time to go in. Shall we?" He extended his arms diplomatically to usher the group inside.

Frank placed his hand lightly on Maggie's waist but she held back. She needed to speak to Cliff. To clear the air. Make things right. "You go ahead, Frank. I'll join you in a moment."

He frowned and looked at her questioningly, but then followed Bethany and Graham inside.

Maggie stood with Cliff and Mandy. "I'm surprised to see you here, Cliff, but I'm pleased to see that you and your family are together." She smiled at Mandy and then her gaze shifted back to Cliff. "I know it's a bit awkward, but don't make it any more so. Please."

"I don't know what you're talking about, Maggie. I was only being sociable."

She pursed her lips. He knew exactly what she meant, but she wasn't about to make a scene. "Okay. Let's leave it for now and go inside and worship. That's what we're here for, isn't it?"

"Yes, you're absolutely right. No other reason at all." He turned to Mandy and took the squirming toddler from her, jiggling her on his hip.

Maggie fought the turmoil of emotions swirling inside her as memories of him holding Serena and Jeremy as toddlers outside this very church flooded back. Where had the years gone? And how had things turned out so badly for them? She prayed silently for Mandy. She was so young and although possibly strong, no one escaped emotional turmoil in a rocky relationship. No one. Maggie guessed she must have loved him enough to take him back, but had things really improved between them? Somehow, she doubted it.

The group walked inside. She was relieved when Cliff chose a pew on the other side of the church from where Frank was sitting with Bethany and Graham. She nodded to the couple as she left them to join Frank. No doubt many eyes were on her, but she didn't care. She kept her gaze down and slid into the pew beside him. He took her hand and squeezed it. She smiled and then drew a slow breath as she prepared herself for worship. She would forget about Cliff sitting behind her and those whose eyes might be on her. She was in church with the man she loved, about to worship God. That was all that mattered.

The worship leader asked the congregation to stand and sing 'Indescribable', one of Maggie's favourite worship songs. She opened her heart to the Lord afresh as the words of the song washed over her soul, comforting her. The Lord was in control, despite the challenges all around. Indescribable, uncontainable, He placed the stars in the sky and knew them by name. Powerful, untameable, amazing. Awestruck, Maggie wanted to lift her hands in worship, but instead, she closed her eyes and lifted her heart to God.

Once the service ended, she felt she should speak to several of her old friends she hadn't seen since she'd stopped attending the church. It would be rude if she didn't. She asked Frank if he minded. He said he didn't. "I won't be long." She squeezed his hand and smiled before making a beeline for the front of the church where her friends Sandra and Julianne were chatting. Their eyes widened as she approached.

"Maggie!" Sandra exclaimed. "I didn't expect to see you here! How are you?" She leaned forward and kissed her on the cheek.

"I'm good. I came with..." She hesitated, wondering what title she should she give Frank. Not fiancé. Not yet, anyway. "With a good friend."

"Oh yes?" Julianne smiled. "Male or female?"

Maggie winced. Of course they'd want to know. The pair had been disgusted with Cliff's infidelity and had, in no uncertain words, encouraged her to move on. She guessed they'd be happy to hear she had. "Male," she whispered with a chuckle.

"Good for you. Where is he?" Sandra asked, craning her neck to see past the crowd.

Maggie turned and spotted Frank exiting with Bethany and Graham. Even from a distance, the sight of him made her heart flutter. "He's leaving now, walking beside the couple holding hands."

"He looks nice," Julianne said. "Is he friends with Bethany?"

"Her brother."

"Not the one who owns the cattle station out in the Kimberley?" Julianne asked.

Maggie nodded. "So, you know Bethany?"

"Yes. She's been coming to our Bible study group. You should come back, Maggie. We miss you." Sandra reached out and squeezed her hand.

"I miss you all, too," Maggie replied. And she did. Since the divorce, her only true friend had been Suzanne, her boss. She'd kept to herself at her new church, not getting involved in any of the study groups. "I'll think about it. So, how are you two doing? How are your families?" She hoped to divert the attention away from her and Frank, and it seemed to work.

They chatted for a while before Maggie felt she needed to find him. "I've got to go, but let's keep in touch."

"Sure. Let's meet for coffee sometime. I'll call you. I've still got your number," Julianne said.

"Sounds lovely," Maggie replied, leaning in for a hug.

She wove her way through the dwindling congregation, keeping her head dipped to avoid any further conversations as she headed for the side exit.

She found Frank standing beside Bethany and Graham and a couple of other people under the shade of the tree, sipping cool drinks. It was too hot for coffee or tea. Frank slipped his arm around her shoulders as she joined him. There was no hiding the fact that they were a couple. Bethany introduced her to the others. Thankfully, Maggie didn't know them. They were new to the church, and Bethany simply introduced her as her brother's friend. She was happy with that.

While she was chatting, she couldn't help but let her gaze wander, but Cliff and Mandy were nowhere to be seen. Relief washed over her. She could do without another confrontation right now. Frank whispered in her ear and asked if she'd like to leave.

She nodded. He stepped closer to Bethany and told her they were off and would see them at their home. He had his own key.

Climbing into the truck, Frank started the engine and cranked up the air-con before squeezing Maggie's hand. "Are you okay, my love?" His eyes were soft and filled with genuine care.

She nodded. "Yes. Just. It was confronting, but in some ways, cathartic. I've been hiding from everyone for so long, it's probably time I started reconnecting with old friends."

"But not ex-spouses?"

She chuckled. "Definitely not ex-spouses!"

CHAPTER 34

After leaving the church, Frank and Maggie drove to Bethany and Graham's house, a modern brick home in the middle of Stuart Park, one of the better suburbs in Darwin. When they arrived home soon after, and while the men cooked the steak on the barbecue, Maggie helped Bethany in the kitchen put the finishing touches to the salads she had prepared earlier.

Bethany was easy to talk with, and when she apologised for not realising Maggie was Cliff Donovan's ex-wife and for the awkwardness it had caused, Maggie waved it off. "It was a shock to see him there, but I survived. I enjoyed the service and catching up with my old friends."

They ate lunch on the deck overlooking the blue waters of Fannie Bay, but while they were eating, the afternoon storm rolled in early and they had to quickly pull down the plastic blinds to keep the wind and rain out. The storm was spectacular. The sky had turned from blue to inky grey in an instant, and claps of thunder made them jump while lightning split the sky. The storm was short-lived but intense, but it did lighten the heavy air.

After they finished eating, Maggie asked if she could see some of Bethany's artwork. She'd noticed some on the walls while helping with the lunch preparation and was intrigued by them. They were mainly landscapes of the Kimberley and the Kakadu, and they were very good.

"Sure," Bethany said. "I don't have many here, only my favourites. Most are on display at the gallery."

Maggie studied the array of paintings with admiration. "I have to admit I can't paint, but I love photography. I took so many shots while I was doing my last assignment."

"When you met Frank?"

Maggie nodded. "Yes. It's beautiful country out there. But I guess you know that."

"Yes, but I left many years ago. I'm well and truly a Darwinite now."

"Which do you prefer?"

"I'm not sure I was cut out to be a country girl although I was born out there. I love it in small spurts, but it can be very isolating at times."

"Frank seems to love it."

"Goddard Downs is his life."

Maggie swallowed hard. She'd figured as much. That he was prepared to spend half his time in Darwin to be with her was humbling but also concerning. What if he didn't cope and grew restless? And what would he do with his time? Would they find enough to do to keep him occupied?

"How did you like it when you were out there?" Bethany asked.

Maggie sensed she was fishing. There was that obvious dilemma of what she and Frank would do if they married. And it *was* a dilemma. Maggie couldn't see Frank living anywhere other than Goddard Downs, but there was Serena. Maggie didn't feel she could leave her just yet, and she had no idea when she would feel okay about doing so. And did she really think she'd be happy being so isolated, especially now that Frank had told her that Olivia and Nathan were leaving? Janella would be the only woman on the station other than the wives and partners of the workers. She'd loved her time out there, and she told Bethany so, but staying a few days was vastly different to living there.

The men came inside and Frank sidled up to her and slipped his arm around her waist. "My sister's pretty good, isn't she?"

"She sure is." Maggie replied, leaning her head against his chest. "I'd love to see the work she has in the gallery."

"We could arrange that. It could be one of the things we do together."

Maggie's heart warmed. He was already trying so hard, but she couldn't see him being happy wandering around art galleries and the like for a week, although they'd had so much fun when they went to the markets a while back.

Bethany offered coffee or tea, but Frank said he'd pass, and if she didn't mind, he and Maggie might take a drive. He suggested they meet up at the markets for dinner and watch the sun set together.

"Oh, I think you two might like to do that on your own." Bethany gave him a wink.

Maggie felt her cheeks warm. Bethany was certainly not blind regarding their relationship.

"Well, yes, but you're more than welcome to join us, aren't they, Maggie?"

She nodded. "Yes, of course."

"Well, that's very kind of you, but we'll pass this time. We're planning our next trip away and we need to do some work on it."

"Oh, where are you going?" Maggie asked.

"Europe. We're planning on spending Christmas with our eldest son and his wife who live in France. We're hoping to have a white one since they live close to Mont Blanc."

"That sounds lovely, but I'd suggest giving Paris a miss."

"Yes, we've been there before so we thought we'd bypass it this time. How is your daughter doing?"

Maggie drew a deep breath. "Not so well, but it's early days."

"I can't imagine what she must be going through. If there's anything we can do, please let us know."

"Thank you. I appreciate that. If you could pray, that would be great. I'm more concerned about her mental and emotional state than her physical, to be honest."

"I can understand that. We'll be sure to uphold her in prayer."

"Thank you."

Frank said he needed to grab something and then they'd head out. Maggie used the opportunity to freshen up, and then, when he returned, she thanked Bethany and Graham for their hospitality before they walked out together to Frank's truck.

"Your sister and brother-in-law are very hospitable," she said as she clipped her seat belt up.

"Yes, they are. I enjoy their company a lot." He reached out and squeezed her hand. "So, my love, where are we headed?"

Maggie glanced at her watch. It wasn't quite three, so they had an hour or so to fill before meeting up briefly with Jeremy and Emma and the children. She'd called them earlier to see if they had some time that afternoon, and they'd arranged to meet at the duck pond in the Bicentennial Park for a short while so Sebastian, their three-year-old could play while the adults chatted. "How about we go to East Point and take a walk?"

"Sounds perfect." He headed the truck in the direction of the point, and when he pulled up a short while later and parked at a spot that overlooked the expansive bay, he leaned over and pulled her into his arms. "I can't help it, Maggie. I just want to hold you."

She chuckled. "It's okay. But I think this handbrake is in the way."

"Oh, sorry about that. The truck's not that comfortable, is it?"

"I told you we should have brought the Jeep."

"I'll be sure to listen to you next time. Okay, let's take that walk."

As their gazes met, she forgot about the handbrake and lifted her hand to his cheek and gazed into his eyes. "I do love you, Frank. So very much."

He lowered his mouth and kissed her ever so gently. She was surprised by her own eager response to the touch of his lips. She didn't want the kiss to end, but finally she couldn't take the handbrake digging into her side any longer and pulled away. "Let's take that walk now," she said, chuckling.

CHAPTER 35

After spending a pleasant hour at East Point, Frank and Maggie headed back to Bicentennial Park to meet Jeremy and Emma. They'd just pulled up in their Toyota Prado when Frank pulled into the car park.

"That's them over there," Maggie said, pointing to the white vehicle.

Frank parked beside them and tipped his hat to Jeremy. He'd grabbed it just before they left Bethany and Graham's, and Maggie had decided she preferred him with it than without it. It truly suited him.

They climbed out and Maggie made the introductions before taking her little granddaughter in her arms. She'd missed the first two months of her life while she was in Paris, so she needed to make up for lost time. "She's growing so quickly," she said, cooing at the baby. She was delighted when the baby girl smiled at her.

Sebastian was clinging to his mother's legs until Jeremy

suggested they feed the ducks. He let go and then ran off happily with his dad in tow. When they reached the edge of the pond, a flock of ducks flew in and landed gracefully on the water and were now paddling quickly to where another young family were already tossing bits of bread to them.

"Come on, let's join them," Maggie said to Frank, smiling.

"Sure. I must say, you look very comfortable with that little bundle."

Maggie smiled. "She's gorgeous, isn't she?" She showed baby Chloe to Frank as they walked.

"She sure is. Reminds me of my grandkids when they were that size."

"How many do you have, Frank?" Emma asked.

"Four. The eldest recently turned thirteen, and the youngest is going on two."

"And they live on the station with you?"

"For now. Two of them will be moving to Darwin soon."

"Oh, well that will give you even more reason to visit."

Frank chuckled as he placed his hand on Maggie's back. "Yes. I can see I'll be doing a lot of driving."

"You could fly."

"I guess I could, but I'm not really a flying man. I don't like being confined for long."

Maggie thought about that. Frank could easily feel confined in Darwin. She'd need to make sure they did a lot of outdoor activities, not just visit galleries.

They stood at the duck pond and fed the ducks with pieces of bread Jeremy and Emma had brought with them. Maggie stifled a laugh when a duck chased after Sebastian, making him cry. Jeremy made him stand his ground, and the duck soon gave up and waddled away.

A little later, they sat at a table under a covered shelter and shared afternoon tea. Emma had brought some homemade brownies and coffee in flasks. Maggie felt guilty. Here Emma was with two small children and yet she still provided the snacks. "I'm sorry, Emma, we should have brought something."

"Don't worry about it," she replied. "I love baking."

"Well, thank you," Frank said. "These brownies are scrumptious."

Maggie wanted to get Jeremy on his own for a minute and quiz him about Cliff. She got the opportunity as they were packing up. He'd walked to the bin and she followed. "I know it's none of my business, Jer, but I bumped into your dad and Mandy at church this morning. Are they back together again?"

He shrugged. "It's on and off at the moment. I never really know what's going on with them." He ran his hand through his hair. "He'll lose his seat at the next election if he's not careful."

Maggie frowned. "What do you mean?"

"He's drinking a lot, and it's becoming a problem."

"He seemed all right at church this morning."

"He's good at covering things up, Mum. You know that."

"Yes, I do."

"I don't hold much hope for their marriage."

"Hmmm… I figured that much. Mandy didn't look particularly happy this morning. Anyway, it's none of my business, I was just curious. On a different matter, I'm hoping Serena will be happy to see you soon."

"Yes, well, that's another story, isn't it? I'm hoping this whole situation might make her look at herself."

"That's what I'm praying for. She seems so depressed. It's like she's a different person."

"I guess it's understandable—she always did like things to go her way. This time it certainly didn't."

"Yes. We can only pray that God will get through to her. David's been great with her. I'm very impressed by him."

"He's a good man."

They strolled back to the cars. Before reaching them, she stopped and faced him. "She's a real mess, Jeremy. She's going to be scarred for life." Her voice hitched and tears welled in her eyes.

He stepped closer and pulled her into a bear hug. "She'll come through it, Mum."

Maggie sniffed. "I know. It's just so sad seeing her like this."

"I can imagine. I'll go see her as soon as she lets me."

Maggie drew back and smiled. "Good man."

After they all said their goodbyes, she gave a last kiss to Chloe before Emma popped the baby and the carry basket into their car. Maggie said she'd come and visit sometime during the week and offered to babysit whenever.

Frank squeezed her hand when they were back in the truck. "Where to now?"

"The markets?"

"I was thinking of somewhere a little quieter."

"Oh? Like where?"

"Fish and chips by the water?"

She smiled. "Sounds great."

The rest of the afternoon and evening passed with pleasant chat and lots of cuddles and kisses. When Frank dropped Maggie back at her apartment just before nine, it was an effort to leave him, but leave him she must. "Thanks for the day, Frank. It was wonderful spending time together."

"And we get to do it all over again tomorrow."

"Yes." She leaned over and kissed him on the lips. "Until tomorrow."

THE REST of the week passed all too quickly. They visited the art gallery and admired Bethany's work that was on display, they went to the movies several times and even played a round of golf. They dined out often, trying different restaurants each time, and occasionally ate with Bethany and Graham. Maggie visited Serena several times, but she still refused to see anyone else, so Frank didn't go with her. David was still doing a superb job and showed no end of patience. Serena was scheduled for more surgery the following week, and they both hoped that would mark a turning point as her right cheek was going to have a major skin graft. It would never look normal, but the doctors were confident it would look better.

One day, Graham took them out on the boat. They had to leave early because of the afternoon storms. No one wanted to get caught in them, and they only just made it back to the harbour before the first storm hit.

But despite all this, Maggie sensed Frank was restless. He said he'd give her as long as she needed, and she knew he meant it, but she felt bad making him wait. Nevertheless, despite knowing she loved him, she still needed time. Was she being selfish? Perhaps. But the marriage commitment was a huge one and she wanted to enter into it without any doubts.

She would use the time when Frank was back on the station to assess her feelings and further seek God's will.

The day before he was due to leave, he told her to dress in her best outfit that night. She was intrigued and quizzed him about where they were going, but he wouldn't tell her.

~

As the time to leave Maggie and return to the station drew nearer, Frank's heart grew heavier. Yes, he'd said he'd give her as much time as she needed, but he'd love to have her commitment before he left and know that she was as committed to their relationship as he was. But despite that, he wouldn't push her. She would commit when she was ready, and not a moment earlier, of that he was sure.

Although not one for flashy outings, he'd planned to take her somewhere special the night before he left. There was little scope for that on the station, and even when he and Esther had dated, they'd enjoyed the simpler things in life, like picnics and fish and chips on the beach.

But Maggie was different. Being married to Cliff, she'd eaten at the finest restaurants and mixed with the top echelon of society. Frank knew she didn't crave that lifestyle. She also enjoyed the simpler things, or thought she did, but he wanted to spoil her again, just like he had on the cruise. He'd booked a table at Sterlings on the top floor of the Arcadia Hotel, the finest restaurant Darwin had to offer. He hoped she'd like it and it didn't bring back bad memories, because no doubt she would have dined there before.

He'd agreed to collect her at seven o'clock and said he was

happy to take her Jeep. He'd had to shop for clothes because he hadn't brought a suit with him. In fact, he hadn't worn a suit since Esther's funeral, and for obvious reasons, he would have been reluctant to wear that particular one, anyway.

He started to get ready a little after five. Maggie had been to visit Serena that afternoon and so he'd had the afternoon to himself. Struggling to relax, he couldn't keep his thoughts from what might be happening on the station. He'd tried to read, but in the end had taken himself for a long walk. When he got caught in the rain, it was refreshing and helped clear his thoughts. He was soaked by the time he returned, so he showered and shaved and put on some casual clothes until it was almost time to go. Despite the storms, it was still hot and humid, and the less time he spent in his long-sleeved shirt and tie before reaching the air-conditioned restaurant, the better. He didn't want to be a ball of sweat before he collected Maggie.

Bethany chatted with him as she prepared dinner for her and Graham. On several occasions, she'd quizzed him about whether he was planning on proposing that night. He couldn't tell her he already had, so he answered the question by saying that he and Maggie were taking things slowly. She simply chuckled. He would have loved to have told her, but it didn't seem right. He'd called Julian during the week and told him that their engagement was on hold for the moment. Fortunately, Julian had only shared the news with Janella and he promised to tell her to keep it quiet.

Finally, the time came to dress before collecting Maggie. He'd chosen a lightweight linen suit in soft grey and a white shirt. He'd deliberated for a long time about what tie to buy, but in the end had chosen one with a bright, tropical design.

He hoped it wasn't too flashy, but the shop assistant had assured him it looked great. Now, looking at his reflection in the mirror, he wasn't too sure. He walked into the kitchen and asked Bethany what she thought.

She smiled. "You look like a million dollars." He guessed that was good enough. She gave him a hug as he went to leave. "I hope you have a wonderful evening, Frank. Give Maggie my love."

He hugged her back. "I will."

As he drove his truck to Maggie's place, his hands began to sweat. For some reason he was nervous, although they'd spent most of the past week together. Tonight reminded him of the afternoon they'd spent on the sunset cruise on Lake Argyle when he'd proposed. He wasn't about to re-propose, but he wondered if perhaps she was wearing the ring. The thought made his heart pound.

∼

MAGGIE HAD RETURNED AGITATED and annoyed from seeing Serena. She knew she shouldn't feel like that. After all, Serena was her daughter and she was in a terrible way physically, but her attitude was appalling. Maggie felt like shaking her and telling her to wake up. Plenty of people struggled with injuries but managed to get on with their lives. They didn't give up like Serena seemingly was. For goodness' sake, she was only thirty-three. She had her whole life in front of her, and she had a wonderful partner in David.

Maggie had to admit that she'd struggled with their loose relationship. It didn't sit well with her, but it seemed to be the way of things for most young people these days. They shied away from marriage, but they also shied away from God, removing the moral foundations that Maggie and Frank's generation had grown up with. Society was becoming more liberal about what was acceptable and what wasn't, and Christian values in general were looked upon as old-fashioned.

However, Maggie knew that God still answered prayer, and that He cared deeply for *all* His children, even those who'd strayed, so she wouldn't give up on Serena finding Him, and she would try her best not to judge her and David. She might not approve of their chosen lifestyle, but she could still love them. That's what Jesus would have done.

But what she was struggling with right now was Serena's unwillingness to see that despite her injuries and permanent scarring, she could still live a worthwhile, purpose-filled life. Maggie had actually grown angry with her and almost walked out this afternoon. She ended up apologising and then had a long chat with David. He'd told her that he believed, in time, Serena would come around and that he'd stand by her, regardless, and would be there for her.

Maggie had told him he was a good man and that Serena should be more grateful. He'd shrugged and said it was okay. She wondered what had made him like he was. Yes, he was a firefighter and had obviously been in some horrific situations, but he had a strength of character that was unusual. She'd like to get to know him better, because all she really knew about him was that his family lived locally in Darwin and that he loved outdoor activities. Her journalistic nose told her there was a story there somewhere.

Arriving home, she only had time to take a quick shower,

not the long one she would have liked. In fact, she'd entertained the idea of taking a bath before her date with Frank. Something about the evening spoke of romance and love, and a long leisurely bath would have been the perfect start. But that wasn't to be. He'd said to dress up and that indicated they were going somewhere special. It reminded her of the cruise he'd taken her on... the night he proposed. There'd definitely been something special about that date.

Was he going to propose again tonight? Her heart beat faster. What would her answer be if he did? Was she ready to commit? She'd told herself over and over that she wasn't, but was fear holding her back? If so, was that fear unfounded?

She loved him, and there was no doubt in her mind that he loved her. He was a kind man and they got on so well. They enjoyed each other's company, and they both loved God. In fact, she loved it when they prayed together, which they did almost every time they were with each other, and they were able to converse easily on a range of topics. Even their silences were comfortable.

After she'd dressed in her knee length black cocktail dress, she looked at the ring Frank had given her the night of the cruise. Simple but exquisite, a solitaire diamond in a white gold band. She'd worn it close to her heart since the night he'd proposed, but could she wear it on her hand tonight to show him she was serious about marrying him?

She sat on her bed and studied the ring as a haze of feelings and desires flowed through her. The only thing she could do was pray, so she closed her eyes and took a moment to steady her thoughts before opening her heart. *Lord, you know I love Frank, and I now have peace about our relationship, but I'm not sure how our marriage would work with Serena so troubled and Frank so far away. Lord, I want to marry him, to spend the rest of my life with him. Can I trust You to work it out?*

No. She wouldn't put the ring on her finger yet, not until she was absolutely certain. She wouldn't do that to Frank. Tucking the ring under her dress, she prayed she'd know when the right time was.

She'd just finished applying her lipstick when the doorbell rang. After taking one last glance in the mirror, she hurried to the door. Pausing, she took a steadying breath before opening it.

When she did, her breath caught. Frank was a handsome man, but she'd never seen him looking quite so dapper. His eyes twinkled as he held out a single, long-stemmed red rose.

Accepting it with a smile, she lifted it to her nose. The perfume was divine, almost intoxicating. "Thank you, Frank. It's beautiful."

"As are you," he said softly as he leaned forward and kissed her lightly on the cheek.

Her heart pounded like a drum. He was so romantic and love for him swelled inside her. "Would...would you like to come in for a drink before we go?"

"That would be lovely, but we have a booking for seven."

"Okay. Let me grab my purse." She smiled at him again before dashing inside to grab her silver clutch.

Before long, they were driving to town in her Jeep, Frank at the wheel.

"How was your afternoon with Serena?" he asked.

She groaned. "Not great. I don't know how David puts up with her."

"That bad?"

"Yes." She sighed. "I despair for her sometimes."

"Her healing will be a slow process."

"Yes. At least she's agreed to see a psychologist."

"That's progress."

"Yes. And David's applying to be her permanent carer so he won't need to go back to work until she can look after herself."

"Where does that leave you?" Frank turned and faced her as he slowed for a red light.

She knew what he meant. Was she needed? That was the question she'd been asking herself for days. She lowered her gaze to her lap. "I'm not sure."

They drove the rest of the way in silence. When Frank turned into the sweeping entrance of the Arcadia Hotel, her eyes widened. "You didn't tell me we were coming here."

"Is it a problem?"

She shook her head. "Not at all." She'd wanted to dine here for a long time. Apparently the view was amazing and the food was to die for. Cliff had always found an excuse not to bring her here, although he'd entertained plenty of his well-to-do supporters in the hotel. Not that she wanted to dine here with him. Not anymore, at least.

A valet opened the door for her and she stepped out and waited for Frank. When he reached her, she laughed when he slipped his arm around her waist and pulled her tight, gazing into her eyes with a twinkle in his. "Frank…"

"You look so gorgeous tonight, Maggie. I don't want to forget what you look like when I go home tomorrow." He lifted a hand and traced her hairline with his finger.

"Nor me, you." She was already dreading the moment when they'd have to say goodbye.

He lowered his mouth and placed it gently over hers. She closed her eyes and responded before remembering the young valet who stood by waiting to park the car.

She stifled a giggle and clung to Frank's arm as they headed to the entrance. The foyer was like a tropical oasis, with large, lush palms reaching all the way to the glassed ceiling, and trickling ponds and fountains scattered amongst them.

They headed for the lift and took it to the top floor. The view was even better than Maggie had expected. The floor rotated and offered 360-degree views, but although the stunning sunset across the sea and the city skyline were amazing, she had eyes only for Frank. She drank in the sight of him as they sat at their table and chatted while they ate. The meal was scrumptious, but it could have been terrible. It didn't matter. Only being with him mattered. When he suggested they dance, she molded into his body as if they were made for each other. His arms encircled her and she nestled her head against his chest as they swayed to the soft music. It was an evening made in heaven and she didn't want it to end. But finally, it was time to leave. "I need to visit the bathroom. Would you wait?".

"Of course, my darling."

Her heart beat a staccato as she closed the door behind her and set her purse on the counter. She drew a steadying breath as she slipped her ring off its chain and slid it onto her finger. Her mind was made up. She was absolutely sure of this. She loved Frank and wanted to marry him. Everything else would somehow work itself out.

Frank couldn't believe it when Maggie returned from the bathroom. He was standing by the floor-to-ceiling window looking out over the city when she sidled up and slipped her arms around him from behind and leaned her head against his back.

He was relishing the feel of her body close to his when he placed his arms over hers and felt the ring on her finger. He spun around, his heart jumping inside his chest. "Maggie…" He gazed into her eyes and cupped her cheeks with his hands. "You're…you're wearing the ring."

"I am." She flashed a smile that made him giddy. Sent his senses spinning.

"I want to marry you, Frank. If you'll still have me." Her voice was soft, tender.

He pulled her close and hugged her, his heart soaring. "It's all I want, my love. You've made me the happiest man alive. I love you so much."

She tipped her head and smiled. "And I love you with all my heart."

Lowering his mouth, he pressed his lips against hers and kissed her tenderly.

NOTE FROM THE AUTHOR

Note from the Author

I hope you enjoyed "Slow Road to Love" as much as I enjoyed writing it. Frank and Maggie's story continues in "Slow Path to Peace". You'll find the first chapter below!

To make sure you don't miss any of my new releases, why not join my Readers' list? (http://www.julietteduncan.com/linkspage/282748) You'll also receive a free thank-you copy of "Hank and Sarah - A Love Story", a clean love story with God at the center.

Enjoyed "Slow Road to Love"? You can make a big difference. Help other people find this book by writing a review and telling them why you liked it. Honest reviews of my books help bring them to the attention of other readers just like yourself, and I'd be very grateful if you could spare just five minutes to leave a review (it can be as short as you like) on the book's Amazon page.

NOTE FROM THE AUTHOR

Keep reading for your bonus chapter of "Slow Path to Peace".

Blessings,

Juliette

Slow Path to Peace - Chapter 1

Frank drove back to Goddard Downs on cloud nine. Maggie was wearing his ring. They were going to be married. They'd talked late into the night after leaving the hotel. Sitting on a bench at East Point, they'd committed their relationship once more to God, and had agreed they would announce their engagement to both families as soon as possible. They'd told Bethany and Graham that morning before he left, and they were ecstatic with the news. They'd also told Jeremy and Emma, and Maggie had said it was time he met Serena and David, regardless of how Serena felt.

He'd been a little anxious on the way there. Maggie had warned him that Serena was still her grumpy self, but he'd found her anything but. Perhaps it was her upbringing that caused her to be polite to strangers, because that's what he was to her. A stranger. A stranger who happened to be marrying her mother. That in itself could have caused her to be wary, but to him she seemed a polite, well-adjusted young woman. Despite her obvious physical injuries and burns, she was an interesting person. Both she and David offered their congratulations and said they would survive without Maggie. Frank knew Maggie would be both pleased and saddened by that sentiment. Pleased she was free to move away but saddened because she wasn't needed. He of all people could understand how that felt.

They would announce their engagement to his family when she came to visit the following week. They thought that was best rather than making the announcement in any other way.

He couldn't wait for her to be back at Goddard Downs. Although they hadn't finalised any details yet, he was hopeful she might agree to move into the cabin until they married.

The drive home seemed shorter somehow, and before he knew it, he was pulling off the main road and driving along the track that led to the homestead. Although he'd only been gone a week, he wondered what awaited him. Would Julian have spent more quality time with Caleb as he'd encouraged him to do? Before he left, he'd suggested they work on a project of some kind together. Julian needed to bond with his son or else he risked losing him. Frank had been quite blunt about that. And were Nathan and Olivia further along with their plans to move? He assumed so. The three months would pass quickly and there was a lot to organise. A job for Nathan for a start, and a place to live.

He pulled up in front of the homestead and climbed out of the truck and stretched. He'd driven well into the night and had only stopped for a short break before hitting the dirt road which had turned to mud now that the rains had arrived. He'd put the seat down in the truck and caught a few hours. He was probably too old to be doing that, but at least he was home in time for breakfast.

As he grabbed his bag from the cab, Isobel raced out of the

house and launched herself at him. "Grandpa! You're home. I've missed you."

Frank gave her a hug and smiled. "And I've missed you, little Issie. What have you been up to?"

"Not a lot. Mummy and Daddy have been doing a lot of talking."

"Have they just?"

She nodded.

Frank wondered if they were rethinking their decision to move to Darwin.

As they walked in together, the tantalising aroma of bacon and eggs wafted through the house and he realised how hungry he was. He hadn't eaten since grabbing a quick dinner at Timber Creek the night before. "Something smells good," he said.

"Aunt Nellie's breakfast," Isobel said.

"I hope there's some left."

"I think there is. Everybody's in the kitchen."

"Everybody?"

She nodded again. "They're very serious."

It was most unusual for everybody to still be in the kitchen at this time of day. Something must have happened. He quickened his pace.

Issie was right. When he entered, the whole family was there and they all looked up at him. The way they glanced at each other made him think he'd caught them by surprise and immediately put him on guard. "What's going on?" he asked.

"You'd better sit down, Dad," Julian said.

"That bad, huh?" He removed his hat and slid onto a chair. Not his chair. Julian sat in that one. "What's up?"

"You haven't heard the news?" Julian asked.

Frank shook his head. He'd been listening to the playlist Maggie had made for him. "What have I missed?"

Olivia leaned forward. "It's not good, Dad. The government has banned live cattle exports for the foreseeable future."

He felt the blood drain from his face. The licensing issues were now irrelevant. This ban sounded the death knell for the station. "When does it come into force?"

"Immediately," Julian replied.

Frank sighed. "I figured something was up, but I hadn't expected this. So that means our last shipment won't go?"

Julian shook his head. "That's right. We're up the proverbial creek. I told you we should have looked at other options."

"Nathan's come up with one," Janella said quietly.

All eyes turned first to her and then to him.

"What are you thinking?" Frank asked.

Nathan shifted in his seat, his expression cautious but hopeful. "I know you're not keen on opening the station to tourism, but what if we offer a cattle driving experience, the old fashioned way?"

Frank narrowed his eyes. "You mean, sleeping out? In swags?"

Nathan nodded.

"We wouldn't have to build anything?" Frank asked.

Nathan shook his head. "No. We'd only need horses and swags. People would pay a fortune for an experience like that."

"Enough to get us out of this pickle?"

"Not on its own. But it would help."

"What do the rest of you think?" Frank cast his gaze around the table.

"I think it could work," Janella said.

Julian shrugged. "Maybe. Although I think we should still develop the station into a complete tourist destination."

"I'm not putting you down, son, but we don't have the funds to do that, and I'm not keen on borrowing."

Julian folded his arms. "I guess that's that, then."

"For now, at least."

"I think the cattle driving experience option is a good one," Olivia said.

Frank turned to Joshua, who was leaning back in his chair, looking disinterested. "Josh?"

His youngest son shrugged. "I'll go with whatever you all decide. It doesn't bother me."

"It should. This is your home and livelihood, too."

"Not for long. Sean and I are planning on going on the rodeo circuit full-time."

Frank leaned forward, his forehead creasing. "And when were you going to tell me that?"

"Soon."

Frank blew out a breath and raked a hand across his hair. "You know your sister and Nathan are leaving, too?"

"Yeah. I know."

"And you don't think you should be staying to help out?"

"I need to do my own thing, Dad. Sorry. I may as well leave you to talk about this without me here."

"If that's how you feel, maybe you should. Although we could sure do with the help."

"We're better off without him if he doesn't want to be here," Julian said, pinning Joshua with narrowed eyes.

NOTE FROM THE AUTHOR

"It won't be forever. I need to get it out of my system, that's all."

Nathan exchanged a glance with Olivia and then leaned forward. "We've been talking, Frank, and we're prepared to stay and help for as long as needed. There'll be a lot of promotion and advertising to do, and a new business plan will need to be drawn up. Livvie can do that." He squeezed his wife's hand and smiled.

Frank was rendered speechless. "I...I don't know what to say. You were so set on leaving..."

"I know. But we won't leave you in the lurch. You're going to need help." Nathan flashed an accusatory glance in Joshua's direction. "It would be wrong of us to leave now when you've done so much for us."

Joshua leaned back and crossed his arms. "Well, that leaves me between a rock and a hard place, doesn't it?"

"Sure does, son," Frank said.

"Well, I guess I could delay it for a while. As long as you're happy to have Seano around for a bit longer."

A general groan travelled around the table before Frank said, "He'd be very welcome. We won't turn anybody away if they're happy to pull their weight."

"So, it's settled, then? Is that what we're doing?" Julian asked. Frank was unsure of his son's tone. It almost sounded like he was put out because the decision was happening around him and not by him, but he could have been wrong.

"We've been praying about this for some time, don't forget," Frank replied. "This is the first and only suggestion that everyone seems happy with, so I'm thinking it might be what we should do. Draw up the plans, Liv, and let's take a look at them."

"Onto it, Dad. I'll need to get some ideas from you all, but it shouldn't take long. I'll modify one I did earlier when we were looking at other things."

"Always on the ball, Liv." Frank chuckled. Maybe he wasn't about to lose his family, or the station, after all. "I think we should commit this to the Lord. Proverbs sixteen three tells us to *commit to the Lord whatever you do, and He will establish your plans*. It's important we don't forget that." He looked at Julian. "How do you feel about leading us, seeing how you're sitting in my chair?"

His son's eyes widened, but he agreed. He cleared his throat before extending his hands and closing his eyes.

Frank smiled to himself as his son led the family in prayer for the first time. It would have been hard if Maggie hadn't agreed to marry him, but now that she had, everything was different, and hearing his son ask God for guidance and assurance that this was the right path to take gave him confidence that the station would be in good hands. Not that he was planning on leaving, especially now that the government's decision had forced their hand. He was just stepping back, that's all. Somehow, it felt right.

Grab your copy of Slow Path to Peace.

OTHER BOOKS BY JULIETTE DUNCAN

Find all of Juliette Duncan's books on her website:
www.julietteduncan.com/library

A Sunburned Land Series

A mature-age romance series

Slow Road to Love

A divorced reporter on a remote assignment. An alluring cattleman who captures her heart...

Slow Path to Peace

With their lives stripped bare, can Serena and David find peace?

Slow Ride Home

He's a cowboy who lives his life with abandon. She's spirited and fiercely independent...

Slow Dance at Dusk

A death, a wedding, and a change of plans...

Slow Trek to Triumph

A road trip, a new romance, and a new start...

The Shadows Series

A jilted teacher, a charming Irishman, & the chance to escape their pasts & start again.

Lingering Shadows

Facing the Shadows

Beyond the Shadows

Secrets and Sacrifice

A Highland Christmas

True Love Series

Tender Love

Tested Love

Tormented Love

Triumphant Love

Precious Love Series

Forever Cherished

Forever Faithful

Forever His

A Time For Everything Series

A mature-age Christian Romance series

A Time to Treasure

She lost her husband and misses him dearly. He lost his wife but is ready to move on. Will a chance meeting in a foreign city change their lives forever?

A Time to Care

They've tied the knot, but will their love last the distance?

A Time to Abide

When grief hovers like a cloud, will the sun ever shine again for Wendy?

A Time to Rejoice

He's never forgiven himself for the accident that killed his mother.

Can he find forgiveness and true love?

Transformed by Love Christian Romance Series

Because We Loved

A decorated Lieutenant Colonel plagued with guilt. A captivating widow whose husband was killed under his watch...

Because We Forgave

A fallen TV personality hiding from his failures. An ex-wife and family facing their fears...

Because We Dreamed

When dreams are shattered, can hope be restored?

Because We Believed

A single mom forging a new life. A handsome chaplain who steals her heart...

Billionaires with Heart Series

Her Kind-Hearted Billionaire

A reluctant billionaire, a grieving young woman, and the trip *that changes their lives forever...*

Her Generous Billionaire

A grieving billionaire, a devoted solo mother, and a woman determined to sabotage their relationship...

Her Disgraced Billionaire

A billionaire in jail, a nurse who cares, and the challenge that changes their lives forever...

Her Compassionate Billionaire

A widowed billionaire with three young children. A replacement nanny who helps change his life...

The Potter's House Books...

Stories of hope, redemption, and second chances. *The Homecoming*

Can she surrender a life of fame and fortune to find true love?

Blessings of Love

She's going on mission to help others. He's going to win her heart.

The Hope We Share

Can the Master Potter work in Rachel and Andrew's hearts and give them a second chance at love?

The Love Abounds

Can the Master Potter work in Megan's heart and save her marriage?

Love's Healing Touch

A doctor in need of healing. A nurse in need of love.

Heroes Of Eastbrooke Christian Suspense Series

Safe in His Arms

SOME SAY HE'S HIDING. HE SAYS HE'S SURVIVING

Under His Watch

HE'LL STOP AT NOTHING TO PROTECT THOSE HE LOVES. NOTHING.

Within His Sight

SHE'LL STOP AT NOTHING TO GET A STORY. HE'LL SCALE THE HIGHEST MOUNTAIN TO RESCUE HER.

Stand Alone Christian Romantic Suspense

Leave Before He Kills You

When his face grew angry, I knew he could murder...

The Madeleine Richards Series

Although the 3 book series is intended mainly for pre-teen/Middle Grade girls, it's been read and enjoyed by people of all ages. Here's what one reader had to say about it: *"Juliette has a fabulous way of bringing her characters to life. Maddy is at typical teenager with authentic views and actions that truly make it feel like you are feeling her pain and angst. You want to enter into her situation and make everything better. Mom and soon to be dad respond to her with love and gentle persuasion while maintaining their faith and trust in Jesus, whom they know, will give them wisdom as they continue on their lives journey. Appropriate for teenage readers but any age can enjoy."* Amazon Reader

ABOUT THE AUTHOR

Juliette Duncan is a USA Today bestselling author of Christian romance stories that 'touch the heart and soul'. She lives in Brisbane, Australia and writes Christian fiction that encourages a deeper faith in a world that seems to have lost its way. Most of her stories include an element of romance, because who doesn't love a good love story? But the main love story in each of her books is always God's amazing, unconditional love for His wayward children.

Juliette and her husband enjoy spending time with their five adult children, eight grandchildren, and their elderly, long-haired dachshund, Chipolata (Chip for short). When not writing, Juliette and her husband love exploring the wonderful world they live in.

Connect with Juliette:

Email: juliette@julietteduncan.com

Website: www.julietteduncan.com

Facebook: www.facebook.com/JulietteDuncanAuthor

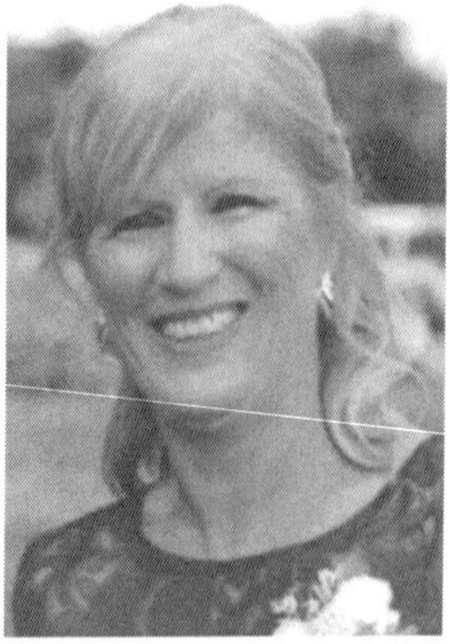

Made in the USA
Columbia, SC
19 May 2021